Ralph Compton:
The Omaha Trail

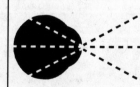

RALPH COMPTON:
THE OMAHA TRAIL

JORY SHERMAN

THORNDIKE PRESS
A part of Gale, Cengage Learning

GALE
CENGAGE Learning·

Farmington Hills, Mich • San Francisco • New York • Waterville, Maine
Meriden, Conn • Mason, Ohio • Chicago

GALE
CENGAGE Learning®

LIBRARY OF CONGRESS CATALOGING-IN-PUBLICATION DATA

Sherman, Jory.
    Ralph Compton : the Omaha Trail / by Jory Sherman. — Large Print
edition.
        pages cm. — (Thorndike Press Large Print Western)
    "A Ralph Compton Novel."
    ISBN-13: 978-1-4104-6715-7 (hardcover)
    ISBN-10: 1-4104-6715-5 (hardcover)
    1. Large type books. I. Title.
PS3569.H43R35 2014
813'.54—dc23   2013046147

Published in 2014 by arrangement with NAL Signet, a member of
Penguin Group (USA) LLC, A Penguin Random House Company

Printed in Mexico
2 3 4 5 6 7 18 17 16 15 14

THE IMMORTAL COWBOY

This is respectfully dedicated to the "American Cowboy." His was the saga sparked by the turmoil that followed the Civil War, and the passing of more than a century has by no means diminished the flame.

True, the old days and the old ways are but treasured memories, and the old trails have grown dim with the ravages of time, but the spirit of the cowboy lives on.

In my travels — to Texas, Oklahoma, Kansas, Nebraska, Colorado, Wyoming, New Mexico, and Arizona — I always find something that reminds me of the Old West. While I am walking these plains and mountains for the first time, there is this feeling that a part of me is eternal, that I have known these old trails before. I believe it is the undying spirit of the frontier calling me, through the mind's eye, to step back into time. What is the appeal of the Old West of the American frontier?

It has been epitomized by some as the dark and bloody period in American history. Its heroes — Crockett, Bowie, Hickok, Earp — have been reviled and criticized. Yet the Old West lives on, larger than life.

It has become a symbol of freedom, when there was always another mountain to climb and another river to cross; when a dispute between two men was settled not with expensive lawyers, but with fists, knives, or guns. Barbaric? Maybe. But some things never change. When the cowboy rode into the pages of American history, he left behind a legacy that lives within the hearts of us all.

— *Ralph Compton*

CHAPTER 1

Dane Kramer, owner of the Circle K Ranch in Shawnee, Oklahoma, rode the whiteface calf down into heavy brush. The calf had been struck by lightning the night before when a violent thunderstorm had swept over the plains, stampeding some of his herds, knocking down trees, and stripping some of their limbs. Some of the roofs on his outbuildings were in tatters, and debris lay strewn along a mile stretch from one tank to another. The tanks were filmed over with dust and leaves and stray branches that would have to be skimmed off with long-handled rakes.

The calf had a streak of raw flesh running from its neck to its tail, right along the spine. The calf needed doctoring or it could die, Dane knew.

He called to one of his hands, Joe Eagle, a Cherokee. "I've got him spotted, Joe. The little feller is caught in that gully full of

7

brambles."

"Be right there, Dane," Eagle replied from the other side of the gully. "Can you get a rope on him?"

"I don't think so. Might take two of us to drag him out."

Eagle spurred his horse, a small dun, with bogged tail and mane, and rode to where Dane waited.

The bulging black elephantine clouds of the early morning had blown east and left only streamers of ash gray clouds in their wake. These were far to the west and the sun had not risen high enough to paint them peach and gold. There was a dankness to the air, the cloying scent of rain that had left glistening beads on the branches and buds in the thick brush where the calf was imprisoned. It was early spring in Shawnee Mission, Oklahoma Territory, and the grasses were still short on the prairie.

Joe Eagle trotted up alongside Dane. He saw the calf struggling with the blackberry vines, kicking its way into even more tangles. Its long tongue lolled from its mouth like a pink ribbon and its brown eyes were rolling in their sockets, flashing shadows and sunlight with a glassy intensity. The calf bawled and flailed with its front hooves as it tried to jump through the mesh of vines and sapling bushes.

"Him heifer," Eagle said.

"Yep, Joe. I saw it happen. She was standin' next to that hickory tree by the home pond. Sky lit up bright as a shiny silver dollar and twined around that tree, then jumped over to the calf. Stripped her back just like that tree, only the tree looks like an unpainted barber pole now. Lightnin' just twined around it and then run the length of that little heifer's back."

"Heap storm," Joe said. "Heap lighting. Heap rain."

"We got to get her out of there and not get caught in that brush ourselves."

"You get head. I get tail. We drag out and rope."

"Good idea, Joe," Dane said. He dismounted and ground-tied the sorrel gelding to a clump of sage.

Joe slipped from his saddle and let his reins trail. The dun was a cow pony and well trained to stay where Joe left it.

The two men walked into the gully, two yards apart. Joe headed for the tail of the calf while Dane forged toward its head and neck. The two waded and clomped down on brittle brush while the heifer bawled and kicked and jumped to escape both from the patch of berry vines and the two humans bearing down on it.

Dane grabbed the calf's left ear and then wrapped his wiry arm around its neck. Joe dived between the hind legs and grabbed them just above the hooves and lifted its rear end waist-high. He grunted as the calf twisted and struggled to free itself. Its legs pumped back and forth, but Joe increased the pressure of his grip and started dragging it toward the rim of the gully.

Dane wrestled the calf's head until it bent down toward his boots and then pulled in concert with Eagle.

They got the calf onto bare land. It was bawling and struggling, kicking with those cloven hooves and bucking like a bronco out of the chute.

"You sit on her, Joe. I'll get a rope."

"You sit on neck. Joe get rope."

Dane grinned. Sweat drenched his face, dripped in streaks from under his hatband. His shirt was plastered to his back, and the armpits of the gray chambray were sweat-soaked ovals, dark as a cow dug.

"Good idea, Joe," Dane said, and bulldogged the calf's head to the ground. Joe released the hind legs and scrambled over the calf and sat on his neck, pinning the animal to the ground.

Dane ran to his horse and untied the

leather thong that held the looped coil of manila rope. He found the loop and widened it as he came upon Joe and the calf.

Joe reached out and grabbed the loop, pulled it over the calf's head clear to the shoulders. Dane pulled on the rope and tightened the loop until it was snug around the calf's neck.

Joe stood up and stepped away from the heifer. It stood there, spraddled, its brown and white curly hide dulled with dust and the detritus of the brush. It looked stupefied and stopped its caterwauling.

Dane handed the coiled rope to Joe. "Hold her tight. I got a tin of salve in my back pocket."

"Hunh," Joe grunted, and grasped the rope. He held the rope in one hand and bent the calf's head toward its chest with the other, holding it in place.

Dane reached into his back pocket, the one that did not hold his tobacco pouch, and pulled out a flat tin box. The tin, which had once held snuff, now was packed with Indian Salve. The original label from which he had drawn this portion proclaimed it to be "vegetable and animal." The ad on the original label said that the salve was "an invaluable specific for the cure of cuts, tumors, swelling, running sores, burns,

11

freezes, chopped hands, and corns."

The price of the salve had been twelve and a half cents when he bought it from a medicine peddler passing through Shawnee Mission. The peddler said the salve was prepared and sold by Merritt Griffin of Glens Falls, New York. And that too had been on the label.

Dane figured that the calf had at least two of the ailments, perhaps three. When he looked at the slashed flesh, he saw that there was some swelling, and it was probably burned and would wind up as a running sore.

"Joe, you hold that calf real steady while I smear this salve over its wound."

Dane twisted the lid off the tin and let it drop to the ground.

Joe sniffed the odor emanating from the salve. "Him stink," he said.

"Yep, it smells to high heaven, Joe, but it's better'n ointment. Last longer, I reckon."

Dane stuck two fingers into the salve and withdrew a dollop of the medicant. He started at the tail and laved the goop on, dipping into the tin for more salve until he had covered the entire pink of the exposed flesh. When he finished, the tin was almost empty and it still gave off a rank odor.

"Okay, Joe, you can let her go. I'll dope

her again in a couple of days and see how she's doin'."

Joe slipped the loop off the calf's neck. It stood there for a long moment, then took one gingerly step, then another. It wagged its short tail and shook its head.

"If she don't lick it off, that salve ought to cure her. A wonder she didn't get electrocuted," Dane said.

The calf made a sound and slowly trotted away toward the pasture in front of the ranch house.

"At least she knows where home is," Dane said.

"Heap smart heifer," Joe said, and ginned.

Joe stood a head shorter than Dane, who was not tall, but barely reached five feet and ten inches. Dane was clean-shaven with straight brown hair that was chopped even all around and did not touch his shoulders. He was all sinew and muscle, while Joe had a slightly bulging midriff, burly arms, and bowed legs from many hours and days astride his dun horse.

Dane picked up the lid of the tin and screwed it back on the container, tucked it into his pocket. Then he wiped his hand on his denim trousers, picked up a handful of dirt, and scrubbed away the stench before rubbing the dust off.

13

Both men saw the calf bolt a few yards to its left. They looked beyond the switching tail and the salve-smeared back and saw a rider heading their way.

"Him come, Randy," Joe said.

"Sure looks like Randy," Dane said. "Wonder what he wants."

"Him hurry," Joe said.

He was right. Randy Bowman was coming at a gallop, slapping the sides of his paint with the trailing ends of his reins, the front brim of his hat bent back from the breeze he was fanning with his speed.

Dane reached into his other back pocket and pulled out a tobacco pouch. He opened it and plucked a clump of it and worked it into his mouth. With his tongue, he evened the tobacco out and began to chew it, savoring the nicotine juices that squirted into his mouth. His brown eyes glistened in the pale sunlight and he wiped the sweat streaks from his brow with the back of his left hand.

Randy rode up and skidded his horse to a stop. "Dane, they's somebody at the house wants to talk to you."

"Who is it? He in a hurry?"

"He's, well, he's mighty anxious. Says he's from Omaha."

"Omaha?"

"Yep," Randy said. "That's what he said.

14

Big feller. Dressed kind of fancy."

"Omaha, Texas?" Dane asked.

"No, sir. Clear up in Nebraska Territory."

"Omaha, Nebraska?" Dane asked.

"Yep, sure enough. I ast him twice. I was shoein' that swaybacked mare in the barn when he come up and called out. Your pa, he was sitting in the front room and I heard him thump his cane like he was rarin' to run out and see who it was rode up."

"What's the feller want?" Dane asked.

"Hell if I know," Randy said. "But when he talks, he bellows, and I hopped on Patches here and got to you fast as I could."

"He asked for me by name?" Dane asked.

"Yes, sir, he done said he come to see Dane Kramer of the Circle K, like it was a real formal visit."

"Randy, you wouldn't know formal from a pie social. What in hell do you mean?"

"I don't know, but he walked right in and is talkin' to your pa in the front room."

"Just walked right in, did he?"

"Like he belonged in your house."

"I think maybe my pap invited him in," Dane said.

"Well, I reckon. I got to get back. That mare's kickin' at her hobbles and might hurt herself if I don't hurry back."

"Run along, Randy. Joe and I will mosey

15

up to the house."

Randy turned the paint and rode off at a gallop.

He was a young man, a drifter, who had come to the ranch about six months before, looking for work. He never said where he was from or talked about his parentage. He slept in the barn and seemed to bond with animals, especially horses. Dane figured him to be seventeen or eighteen. He paid the boy ten dollars a month and fed him. He was cheap help at that, because he hauled food from Shawnee Mission when asked and fixed fencing, could set a pole in hard ground, and knew how to tack on shoes to unshod horses or replace worn ones with new.

Eagle and Kramer lifted themselves into their saddles.

"Well, let's see what the man from Omaha has to say. He must have something on his mind to come all this way a-lookin' for me."

"Maybe," Joe said, "you owe him money."

He said it as a joke, but Dane's face clouded up and his lips clamped tight. He spat a stream of tobacco juice out of the side of his mouth. "Only man I owe money to is Throckmorton, that greedy banker in the Mission. If Mr. Omaha is here to buy me out, I'm going to throw him out on his ear."

"Heap big man, Randy say," Eagle said.

"You know, Joe, a boot in the nuts can make a man mighty small mighty quick."

Joe Eagle laughed.

"That true," he said, and the two rode on as the sun rose and the heat began to burn through their clothes and dry the sweat on their faces.

CHAPTER 2

Thorvald Kramer pumped his cane up and
down. It thumped on the oak floor of the
front room. It was, to him, a mighty cane,
because his son, Dane, had crafted it from
the penises of bulls he had raised and
butchered. He had glued them all together,
shellacked them so that the cane was a
single piece of hard, straight flesh with a
metal tip made from melting down and
shaping an iron horseshoe.

"Tell the man to come inside the house,"
Thor shouted as he pounded on the floor
with his cane.

Thor was bent over in his chair. His spine
was bowed so that his back formed a paren-
thesis, bowed so much that he appeared to
be a hunchback. He was eighty-five years
old, but his mind was as sharp as a barber's
razor. His balding head was streaked with
strands of gray hair, swept back by his
brush, so that his head appeared stream-

lined, especially with that hunched-over stance when he stood up from his over-stuffed rocking chair.

The door opened and a large, heavyset man had to duck to enter the room.

"Who be ye?" Thor demanded when the man was clear of the door and stood up straight.

"The name's Himmel, sir. Otto Himmel."

"Well, set down on the divan there, Mr. Himmel, and tell me your story. Why are you here and what do you want with my son?"

Randy stood there, gape-mouthed, in the doorway.

Thor shook his cane at the young man and growled at him in his gravelly voice, "You ride out and find Dane, young feller, and tell him to get his sorry ass back here pronto."

"Yes, sir, Mr. Kramer," Randy said, his sharp-pointed Adam's apple bobbing up and down, threatening to puncture the skin of his skinny throat. He wheeled and went out the door, easing it back so that it wouldn't slam. If it had made a noise, he knew he would feel the explosive wrath of Thorvald, complete with snarl and invective.

Otto Himmel sat down on the divan and

looked around the room. Above the fireplace, he saw a Kentucky long rifle with its polished curly maple stock, hanging on wooden pegs. Next to it was a powder horn dangling from another peg. There were tintypes in frames of prairie scenes and some Currier & Ives colored prints of horses and carriages, exotic fountains, and buildings. There was also a photo, faded to a yellowish brown, that looked very old in an oval frame.

"That's my ma," Thor said, pointing with his cane at the picture. "Danish woman. My pa was German. Like you, eh, Mr. Himmel?"

"I am of German heritage, yes. My parents were both born in Andernach, Germany. They came to this country in 1815. I was born in Pittsburgh. They never did speak English very well and I never learned the German language."

Himmel was a huge man, topping six feet, with rounded shoulders and a belly as big as a Chicago stove. His boots were polished and seemed to have the same sheen as his dark hair and the handlebar mustache beneath his nose. His eyes were small and porcine, as blue as a June sky, as penetrating as sharp-pointed darts.

"Handsome woman," Himmel said. His

tone was polite but wary.

"You want some coffee, Himmel?" Thor asked.

"I don't want to put you to any trouble, Mr. Kramer."

"Call me Thor. No trouble. Ora Lee keeps a pot goin' all day long. I got to have my coffee every mornin' and through the day."

"That would be fine," Himmel said.

Thor thumped his cane on the floor several times.

"Ora Lee. Ora Lee," he called.

Seconds later a large dowdy woman came down the hall from the kitchen and entered the room. She wore a blowsy dress of soft linen, dyed mauve, with streaks of gray in her bundle of hair piled atop her large head. She had puffy lips faintly brushed with a light rouge, rouge circles on her checks. She had at least three chins that looked like a bloated accordion. Short, with stocky legs covered in blond stockings. Her shoes were the type worn by nurses and washerwomen, black, with large sturdy heels and white laces.

"Yes, sir, Mr. Thor," she said. "More coffee?"

"More for me and a fresh cup for Mr. Himmel, Ora Lee, if you please."

"I didn't know we had a visitor," she said

to no one.

"Ora Lee's been with me for better'n two years, Himmel. She cooks and cleans and makes my bed. Sometimes she rubs my back."

Ora Lee's face flushed a bright pink and she left the room, waddling down the hall on those functional black shoes of hers.

Himmel cleared his throat and looked up at the beamed ceiling of the log home, the cobwebs in two corners that looked like swamp mist.

Thor swung his attention to Himmel as if trying to figure out what brought him to the Circle K.

"Just what did you want to see Dane about, Himmel?" he asked. "Earl send you out?"

"Earl?"

"Earl Throckmorton. Runs the Prairie Land Bank over at the mission."

"Never heard of him," Himmel said.

Ora Lee Gibson returned to the front room carrying a small wooden tray. She set it on the little table next to Himmel's chair. She lifted a pot and poured coffee into a cup, then carried the pot to Thor, who held out his almost-empty cup. She poured steaming coffee to within an inch of the brim. He nodded to her and she set the pot back on the tray.

"There's some fresh cream there," Ora Lee said to Himmel, "and some sugar in that bowl with the teaspoon."

"Thanks," Himmel said. "I like my coffee black."

"Suit yourself," Ora Lee said, and left the room on stout muscular legs, her shoes clacking on the hardwood floor of the hallway.

"Ora Lee follered us from Texas," Thor said. "We pulled up stakes in the Rio Grande Valley when Cap'n King started buyin' up all the land and we figured that if we stayed in those parts, he'd eventually swaller us up, lock, stock, and barrel."

"I've been there," Himmel said as he lifted the coffee cup to his lips.

"Where?" Thor asked.

"The Rio Grande Valley. Lots of cattle. Lotta land."

"You got that right. You sure Earl didn't send you out here?"

"I'm sure, Mr. Kramer. Er, I mean, Thor."

"Well, what do you want to see Dane fer?"

Himmel worked the coffee around in his mouth to cool it before he swallowed it. "I prefer to conduct my business with Dane Kramer, sir, with all due respect."

"Hell, I'm his pa. Him and me don't hold

23

no secrets from each other." Thor seemed to bristle as he leaned his bent frame forward in the chair.

"It's just my policy, sir. No exceptions."

"Dang it all, you got my curiosity all perked up and won't tell me why you come out here."

"I'm sorry, Thor. It's just my policy. I deal with a lot of parties and it seldom pays to discuss business with anyone except the principal. I hope you understand."

Thor leaned back in his chair and sipped his coffee after blowing on it with bloodless pursed lips. "Parties and principals, eh? Well, out here we talk man to man, 'thout'n no formalities. Where did you say you was from, Mr. Himmel?."

"Why don't you call me Otto, Thor? We might become friends, you and I. I'm from Omaha, up in Nebraska, and I've come to see your son, Dane. On business."

"I don't know how you do business up in Omaha, but we lay it all out on the table down here. I don't think Dane is much interested in any business you got in Omaha."

Himmel flashed a weak smile at Thor and took another sip of coffee, as if to stop any further conversation that might issue from his mouth.

The two sat in silence for several minutes. They drank their coffee and seemed oblivious of each other.

They heard hoofbeats a few minutes later.

"That would be Randy comin' back from tellin' Dane you was here," Thor said.

"So Dane can't be very far away," Himmel said.

"Nope. He had to chase a calf down what got itself struck by lightning early this mornin'."

"I was in that storm," Himmel said. "Got soakin' wet. My bedroll's still damp, I suppose."

"You rode down here on horseback all the way from Nebraska?"

"I did," Himmel said. "A buggy wouldn't have made it and I have a good horse. No trail along the Missouri River."

"Well, I swan. All the way down from Omaha. Just to see a principal party." Thor shook his head in mock disbelief.

"It was quite an experience," Himmel admitted.

"I reckon so."

They had finished drinking their coffee when they heard more hoofbeats coming toward the house at a rapid pace.

"That would be Dane and Joe Eagle," Thor said. "Won't be long now before you can state your business to the principal."

Himmel ignored the sarcasm and finished his coffee. He tapped a pocket of his vest but did not take out his pipe or tobacco. It was just a reassuring pat in case his meeting turned out to be successful and he could light his pipe.

"I've got a satchel outside on my horse," Himmel said. "I'd better go and get it."

He set his cup down and walked to the door without Thor's approval and went outside.

He saw the two riders as they pulled up at the hitch rail. He walked to his horse and untied the leather thongs that held his leather satchel. He had it in hand when Dane and Joe Eagle dismounted and started toward him.

"If you're from the Prairie Land Bank, mister, you can just put that satchel back on your horse."

Himmel turned around, his hand midway through the untying.

"I am not from any bank, sir," Himmel said. "Are you Dane Kramer?"

"I am."

Joe Eagle walked up. Both men were packing sidearms and Himmel looked down at the butts of their pistols.

"I'm Otto Himmel. I rode here from

Omaha up in Nebraska, and I've got a proposition for you. I've met your father. Drank a cup of coffee with him, in fact."

Dane stuck out his hand.

Himmel took it and the two shook hands "This is one of my hands, Joe Eagle," Dane said, stepping a half foot away.

Himmel held out his hand, but Joe merely nodded. Himmel withdrew his hand as if it were suddenly an unwanted appendage.

"Come on in the house," Dane said. "I'll listen to what you have to say as long as you weren't sent out here by Throckmorton."

"I was not, nor have I ever met this Throckmorton, Mr. Kramer."

"Call me Dane. Should I call you Otto or Mr. Himmel?"

"Otto is fine."

"I put up the horses," Joe Eagle said.

"Come on in when you're through, Joe," Dane said.

Joe Eagle grunted a guttural "hunh" and led the horses to the stable about two hundred yards in the back of the house.

Himmel hefted his satchel and followed Dane into the house. The door, on a sash-weight spring, closed behind him.

"Pa," Dane said, nodding to his father. "You and Mr. Himmel have a good talk?"

Thor thumped his cane on the floor and

growled at his son, "He don't say much. Wouldn't tell me nothin' 'bout why he come here all the way from Nebraska."

"Well, clean out your ears, Pa, and listen. We'll both hear what Mr. Himmel has to say."

"Harrumph," issued from Thor's mouth, and he leaned back in his chair, his cane across his lap.

"Have a seat, Mr. Himmel," Thor said. "If there are foreclosure papers in that satchel, you might be carrryin' them back outside in a different location."

Himmel sat down and set the satchel on his lap. He did not open it.

"Mr. Kramer," Himmel said, "I assure you there are no foreclosure papers in my satchel. I've come to you with an urgent request and a proposition."

"You want coffee, Dane?" Thor asked.

Dane shook his head. "No, not yet, Pa. Let's hear what the Omaha man has to say."

"I'm all ears," Thor said.

Dane laughed. Himmel wore a serious look on his face.

"Mr. Kramer," Himmel said, "I looked up your brand in the register and I saw that you have better than ten thousand acres here in Shawnee Mission, and that you have had difficulty in getting your cattle to market because of the late start last summer and the harsh winter we all had."

"That's true. We got turned back from Kansas by an early blizzard last fall and now I'm ready to try again when the grass gets higher."

"That's why I'm here, Mr. Kramer," Himmel said.

"Better call me Dane or I'll think you're talkin' to my pa here."

"Very well, Dane. I need three thousand head in Omaha. I'm prepared to pay you twelve dollars a head if you can deliver the herd by midsummer. It's a long drive up the Missouri. A small advance, say a thousand dollars, to get you started and buy grub for your chuck wagon, and the balance on delivery. Fair enough?"

"Not quite, Mr. Himmel," Dane said. "I know how far it is to Omaha, and it's a dangerous trail with Indians and cattle thieves from here to Kansas. I'll need more money."

"How much more? That's a fair price."

"It's fair if I was going to Salida or Kansas City. Omaha's a different matter."

"Let me think for a minute," Himmel said.

Dane waited, with a look of unconcern on his face. He examined his hand that still bore traces of salve under the fingernails of two fingers and streaks of it along the side of his thumb.

"Tell you what," Himmel said. "If you can deliver three thousand head to my stock pens in Omaha by June first, I'll pay you fourteen dollars a head."

"Fifteen," Dane said.

Himmel's throat swelled and his face colored from infusions of sudden blood into his corpuscles. He appeared almost apoplectic.

"In that case, I'll meet your price, Dane. Fifteen dollars a head for three thousand head by early June. But there is another matter that is now on the table."

"Another matter?"

Himmel cleared his throat and the rosy hue on his face subsided. "I need a big favor from you and I'm prepared to pay."

"You be real careful, Dane," Thor said. "I think there's a snake in the woodpile with this feller."

Dane looked at his father, then back at Himmel.

Himmel opened his briefcase and the silence in the room deepened with suspicion and anticipation. Thor lifted his cane from his lap and glared at Himmel as if ready to do battle.

Dane thought of driving three thousand

30

head of cattle all the way to Omaha, and his stomach churned with something that might have been called fear in a lesser man. Bile roiled in his belly like writhing snakes and he waited for Himmel to take something out of that fat satchel of his.

And Himmel was taking his sweet time for some unknown reason.

CHAPTER 3

Before Himmel reached into his satchel, he looked over at Dane, then at Thor. The expression on his face was one of curiosity and his eyes widened.

"Just curious," Himmel said. "About that man who rode up with you. Joe Eagle, I believe you said, was his name."

"Yeah, that's what we call him."

"He's an Injun, isn't he?"

"Yes. Full-blood," Dane said.

"May I inquire what tribe he's from?"

Thor cackled from his chair.

"He's a Cherokee," Dane said. "But that's not what his tribe is called in his own language. Cherokee is a Creek word and somehow it stuck. In his language he is a Tslagi, and his name is really Awohali, their word for eagle. So we call him Joe Eagle. He was half-dead when we found him, starving, just skin and bones. He had been captured by a snake oil peddler who used him as a kind of attraction. Didn't feed him well, and beat him regularly. Kept him in chains. We took him in and run the drummer off. I taught him the cow business and he's a damned good hand."

"Reason I asked was I never saw a real Indian up close before. We got Omahas in Nebraska and Kiowas."

"Well, between here and Kansas, you got renegade Comanches and maybe some Apaches what won't stay put on any reservation. They think a cattle drive is manna from heaven, that God is bringing them food and money."

"I know," Himmel said.

Then he drew a sheaf of papers from his satchel, closed it, and set it on the floor beside his chair. "The favor I'm asking you is this. I have about nine hundred head in Kansas City. I'm paying out feedlot prices to hold them there. I want you to pick those cattle up and drive them up to Omaha with your herd. I'll pay you two dollars a head on those. They carry the trail brand of the Three Bar Two. Here's the manifest that you will show to the owner of the feedlot in Kansas City, a Mr. Chester Dowd. I'll give you a bank draft to pay the remainder of the bill there so that he'll release the cattle to you."

Himmel leaned from his chair and handed the papers to Dane, who scanned them for a few seconds.

Dane looked up from the paper.

"That's an extra nine hundred head," he said. "Big responsibility. Do you know how far it is from here to Omaha?"

"It's nigh on to five hundred miles by my reckoning."

"We have to figure on ten miles a day. There's no way we could drive the herd that far, pick up your strays in Kansas City, and make it to Omaha by mid-June."

"Let's say July, then," Himmel said. "Look, I have stock pens there and both a slaughterhouse and packing plant. I employ a number of Poles to butcher the cattle and it will be a stretch to keep them there that long if I don't have work for them."

"Three dollars a head for the K.C. herd," Dane said.

"Ouch," Himmel said. "I've already paid for that small herd, plus I've got the feedlot bill for maybe two months. If I add three dollars, those cattle will cost me dearly."

"Your choice, Otto," Dane said. "And I'll need more than a thousand dollars in advance. With that many cattle I've got to hire drovers at thirty a month and found, plus buy or build a bigger chuck wagon.

The men I pick not only have to be good drovers, but be able to shoot both pistol and rifle. The pickin's around here are mighty slim."

"I can advance you another five hundred, Dane," Himmel said.

"Make that bank draft for another five hundred that I can cash in K.C., and we have a deal."

"Why so much?"

"You might as well know what I'm facing here," Dane said. "It's ugly as hell and if I don't make a bank payment, Throckmorton is ready to grab my ranch and all the cattle on it. And that's not the end of it. When I finish the drive, I have to pay off the mortgage by the first of September or I lose everything."

"I see," Himmel said. "I hate to lay out so much money after what happened to the cattle now sitting in Kansas City, eating up my meager profits."

"You must have a market for good beef in Omaha," Dane said.

"I do, but I'll lose all my workers if you don't bring me all those cattle by mid-July at the latest."

" 'Pears to me, Otto, you and me got similar hitches at stake. You might lose your Polish workers and I could lose my ranch."

"Haw," Thor exclaimed. He slapped his knee with a whack of his hand. "You done hit the nail square on the head, Dane boy. Otto's twixt a rock and a hard place. You're twixt a hard place and a harder place, by golly."

"So," Himmel said, "we might just as well throw in together and solve both problems. I have a contract here that you can look over after I fill it out. We can both sign it, your daddy can witness it, and I'll take it to a notary public this afternoon and it will all be legal and binding."

"If you agree to my terms," Dane said, "I'll go along with your'n."

"Fine. Now, if I can sit at a table or desk, I'll fill in all the blanks."

"I figure we can make ten miles a day, fifteen on good days, and bring you the herd about as fat and sassy as when we leave here."

"Say fifty days," Himmel said, "but allowing for some slow days and some faster, we'll say sixty to eighty days. That sound about right?"

"Barrin' storms, floods, Injuns, and cattle rustlers, I'd say that's about right," Dane said.

"Good," Himmel said, and stood up, the

papers rattling like blowing leaves in his hand.

"There's a desk yonder, ahind you, Otto. Where I do all my tallyin' and figgerin'," Dane said. "Make yourself to home."

Himmel turned around and saw the small rolltop desk with a cane chair shoved beneath it. There was a small throw pillow on the seat. He walked to the desk, pulled out the chair, and sat down. He rolled up the accordion cover and laid the papers flat on the desk's surface.

"You'll find ink and a quill pen or two in one of them cubbyholes," Dane said.

As Himmel started to write on the paper after he dipped a pen in an inkwell, Ora Lee entered the room, a look of consternation and exasperation on her face.

"That boy," she said. "He's been listenin' outside that front winder yonder. Ain't the first time I've caught him at it neither."

"What the hell?" Dane said as he rose to his feet. "He still there?"

"No, I was emptyin' the dishwater out and spotted him. I run him off. He went back to the stables, I reckon."

"Thanks, Ora Lee," Dane said. He walked to the window next to the fireplace and looked out at the barn. He saw Joe Eagle talking to Randy but could not hear what

37

he was saying.

"The little sneak," Ora Lee huffed, and waddled back down the hall, rubbing her hands on a dish towel.

"That young whippersnapper ain't got no business listenin' at that winder," Thor said.

"No, he doesn't," Dane said. "I'll get to the bottom of it."

"You take in strays, that's what you get," Thor said.

Dane walked back to his chair but did not sit down. He looked at the large man at the small desk and could hear the pen scratching across the paper. He set the papers in his hand down on the seat of his chair and walked to the door just in time to open it for Joe Eagle.

"Come on in, Joe," Dane said. "You see Randy listenin' at the window a while ago?"

"Me see Ora Lee come out and shoo him away."

"What did you say to him?"

"Me tell him to finish shoeing the mare. He say he lost something and him look for it by window."

"He was spying on us, I think. I wonder why. What did he say he lost?"

Joe Eagle stepped inside and closed the door behind him. "Him say quarter. Two bits."

Thor slapped his knee again and leaned forward in his chair. "That kid ain't seen two bits since he drew his pay last month. He's a damned liar."

"Take it easy, Pa," Dane said. Then he looked at Joe Eagle. "Go fetch Paddy, will you, Joe? I need to talk to him right away. I think he's finishing up the branding on the West Forty."

Paddy O'Riley was Dane's ranch foreman. Spring roundup was over and he and two other men, Jim Recknor and Donny Peterson, were still branding calves that had dropped a few weeks before. Good men, he knew, but he would need more men for the drive north.

"Me go," Joe Eagle said, and glanced at both Thor and Himmel. "I help Paddy when he come."

"No, you come back with him. We've got work to do. We're going to round up three thousand head and drive 'em north. Way north."

"Me go north?"

"You bet, Joe. You'll work your Cherokee ass off, but there'll be some sugar in your pay when we settle up in Omaha."

"Where Omaha?"

"Far to the north, Joe. Five hunnert mile, near as I can figger."

39

Joe grinned. "Long ride," he said, and then went out the door.

"A damned long ride," Thor said. "Wisht I was goin' with you, son."

"I'll need you to look after Ora Lee and the hands I leave behind, Pa."

"Haw. Me look after Ora Lee? It's the other way around, you ask me."

"Keep her busy, Pa, and see that she has plenty of starch to chaw on."

Thor laughed.

Ora Lee was addicted to starch and Dane always saw to it that she had several boxes to dip into. She made a mouthful last most of a morning, but was a harridan on wheels when she ran out. It was, he thought, a strange addiction, but harmless enough.

Dane started for the door.

"I'll be back in a few minutes, Otto," he said. "I've got to get that boy to work on making me some trail brands. We'll have to brand three thousand head before we start out."

Himmel turned around and looked at Dane.

"That boy who was eavesdropping at the window?" he said.

"Yeah, that boy."

"Can you trust him?" Himmel asked.

"No, but I can keep the little bastard busy

until I fire him."

Dane walked out the door and Himmel returned to his pen and ink and legal papers.

Thor's eyes clouded up and he slumped in his chair. He was tired. It had been a busy morning and a worrying one. And now his son was going on a long trail drive in a few days and he would be left all alone with Ora Lee. He looked over at the picture of his mother on the wall, and tears welled up in his eyes.

All alone, he thought.

And Earl Throckmorton breathing down their necks like a fire-spewing dragon.

CHAPTER 4

Randy Bowman was just finished with shoeing the bay mare when Dane walked up on him.

"Find your quarter, Randy?" Dane asked.

"Huh?"

"The two bits you told Joe Eagle you lost."

"Uh, oh no, I didn't find it."

"Lost it under the window of my house, did you?"

"Uh, I don't know where I lost it."

"What did you hear when you were listening at my window?"

Randy looked sheepish. He poked the fire he had used to heat the shoes to make them fit. "Nothin'. Honest."

"Bullshit, Randy. You heard every damned word. I'm just wondering why you were listenin' in on us."

"I didn't hear nothin', honest, Dane. I was lookin' for that two-bit piece I lost."

"You're not a very good liar, Randy."

Randy said nothing. He hung his head when Dane gave him a withering look of contempt.

"Well, I'll get to the bottom of it, I reckon. Meantime, I've got a job for you."

"Yes, sir. I finished shoeing the mare. I was goin' out to fix the corral. One of the poles got knocked down in last night's storm."

"I need four brandin' irons, Randy."

"Circle K?"

"No. These are for trail brands. As you probably heard, I'm takin' a herd of cattle up the Missouri."

"No, sir. I — I didn't know."

"Never mind. I need those trail irons right away. Four of 'em."

"What's the brand?" Randy asked.

"Make it a Box D. Can you do that real quick?"

Randy looked down toward the back end of the eight-stall livery stable at the tack room. There were a number of straight irons hanging on the wall there. "If you want 'em real quick, I'll have to make two brands, one with a square, and then you can burn the D inside it. That be okay?"

"Whatever it takes."

"I'll stoke up the fire and add more wood so's I can weld the brands on the end of those irons. It'll take me a while."

"I want them first thing in the morning, Randy."

"I'll do 'er, even if it takes all night."

Dane started to leave. He stopped at the pen doors and looked back.

"I hope you find that two-bit piece," he said.

CHAPTER 5

When Dane got back inside his house, Himmel was waiting for him at the desk.

"Papers are ready for you to look over and sign, Dane," Himmel said.

"Just leave 'em on the desk and take a chair, Otto. I'll get right to it."

"What did the kid have to say?" Thor asked, thumping his cane on the floor, softer than usual.

"He lost a quarter."

Thor snorted.

"Let me look through these papers, Pa," Dane said. Himmel sat down and folded his hands on his lap.

"I'm putting the trail brand on these papers, Otto," Dane said. "Box D."

"Good," Himmel said. "That will cinch it."

A few minutes later, Dane signed the two documents.

"All done," he said.

"Thor, if I bring the papers to you, will you sign them as a witness?" Himmel asked.

"I can walk to the desk," Thor said.

He ejected himself from the chair and stood on shaky legs. He balanced himself with the cane and thumped over to the desk. Himmel got up and stood beside him. He pointed to the blank line where he wanted Thor to sign.

"Put your John Henry right there," Himmel said.

"I'll put Thorvald Kramer there," Thor said with a grin. He hunched over, which was not much of a stretch for him, and affixed his signature to one paper, then the other.

"When does Dane get some money on this?" Thor asked.

"First advance right now," Himmel said. He walked to his chair, lifted his satchel, and pulled out a stack of one-hundred dollar bills. He counted out ten of them and handed them to Dane.

"Thank you, Otto."

"I'll go into town right away and find a notary," Himmel said. "I'll bring the papers back and give you two bank drafts for Kansas City. One for the feedlot, the other for you."

"That will be fine," Dane said. He es-

46

corted Himmel out the door after Otto had put the papers back in his satchel. Dane watched him ride off as Thor hobbled back to his easy chair.

"Now you can stave off Throckmorton," Thor said as he settled into his chair.

"I'd like to stuff these bills down his greedy throat," Dane said.

"He ain't gonna like it none. Earl wants this ranch bad and all the cattle on it."

"Well, he's not going to get it."

"I wouldn't put nothin' past that schemin' bastard," Thor said.

"Neither would I," Dane said. He walked to the front window and looked out at the prairie beyond the yard. In the distance, he saw two riders break the empty horizon.

"Paddy and Joe Eagle will be here in a few minutes," he said to his father, and walked back to the chair Himmel had sat in.

"Well, the big man didn't break it," he said as he sat down to wait for his foreman.

"He probably bent a few springs, Dane. He must weigh close to three hundred pounds."

Dane laughed. "Easy," he said.

A few minutes later, they heard hoofbeats, and then Paddy and Joe Eagle knocked on the door.

"Come in," Dane called.

Paddy O'Riley entered first. He was a small barrel keg of a man with flowing rusty locks that strung to his shoulders. He was silted over with dust and his face bore a thin sheen of sweat. He wore striped serge trousers and a chambray shirt. His boots were caked with mud and cow shit, and the pistol he wore hung low, to a point just above his right knee.

"What you got, Dane?" Paddy asked as Joe Eagle sidled around him and sat in a straight-backed chair.

"Set down, Paddy," Dane said, pointing to a cane chair nearby.

"I don't mind settin' down for a bit," Paddy said.

He scraped the chair as he moved it closer to where Dane sat and plumped his bottom down on it. He wiped his forehead and took off his hat.

"Paddy," Dane said, "we're going to drive three thousand head of beeves right on up the Missouri River, clear to Omaha."

Paddy let out a low whistle of surprise. "Boy oh boyo, that's some drive, Dane. We ain't got hands enough for that many cattle."

"I know. Can you find me some hands that can take care of themselves if we run up against Injuns or rustlers?"

48

Paddy crossed his legs and put his hat back on his rusty head. He scratched his chin. "Well, there's some we had to let go last fall, what might like to ride with us. One of 'em's a swamper in the Mission Saloon. The other'n was haulin' freight from Tulsa last I heard."

"We'll need more than two extra men," Dane said.

"Me know three Mexicans in town," Joe Eagle said. "They ride and shoot good."

A wavelet of recognition passed across the blue moons of O'Riley's eyes, and his face brightened with a sudden flush of rose-hued color. "Joe's right. We had them Mexes on our drive two years ago when we ran them five hunnert head to Abilene. Good boyos, they were, and they can pop the head off a prairie dog at seventy-five yards, or stand off a bunch of Comanche rustlers without soilin' their pants."

"Yeah, yeah," Dane said. "I remember them. Can't recollect their names right off. Where can you find them?"

"Carlos, him got horse ranch. Me know where."

"Fine, Joe. Tell 'em I want to see them. How's the horse ranch faring?"

Joe shook his head. "No good. No one buy. But good horses."

"We can use the horses too, in our re-muda," Dane said. "Things are starting to shape up right nice."

"I 'spect we can get some good hands from hereabouts," Paddy said. "There's plenty of boyos out of work right now this early in the spring."

Something outside the side window of the house caught Joe Eagle's eye. He got up and walked to the window while Paddy and Dane put their heads closer together and conversed in low tones. Thor strained to hear, and cupped a hand to his right ear. Ora Lee made a clatter in the kitchen as she dried dishes and slammed cabinet doors.

Joe stood at the window, then saw the quick flash of a horse and rider. They were visible only for a split second, but he knew that Randy was going somewhere in a hurry. He turned from the window and walked over to where Dane and Paddy were bent over in a small huddle.

"Him go," Joe said. "You send Randy to town?"

Dane sat up straight and looked up at Joe. "No, he's supposed to be smithin' out in the stable, makin' trail brands."

"Him go. Him gone. Mighty fast," Joe said.

Paddy looked at Joe. Then back at Dane.

"The kid lit a shuck, did he? Not surprisin'," Paddy said.

"What do you mean, Paddy?"

"He's a sneaky sort. I caught him countin' cows once or twice, keepin' a tally on a little tablet he carried in his hip pocket."

"What?" Dane exclaimed.

"I ast him what he was a-doin'," Paddy said, "and he told me you wanted a tally on all the herds in pasture."

"I'll be damned if I did," Dane said.

"I took the boy at his word," Paddy said.

"So he's been tallyin' my cattle and sneakin' up to hear what we say in here," Dane said. "Seems I misjudged the little rascal."

"Haw," Thor exclaimed as he poked the air with his cane, "I warned you about takin' in strays, Dane. Never did trust that boy, no, sirree."

"Well, the damage is done. I have a hunch Randy is headin' for town to report our doin's to Throckmorton."

"What can Throckmorton do?" Paddy asked.

There was a silence among the men in the room.

"I don't know," Dane said, finally, "but I don't like it none."

"Throckmorton's a damned snake," Thor spat, emphasizing his words with a thump of his cane on the floor.

"Seems we got more'n one snake in the woodpile," Dane said.

Then he looked at Paddy. "Let's get back to business, Paddy. I'll get us a map tomorrow when I go in to see Throckmorton. You start separating our best cattle from the rest of the herd."

"What about the trail drive irons?" Paddy asked.

Dane paused in thought. Then his eyes brightened.

"We've got those running irons we got from those rustlers last year," he said. "We can add to the Circle K with some kind of mark."

"That would surely work," Paddy said.

"Save us a lot of time at that. Maybe the kid did us a favor after all."

Paddy laughed.

Joe Eagle scowled, as did Thor.

"We'll gather some hundred or two hundred extra head," Dane said to Paddy. "In case we lose a few on the drive."

"My aim is not to lose a single head," Paddy said.

"That's the kind of talk I like to hear," Dane said, and reached into his pocket for his tobacco pouch. "Joe, go tell Ora Lee to make us a fresh pot of coffee. And tell her to make it strong. We got a lot of figurin' to do before Himmel gets back with them papers."

Paddy looked up at Joe. "Tell Ora Lee to make that coffee so strong I can float a horseshoe nail in it."

Joe grunted and left the room.

Dane stuck a wad of chaw in his mouth and reached down to drag a brass spittoon closer to his chair.

There was an excitement in the room. A trail drive could be hell, but it was also an adventure, an adventure into the unknown. There would be new lands to see, weather, all kinds of obstacles. But those were what tested a man and made him stronger. And at the end of the drive was the golden chalice, the treasure, money to pay the hands, and money to pay off the accursed mortgage. There was, Dane thought, new-found freedom at the end of every trail drive. And he was determined to make this one work.

CHAPTER 6

Earl Throckmorton was a small weasel of a man, with liverish thin lips, a thin mustache, a thick shock of coal black hair, and shifty porcine eyes that were pale blue. He wore a pin-striped gray suit of flannel and sported a plain black vest with a gold watch chain dangling from a button hole and dripping into a small pocket. He sat at his cherry-wood desk, a few papers in front of him, and stacked trays that represented in- and outboxes.

His secretary, Linda Watson, tapped on his door with the opaque glass window bearing his name and position at Prairie Land Bank.

"Come in," he said.

"That young man is here, Mr. Throck-morton."

"Randy?"

"Yes."

"Send him in," Throckmorton said.

"He seems awfully agitated, sir."

"Well, he's young and gets excited quite easily."

Throckmorton's diction was precise and his words crisp as newly minted greenbacks. He pretended to be busy when Linda ushered Randy into his ornate office, with its world globe, territorial maps framed on the wall, and a large window that looked out on a small green patch of lawn at the rear of the bank with a bench covered with pigeon droppings. The bench was painted green and dotted with white and black globs dropped by perching pigeons.

"Hello, Mr. Throckmorton," Randy said, hat in hand. "I got some news for you."

"Sit down, sit down, Randy. I want to hear all about it."

Randy sat down in a maple chair padded with leather at the seat and back. He looked up at Throckmorton in his raised chair, with his hair slicked back and parted in the middle.

Out of politeness and respect, Randy removed his dirty, misshapen hat and crossed his legs in an attempt to hide his scuffed boots. "Well, Mr. Throckmorton, Dane Kramer is going to drive three thousasnd head of cattle clear up to Omaha."

"You don't say. When?"

"I don't know. A man from up there came to see him and offered him a lot of money. And that ain't all."

"Go on, son, go on," Throckmorton said.

"They's more cattle in Kansas City and the man from Omaha will pay Dane to drive those up to Omaha too."

"My, my, that's interesting news, Randy. Who is this man from Omaha?"

"He said his name was Himmel. Otto, I think. He's rich, I think."

"Anything else?" Throckmorton asked.

"Well, I can't go back and work there no more. I got caught listenin' at the winder."

"I see. What are you going to do?"

"I don't know. I was hopin' you'd pay me extry for this information, Mr. Throck-morton."

Throckmorton leaned back in his chair. He put his hands together and made a steeple with his fingers. "How much do you think this information is worth, young man?"

"Oh, an extry ten or twenty dollars, maybe."

Throckmorton smiled condescendingly. He leaned forward and propped his elbows on his desk.

He picked up a piece of paper and wrote

56

a message on it with a sharpened pencil.

He held it out for Randy. "Take this to Miss Watson out there and she'll give you twenty dollars."

Randy stood up and took the paper from Throckmorton's hand. He put his hat back on and backed away from the desk. "Thank you, Mr. Throckmorton. You ever need me, I'll be takin' a job at the general store. I saw a sign there this mornin' sayin' they needed help."

"Good luck to you, Randy," he said. "And when you see Miss Watson, please tell her to come into my office when she's finished with your transaction."

"I sure will, sir. Thanks again."

Randy left the office and stopped at Linda Watson's desk. Throckmorton could see their shadows through the opaque pane. He stood up and walked to the window and looked out at the pigeon-spattered bench.

When Linda entered his office with her steno pad and pencil, Throckmorton turned away from the window.

"Yes, Mr. Throckmorton," she said. "Do you want to dictate a letter?"

"No, Miss Watson. I want you to tell the messenger to come in here."

"Bobby Fremont is on an errand at the moment," she said.

"As soon as he gets back, I wish to see him."

"Yes, sir," she said. "He should be back at any moment. I had to notarize some papers that were sent over by attorney Mel Bishop a while ago."

She had started to leave when Throckmorton called her back.

"Mel sent some papers over from his office?"

"Yes, sir. I'm a notary, you know."

"Yes, yes, I know. What were the papers?"

"Legal documents regarding a cattle sale involving Dane Kramer and a Mr. Otto Himmel. Mel sent a note over that the signatures were legitimate, so I notarized the documents."

"Do you remember the contents of those documents?" Throckmorton asked in a level tone that gave no indication of his extreme interest in the documents she notarized.

"There was to be a cash advance on a herd of cattle, with the balance due in Omaha, plus a provision for Mr. Kramer to pick up an additional herd in Kansas City for delivery to the Himmel stock pens in Omaha, Nebraska."

"Very well, Miss Watson. Do you recall the amount of the advance and the cash due on delivery?"

"I believe there was one thousand payable in advance, with an additional five hundred to be paid by a bank draft in Kansas City."

"What about the price of the cattle?"

"I don't recall the amount per head, Mr. Throckmorton, but I believe it was something like fifteen dollars a head for Mr. Kramer's cattle and a smaller sum, two or three dollars, for the herd he is to pick up in Kansas City. I'm sorry I can't remember every detail. Mel wanted the documents back right away and Bobby was standing by my desk waiting to run them back to Mel's office."

"Very well, Miss Watson. Thank you. Please send the messenger in as soon as he returns."

"I will," she said, and left the office, closing the door behind her.

Throckmorton sat down behind his desk and took a blank sheet of paper from his drawer and began to write down figures. He wrote down three thousand and multiplied it by fifteen. Then he tore the paper into small pieces and threw them in the wastebasket under his desk. He frowned as he stared at the opaque glass in the door as if waiting for shadows to appear beyond it.

"The bastard can pay off his mortgage and then some," he said to himself. "He's slipping through my fingers like a trout on the end of my line."

Several minutes later, Linda opened the door to Throckmorton's office and peeked in. "Bobby's back, Mr. Throckmorton. Should I send him in?"

"By all means, Miss Watson."

She nodded and a moment later a young man dressed in a dark shirt and a messenger's billed cap entered Throckmorton's office.

"You wanted to see me, sir?" Bobby asked.

"Yes. Don't sit down. This won't take long, and it must remain a confidence between us, you understand?"

"Yes, sir, I understand."

"I want you to run over to the Prairie Dog Boarding house and find a Mr. Concho Larabee. Do you know the place?"

"Yes, sir, it's right next to the Prairie Dog Saloon."

"Do you know Mr. Larabee?"

"I don't know him, but I know what he looks like. I've seen him at the saloon on Saturday nights when I go there to play cards."

"Fine. It's urgent. Bring him back with you if necessary. Tell him . . . tell him just to hurry, will you?"

"Right away, sir," Bobby said, and then

left the office.

The door slammed shut.

Throckmorton opened one of the bottom drawers of his desk and took out a small metal strongbox. He reached in his pocket and brought forth a ring of keys. He separated a small one from the bunch and inserted it into the lock of the strongbox, turned it, and opened the lid.

There was a stack of large greenbacks inside the box. Throckmorton leafed through them and took out a crisp new hundred-dollar bill. Then he closed the box, relocked it, and put it back in the drawer.

He laid the hundred-dollar bill on his desk and patted it.

"Now, Dane Kramer," he murmured to himself, "we'll see how far you get with your herd of cattle."

He reached over to a humidor on his desk and extracted a cigar. It had been rolled in Havana and shipped overland by freight at his request, He took out a small pocketknife and sawed off the end. Then he stuck it in his mouth, opened a box of lucifers, and struck a match on the sandpapered side of the box. He lit the cigar and blew a perfect smoke ring after he drew on it. He watched the ring quaver and swirl with blue smoke and smiled as he took another drag on the stogie.

He looked down at the bill on his desk.

"Money," he said to himself, "that's what makes the world go round, and this should get the ball rolling."

He filled his office with smoke and the scent of dried tobacco and Spanish fingers that lingered on the leaves like dried sweat.

CHAPTER 7

Concho Larabee was a gunfighter. He was also a drifter who sometimes worked on a ranch, or robbed wayfarers or drunks. He was good with his fists and adept with knife and gun. He sought out small prairie towns where he could both blend in and stand out as somebody to be reckoned with. He used intimidation like a weapon. He was fast on the draw and he could cut a man to ribbons with that big bowie knife he carried on his right hip.

He drank in the Prairie Dog Saloon because he was out of work and looking for any unsuspecting pilgrim he could beat at cards or rob come nightfall. He drank warm beer and looked at the sad faces of men who sat at the bar or at tables. He hadn't done another job for Throckmorton in nearly a month when he had run a sodbuster off a piece of land Throckmorton had wanted. That was about all he had done of late, scare off poor folks who couldn't keep up with their mortgages or were on land that Earl wanted to own.

A man pushed open the batwing doors of the saloon and walked bowlegged up to Larabee. He too was wearing a pistol slung low on his gun belt so that he could just slide his hand over and draw the weapon without having to kink up his arm. He was mindful that most lawmen wore their pistols high on their gun belts so that they had to lift their arm to draw. That made them a mite slower and gave him and men like him a distinct advantage in a gunfight.

"Mornin', Concho," the man said. "You wettin' your whistle kinda early, ain't you?"

"Couldn't sleep. Your snoring kept me awake in the next room, Lem."

"Well, tit for damned tat, Conch. Your bedsprings on Saturday night keep me awake. You ought to put some oil on 'em when you bed a glitter gal."

"Pull up a stool, Lem, and I'll buy you a glass of suds. That might make you keep your trap shut."

"I'll have a shot of rye, Concho." Lemuel Norton pulled out a stool and sat down. "I come to tell you they's a feller from the Prairie come to the hotel askin' for you. Some kind of messenger boy."

Concho looked around and at the still-quavering batwing doors. "Well, where is he?"

"I sent him on back," Lem said.

"Hell, that was right kind of you, Lem. He might have put money in my pocket."

"I got the message from the lad before I sent him packin'."

The bartender, one Walt Cleary, sauntered over, a bar towel in his hands. He looked half-asleep. "Lem, you want somethin' to drink, or are you just warmin' up one of my stools for a payin' customer?"

"Bring him a rye, Walt," Concho said. "And put a chili pepper in it."

"We're all out of chili peppers," Walt said. "How's about me droppin' some rat shit in it for extry flavor?"

"Hey, I don't need no food, Walt. Just some good old rye whiskey to get my eyes open all the way."

"Two bits, Concho," Walt said.

"I want four fingers, not a teaspoonful," Lem said.

"Four bits, then," Walt said. He brought a large shot glass and a bottle of house rye and poured it into the glass, filling it to a quarter inch just below the rim. He was a good barkeep.

Concho plunked a fifty-cent piece onto

the bar and Walt wiped it up with his free hand and carried it to the register in the middle of the back bar with its painted lady sprawled on a bearskin rug half-naked, with alluring eyes and a scrap of a scarf over her loins.

"Well, Lem, you goin' to tell me what Messenger Boy wanted, or are you just agoin' to sit there and swill your whiskey like a damned tarbaby?"

Lem lifted his glass in a silent toast to his friend, then drank half of it in one gulp. "Messenger Boy said you was to skedaddle over to the bank right away. Said Throck-morton wanted to see you pronto."

"That's money in my pocket, Lem. Maybe yours too."

"That's what I figured, which was why I come over to cadge a mornin' drink from you. I'm damned near broke after our last job for Throck."

Concho drained his beer and slid his stool away from the bar. He nodded to Walt and started to leave.

"Don't go too far, Lem. If Earl's in a hurry, he must have something real big for me to do."

"I'll be either here or back at the hotel," Lem said. "Got another four bits? I might have another shot of rye."

"Tell Walt to put it on your tab," Concho said.

"I don't have no tab," Lem said.

"Tell him you'll wash dishes."

Lem made a sound of disgust and Concho walked out of the saloon. In moments, he was at the bank. He walked straight over to Miss Watson's desk. He leaned over and admired her trim body, the tight bodice covering her firm breasts. Linda was nearing thirty and still unmarried, but had rebuffed Concho more than once when he asked her to supper or a pie social.

"Earl sent for me," he said.

"I know, Concho. He said to send you right in when you arrived."

She leaned back away from the scent of his breath and he stood up to his full six feet two inches and hitched his belt.

"Well, I'll just go right on in, then," he said.

"Please knock first, Mr. Larabee," she said.

"What happened to Concho?" he asked.

"It was just a slip of the tongue, Mr. Larabee. I forgot my manners."

"If you had a little less manners and more gumption, you'd let me take you dancin' once in a while."

"Thank you for the invitation," she said.

67

"Mr. Throckmorton is waiting."

Concho walked to the door with Throckmorton's name on it and rapped loudly.

"Come in," Throckmorton called.

Concho opened the door and stepped inside Throckmorton's office. He stood there for a moment until his eyes adjusted to the change of light.

"You sent for me, Earl?" he said.

"Take a chair, Concho. I have something for you."

Concho walked to the desk and sat down in one of the chairs.

Throckmorton picked up the hundred-dollar bill and held it between both hands.

"What's that?" Concho asked.

"Earnest money, Concho. Earnest on my part, that is. I have a job for you. A very big job this time and there's nine more of these if you take it on."

Concho rose from his chair and reached for the hundred-dollar bill.

Throckmorton snatched it away, out of Concho's reach. "Not so fast, Concho. First, listen to what I have to say and then if you agree to do the job, I'll give it to you. And a lot more when you start the task I have for you."

"A lot more?"

"Yes. This is a big job and you'll need

68

plenty of help."

"What's the job?" Concho asked as he sat back down.

Throckmorton looked past him to the plaque that hung high over his door. He looked at that plaque often during each day.

The plaque in a wooden frame read LAND IS THE BASIS OF ALL WEALTH.

CHAPTER 8

Throckmorton shifted his glance from the saying over his door and to Concho.

"Concho," he said. "I want you to stop a cattle drive."

It took a moment or two for Concho to react to the statement. "Stop what?"

"Dane Kramer plans to drive three thousand head of cattle up to Omaha. Probably take him a week or so to get his crew ready, make the gather, and head out. I don't want it to happen anywhere around here, so you'll have to follow the herd and find a place to put out his lamp, run off his drovers, or stampede the cows back to their home range."

"Shit, Earl, that's a damned job for an army."

Throckmorton waved the hundred-dollar bill in front of his face as if were swatting at an insect. "Look, Concho, you know cattle and you know Nebraska. Don't you hail from there?"

"Wahoo. But it ain't much of a town and I ain't been back in a long while."

"I've been studying the map and you have about four hundred and ninety miles to turn back that herd. Likely, Kramer will go up along the Missouri so he's got plenty of prairie grass and water. And he has to stop off in Kansas City to pick up nearly another nine hundred head or so. If you have good men, you can do what I ask."

"You want Circle K bad, don't you, Earl?"

"Yes. Kramer has some ten thousand acres of land and he's planted it in good grass. And he has around five thousand head of cattle at last count, plus a bunch of calves dropped recently."

"Grass ain't growed tall enough for a cattle drive just now."

"It's already started and the rains will make the grass grow fast. Another week or so and he'll have plenty of fodder for those cattle."

"I reckon," Concho said, without enthusiasm.

"Study his actions out at the ranch. Don't let him see you or your men. You'll know when he's ready. Study the map I'm going to give you and pick some places where you can bushwhack Kramer and his hands. Take

71

your time and strike when you think you've got him where you want him."

"From what I hear, Kramer's a tough chunk of leather."

"Oh, he's good with a gun and he fought in the war. But he was just a kid then."

"Kids grow up," Concho said.

"You can handle him. You're tough as a boot yourself."

"It's gonna cost you dear, Earl. The men I get to help on this job don't come cheap."

"I know, Concho. You just tell me how many men you will need and I'll take care of the payroll."

Throckmorton leaned back in his leather baronial chair and clasped his hands behind his neck. His piglike eyes narrowed as if he had been injected with a brain-numbing drug, and his facial features tightened over his skull so that he wore a mask Concho had never seen on him before.

"I was an orphan, Concho. Not just an orphan. I was abandoned by my mother, who never wanted me, never cared for me. My father owned a hardscrabble farm in Pennsylvania. He was left with five of us and we all had to work the farm. After my mother left us, he started trying to sell off his land because the farm wasn't paying for itself. We were all little kids and we worked until we dropped at night. One day, a banker, a constable, and another man came out and served my father with papers that said he no longer owned any of the land. The court put all of us in orphanages. I never saw my two sisters or my two brothers again, and I finally ran away and got a job selling newspapers in New York City.

"I saved my money," Throckmorton went on, "and when I heard about the West opening up, about the land rush out here, I packed up and came to Oklahoma."

"So, you was one of them Sooners yourself," Concho said.

"No, I wasn't that stupid. I watched the covered wagons and the homesteaders on horseback and mules all run out hither and thither to stake their claims. Then I followed after them and bought up cheap land around the Mission here. I built this bank and offered loans to hard-up people who needed cash to buy plows, mules, seed, and feed. I vowed that I wasn't going to end up like my father, Waylon Throckmorton, flat broke and deep in debt."

"Well, you did it, Earl. I got to hand it to you."

"Not quite. My father walked in one day and asked for a loan. He didn't recognize me, and he didn't even remember my name or the names of my brothers and sisters. He didn't have a dime and when I told him who I was, he turned around and walked out."

"Did he say anything?" Concho asked.

"Yes. He said that I and his other children had been the cause of him losing his farm. He said we hadn't worked hard enough and there were too many of us. He also said we were the reason our mother ran off with a drummer from North Carolina."

"What happened to your ma?" Concho asked.

"She killed herself, I found out. Had another child and her husband left her. So she hanged herself in a cheap hotel room and was buried in a potter's field somewhere."

"So, why do you want Kramer's ranch and his cattle?"

Throckmorton leaned forward in his chair. He unclasped his hands and looked at the plaque over the door before he set his gaze back on Larabee and huffed in a deep breath. "Because Dane's father, Thorvald Kramer, was the man who ran off with my mother. He never married her, but left her for another woman after she gave birth to another child. My mother not only took her own life, but she killed the child she had with Thor Kramer. He married a woman named Olga, who was rich and gave him the money to buy the Circle K. She died after the money ran out. Dane bought the ranch from Thor and came to me for a loan in 'seventy-six so that he could buy cattle in Texas."

"Dane had nothin' to do with your troubles, Earl."

"No, but his father did, and when he became the biggest landowner in this territory, I vowed that I would one day own the land he sold to his son."

"What happened to your pa?" Concho asked.

"He died in Virginia City while he was prospecting for gold in Alder Gulch. He had consumption and just strangled to death, from lung disease."

"How'd you find out?"

"A man came to me with a letter from my father, written just before he died."

"What did he say? Was he sorry for what he done to you and your kin?"

"No, he didn't say he was sorry. He just wrote and told me to hold on to the land no matter what. So, in a sense, he gave me that gift. I never worked land again, for myself or anyone else. Instead, I buy it up and rent it out. Let others break their backs like my father did and we children did. It's just the land I want."

"So, what will you do when you have all of Kramer's cattle and his land?"

"I'll sell the cattle in Texas or Kansas and divide the land up into smaller sections and lease them. I'll keep the ranch house and the acres around it for myself."

"That's a mighty big cud to chew," Concho said.

"I think big, Concho. Now, are you going to take on this job or not? If not, I can seek help for the task somewhere else. I have connections all over the territory."

Throckmorton picked up the hundred-dollar bill and held it out for Concho.

"I reckon me and some friends can tangle with Kramer, drive his herd back here in a month or so."

Concho stood up and snatched the bill from Throckmorton's hand. He folded it in half and slid it in a front pocket.

"Remember, Concho, you have to do all this far away from Shawnee Mission."

"I know. Get me a map and I'll study on it."

"When you get back with the cattle, I will have another job for you. That's dependent on your killing Dane Kramer of course, somewhere along the trail to Omaha."

"What's the job pay?" Concho asked.

76

"One thousand dollars."

Concho looked down at Throckmorton. He whistled. "What's the job?"

"I want you to kill Thorvald Kramer," he said.

"That old man? Hell, he ain't long for this world no-how."

"I want him to know why he's being killed when you do it. I want you to tell him my mother, Earlene Throckmorton, wants him dead."

Concho took in a deep breath. "Boy, you carry a grudge a long time, Earl, don't you?"

"A long time, Concho," Throckmorton said. "All the way to the grave."

CHAPTER 9

Paddy, Joe Eagle, and Dane looked at all the branding irons hanging on the stable wall of the tack room. Paddy took one down and examined it.

The brand was a crooked S that could be used to alter any number of brands. Joe took one down that was a half crescent. Dane picked out one that was a straight bar.

"This might work," Dane said. "Make an X with it."

"So many trail brands use an X," Paddy said. "Even regular cattle brands, like the XO down in Texas."

"So we have a Circle K and next to it a Bar X," Dane said.

Paddy looked closely at the iron in Dane's hand.

"Three burns would do it," he said. "Should work."

"So we go with a Bar X," Dane said. He pulled down three more running irons that had a bar on the hot end. "That do you?"

"Be fine, Dane," Paddy said. "I'll get right on it. Joe, you willin' to do either some brandin' or some ropin'?"

Joe nodded. "Me do both," he said.

Paddy slapped him on the back.

"One more thing, Paddy," Dane said. "The chuck wagon."

"What about it?"

"I want to ask Barney Gooch if the wagon can make the trip to Omaha. Tell him we can resupply along the way. I don't really want to haul an extra wagon. Be hard enough just to lug the chuck wagon over rough prairie."

"I'll ask him," Paddy said.

"Tell him he'll have to feed maybe a dozen hands three times a day. He'll meet us at our stopping points with a hot kettle and clean plates."

"Barney ain't gonna like it none," Paddy said. "He gripes about flies and skeeters and prairie dog holes, not to mention our appetites."

"Tell Barney I'll find him a helper," Dane said.

"You ain't gonna get no volunteers from among the hands," Paddy said.

He looked hard at Joe Eagle. Joe shook his head.

"See what I mean?" Paddy said.

"Well, you tell him that anyway. Likely he won't have a helper."

"He probably don't want one anyways," Paddy said. "Barney's what we used to call a loner. He's an ornery one at that."

"Barney good cook," Joe Eagle said.

Paddy snorted.

"Yeah, if you like rock-hard biscuits and thin gravy," Paddy said.

"Bear claws," Joe said.

They all laughed.

"Yeah," Dane said, "Barney's bear claws are world-famous, I reckon. I've seen hands from other ranches ride miles to bribe Barney into cooking up a batch of bear claws."

"Hmmm," Joe murmured, and rubbed his belly, smacked his lips.

"Let's ride out, then, and start the gather," Paddy said to Joe.

He divided up the running irons and gave two to Joe and kept two for himself.

"I'll ride out to see you in a day or two," Dane said.

"I'm going to run the trail herd down to the East Ninety. Got plenty of chutes and small corrals, and the grass ain't been touched."

"Good idea," Dane said. "Land's free of a

lot of brush and no prairie dog towns."

"We call that Ninety Sunnyland," Paddy said. "Wide-open prairie, barely a tree on the section."

"Yeah, I know," Dane said. "We call it that too."

Dane watched them ride off. It would take them a week or more to make the gather from several of his pastures. He trusted Paddy to assemble the biggest and best cattle for the long drive north. He wished he were out there with them, but he had to wait out the day for Otto Himmel to return from town with the notarized documents.

He did not have long to wait. He saw the rider break the horizon line and become gradually larger.

When Himmel got close, Dane saw that the man had changed clothes. He was now wearing a fringed buckskin jacket and he saw a yellow slicker covering his bedroll behind the cantle. He noticed too a rifle sticking out of a scabbard and a holster just below the hem of his buckskin shirt. He wore sturdy duck pants, coal black, and a wide-brimmed Stetson, which shaded his face.

His respect for Himmel raised itself several notches.

"Howdy, Otto," Dane said when the

Omaha man rode up. "Got the papers?"

"Yes, all notarized." Himmel swung down out of the saddle and untied his satchel.

The two walked toward the house after Himmel wrapped the reins around a long hitch rail out front.

"Saw that boy Randy when I rode into town," he said.

"That must have been a big thrill, Otto."

"He was coming out of the Prairie Land Bank. Walked over to the general store. I spoke to him."

Dane stopped walking. Himmel halted beside him.

"You did? What did you say to him?"

Otto looked down at Dane with a mischievous grin on his face. "I asked him if he'd had a good talk with Throckmorton at the bank."

Dane jerked his head back in surprise.

"He did what you just did, Dane. He jerked his head back as if he'd been struck by a lightning bolt."

"You caught him by surprise, then."

"I'll say. The look of shock on his face was something to see."

"Did he admit to anything about Throckmorton?" Dane asked.

"He mumbled something, but I couldn't understand what he said."

"So that was it," Dane said.

"Before I let him go, I asked him if he had found his quarter."

"And?"

"He looked at me as if I'd mentioned sleeping with his mother and shook his head. Then he ran off toward the general store and I saw him go in."

"I think he worked there once. Before he became a spy for Throckmorton."

Himmel laughed.

The two entered the house and Himmel spread all the notarized papers on the desk.

Thor had fallen asleep in his chair and did not stir. The men spoke in whispers to keep from arousing him.

"I got a change to make," Dane said. "The trail brand won't be a Box D, but a Bar X. Can we change it?"

"Yes, make the changes and write your initials next to them and I'll add mine."

Dane read the papers and made the changes. Himmel countersigned the changes.

"Here's a copy for you, Dane," Himmel said. "And I'll have a copy to take with me. Carry it along in your kit in case anyone wonders what you're up to with that many cattle. And I'm giving you two bank drafts. One is for you to cash in Kansas City. The other is for the feedlot charges. I left the amount blank and you can fill it in when you get the bill."

"All right," Dane said. He put the papers together and the bank drafts on top."

"I'll be on my way, then. I'll stop off in Kansas City to tell my man there that you'll pick up those nine hundred head in a month or so."

"I'll walk out with you. Looks like you got a mighty fine roan there."

"He's long-legged and got a good deep chest. I call him Raspberry."

"The gelding's a strawberry roan," Dane said as the two walked out of the house and toward the hitch rail.

"I didn't like the straw part. For short, I call the horse Razz."

"Makes sense," Dane said.

The two men shook hands. Himmel tied his satchel with thongs dangling from mid-saddle and stepped into a stirrup.

"See you in Omaha," he said as he looked down at Dane.

"Lookin' forward to it, Otto," Dane said.

He watched the big man ride off. He looked like a mountain man, a fur trapper, in his buckskin shirt. All that was lacking was a fox or coonskin hat.

Dane liked Otto Himmel. The man knew

where to find good cattle and size up a man to make the long drive. He gave him a lot of credit for that. He was sure that Otto had looked over his herd before riding to the ranch house. He was smart, not too talkative, and knew where to go to get things done. Otto was the kind of man Dane admired. Honest and true, but sharp and experienced in business. He hoped the drive would open up a steady market for his beef, either in Omaha or in Kansas City.

He walked back into the house.

His father was just waking up. The old man rubbed his eyes and looked at his son.

"I heard some of it," Thor said. "So, Otto's on his way, and you got the contracts."

"That's about the size of it," Dane said.

"When you hit the trail, son, you better have an extry man or two watchin' for bushwhackers and Injuns."

"I'm takin' drovers with me, not gunfighters," he said.

"A gunfighter or two wouldn't hurt none. I don't trust Throckmorton when he finds out you're drivin' cattle to market."

"I think he already knows," Dane said. "Otto ran into the kid comin' out of the bank."

"Randy?"

"Yeah. He ain't lookin' for his two bits no

85

more. He likely told Throckmorton how many head we were driving and where we were takin' them."

"Throckmorton, for all his puny size and greedy appetite for land, is a dangerous hombre, Dane."

"He can't do much settin' behind that big old desk of his in the bank."

"No, maybe not, but he knows gunslingers in town and my hunch he's used some of 'em to grab up land from sodbusters. Ora Lee tells me all the stories she hears in town."

"Nothing's ever been proved, Pa."

"He's slick too."

"How come you know so much about Throckmorton? You never talk about him much."

"Him and me go back a long ways, son. I don't like to talk about it too much because I'm ashamed of some of the things I've done when I was a young sprout."

"You knew Throckmorton before he came to Shawnee Mission?"

"I knowed who he was. I didn't know him. But he was on my back trail and I think he wants this ranch as much as he wants to see me suffer."

"You never said anything like this before."

"Didn't want to drag you into my little

pile of troubles," Thor said.

"Did it involve my mother?"

"No. Scarlet knew nothing about any of this. Someday, maybe soon, I'll tell you all about it. You get your drive goin' and when you come back from Omaha and pay off the mortgage, I'll tell you the whole ugly story."

"You're a man of many secrets, Pa," Dane said, fixing his father with a hard, shrewd look.

"Every man has his secrets, Dane. And women have even more of 'em."

Dane was left to chew on that statement while he went to the desk and riffled through the papers Himmel had left. Among them was a map that showed the route up the Missouri to Omaha. It was hand-drawn and must have been the way Otto had traveled to get to the Circle K.

The man was thorough too, Dane thought. The map was well drawn and showed watering holes, grasslands, and barren places to avoid. All of the towns and places were written in crisp block letters with a lead pencil.

Dane sucked in a deep breath.

It was a long way to Omaha, and Otto had written down distances as if he knew there would be a drive right through wild, empty land fraught with many perils, including rustlers and Indian renegades.

The task seemed daunting at that moment, especially since his father had indicated he had some kind of history involving Throckmorton.

When he thought back, he remembered that his father had tried to stop him from going to Throckmorton to borrow money and sign mortgage papers for the Circle K. He had put up quite a fuss, in fact.

Now, he thought, it was clear why his father had been so against his becoming beholden to Throckmorton.

But the exact reasons were still a mystery, locked somewhere in that eighty-five-year-old mind of Thor's.

Dane looked over his shoulder.

His father had gone back to sleep and he could hear the patter of Ora Lee's feet out in the kitchen where she was probably preparing their noon meal.

And Dane wasn't the least bit hungry.

CHAPTER 10

Paddy took charge. As soon as he and Joe Eagle rode up on the branding fires, he began to issue orders to the men who were finishing up and returning the newborn calves to their mothers.

"Donny," he said to Peterson, "I want you to go over to the Sunnyland range and haul hay in there and fill those ricks. Get Cal Ferris to help you. Check all the corrals and gates. We'll be drivin' cattle in there next week. And mosey on over to the hundred-acre spread and check the graze. Hop to it."

Donny saddled up and rode off to complete his assignment.

"Jim," Paddy told Recknor, "go get us a half dozen cuttin' horses from the home pasture and bring back Steve Atkins and Chub Toomey off the North Grand. Tell 'em to get their thumbs out of their butts and help you round up the best cutters."

"Damn, Paddy, that's a good two-hour

ride to the North Grand."

"Get movin'."

Then he spoke to Joe Eagle. "Mosey on over to the chuck wagon with me, Joe. We got to ask Gooch if he can make the trip in that rickety old wagon of his."

"You got tents to strike too," Joe said as he looked at the canvas shelters that housed the hands while they were making the gather and branding calves.

"Least of my worries. We'll bunk out here while we cut out the good cows and drive 'em to the Sunnyland spread."

"Many cattle. Small pasture," Joe said.

"When we finish the tally, we'll take the trail herd over to the Two Grand and I'll give out assignments to the hands. Can you get them Mexes before then?"

"Me get," Joe said.

The two rode over a hump in the land where there were more tents and a lean-to built by the cook, Barney Gooch. Gooch was cussing and ragging at his mule, Possum, a flea-bitten, sway-backed animal that stood like a statue while Gooch was trying to push him backward so that he could harness him. He had packed up all his cooking irons and kettles, drenched his fire, and covered the pit with dirt.

"Hey, Barney," Paddy said as they rode

up. "You feed Possum too much sugar and not enough quirt."

"Paddy, you damned bowlegged Mick, wouldn't know a mule from a jackass."

"What's the difference?" Paddy asked as he swung out of the saddle. Joe Eagle dismounted as well, and walked over to the mule's head and stroked his face.

Paddy and Barney squared off. Barney's hair leaked out from under his hat brim in unruly strands and spikes. When he spoke, his bushy mustache looked like a small burrowing animal streaked with yellowish stains from eggs and specks of flour dust. He was fat enough so that his potbelly spilled over his belt, and his trousers, grimy and stained, were tucked into stovepipe boots that had long since lost their shine.

"Barney, can that wagon of yours go another thousand miles?" Paddy looked at the wagon, which was all battened up as if waiting for another rainstorm.

"With some greasin' and oilin' she can do twice that with nary a squeak," Barney said. "Why? We goin' somewhere?"

"Omaha," Paddy said.

"Omaha, Texas?"

"Nebraska," Paddy replied.

"Land o' Goshen, land of grasshoppers. That's a fur piece."

91

"Five hunnert miles right up the old Missouri," Paddy said.

The mule backed up and Joe put him deftly in harness. He patted Possum on the withers and stroked his neck. The mule brayed in contentment.

"What, a couple hunnert head?" Gooch asked, blowing a strand of graying hair away from his mouth.

"Three thousand head and better," O'Riley said. He watched Gooch's face for his reaction.

"Hell, you're gonna need half a hunnert men to drive that many head," Barney said.

"Plus, we're pickin' up another nine hundred head in Kansas City," Paddy said.

Gooch's face began to purple. His neck swelled and his mustache wriggled over his pudgy lips.

"We'll need two more wagons just for staples," Barney said. "And I ain't cookin' for no fifty-odd hands."

"We're going to try and make it with, at most, a dozen hands."

"Hell, you got to take a remuda. That's another couple of hands. You got long flanks and a man or two ridin' point, a couple more ridin' drag, and if the herd ever spooks, you'll have cows scattered from hell to breakfast."

"Dane figures on makin' ten miles a day. A slow, quiet drive and we'll bunch 'em all up at nightfall."

Barney stamped one of his boots on the soggy ground. Water spurted from the lumps of bog.

"I 'member a drive up to Montana oncet when I was a young sprout," Barney said. "Better'n fifteen hunnert head and just a half dozen drovers and one wrangler. It was pure hell, over snowy mountain passes, crossin' ragin' rivers and fightin' off wolves and rattlesnakes. We lost three hunnert head before we reached the Yellowstone and all the men were ready to kill each other."

"It won't be that way, Barney," Paddy said. "You in or out?"

"Let me study on it for a minute or two, will you, Paddy?"

Paddy walked around the wagon and then stood beside Joe, who was still soothing the mule with his hands and voice.

"Wagon needs some paint slathered on it," Paddy said.

Joe just grunted.

Finally Barney turned around and walked over to where Joe and Paddy were standing.

"I'll paint the damned wagon," he told Paddy. "A bright red. A fire engine red."

"A schoolhouse red, maybe," Paddy said.

Barney didn't laugh.

"Barn red," he said, "and I'll make the trip if there's places where I can restock."

"There will be, Barney. Dane's a planner."

"Dane ain't never driv a herd that far before," Barney said. "And never that many head of cattle."

"There's a first time for everything," Paddy said.

"And maybe a last."

Paddy blinked and fixed his glance on Barney's furry mustache. It rippled as if ready to jump off his mouth and dig a hole in the ground so that it could disappear into the earth.

"Take the wagon over to the Sunnyland spread, Barney," Paddy told him. "I'll send a wagon with whatever you need for the next two weeks. You got to cook for eight or ten men while they spank on trail brands."

"Three thousand head ain't gonna fit in that ninety acres."

"No, that's just for brandin'. We'll run 'em all over on the Two Grand and make the drive from there."

"Still goin' to be crowded as the devil."

"You let me worry about that, Barney. Now give me a list of the grub you're gonna need for the next coupla weeks and I'll take care of it."

"I'm out of chewin' terbaccky, just about," Barney said.

"Make out your list. Joe and I have things to do."

"All right. Gimme a minute."

Barney walked to the wagon and fished around under his seat until he found a tablet and a stub of a pencil. As Joe and Paddy watched, he wrote down what he needed from town. It took up three pages because Barney wrote big block letters for every item. He tore off the pages and handed them to Paddy.

Paddy glanced at just one page of the list. He trusted Barney, who could figure what every hand needed to keep his stomach full and not waste any grub.

"In the meantime, Barney," Paddy said as he folded the papers and tucked them into one of his shirt pockets, "you figger out what you'll need when we pull out on the drive. Figger two weeks of grub for a dozen hands."

"Gonna be a mite heavy on the wagon springs," Barney said.

"We'll carry some extra wheels, spokes and such."

"You're too kind, Paddy. Now get on outta here so's me and Possum can haul our asses over to the Sunnyland."

"See you, Barney," Paddy said as he grabbed up his reins.

"Good mule," Joe said, and walked to his horse. "Possum good."

"Why, thank you, Joe," Barney said. "You got more sense than most folks around here."

Paddy and Joe rode back to the branding camp.

"I'll need those Mexes in about a week, Joe. Can you bring 'em out to the gather?"

"Me do," Joe said.

Paddy looked over the surrounding land. There were cattle scattered in all directions. They were grazing on short grass and moving along slowly, each following a leader in separate bunches. Cows with calves were ambling over the soggy ground, snatching up the young shoots. The calves, some of them, were punching their mothers' dugs with their muzzles and drawing milk from their teats. He figured there were at least four thousand head in full view, but not all of them would be making the trail drive.

Soon, he knew, they would all start cutting out the cattle and burning trail brands into their hides before driving them over to Sunnyland. It would be a long and brutal task under a blazing sun with heavy cattle fighting to avoid the rope and the branding irons. They would have to separate the herd bulls from the steers and the mothers with calves.

"What are you thinkin', Joe?" Paddy asked when they had dismounted and were laying out the running irons.

"Me think we got big job. Much work."

"You got that right, Joe. But the work will go well because I'm an organizer and so is Dane. You like work?"

"Me like work."

"I'll see to it that you get plenty. And maybe tonight or tomorrow you can look up those Mexes and bring 'em out."

"Me do," Joe said.

Paddy smacked his lips in satisfaction.

"Meantime," he said to Joe, "let's get some fires started and cut out a few head to see how quick it goes with these running irons."

Joe grinned.

Then the two men began piling up kindling and stacking wood from the woodpile next to the shallow stone pits.

"We shoulda got us a sandwich from Barney," Paddy said. "I'm right hungry."

"Me got grub in saddlebags," Joe said.

"Sandwiches?"

"Rabbit," Joe said. "Me kill. Me cook. Good meat."

Paddy's stomach roiled with both hunger and a tinge of revulsion. He knew that Joe Eagle hunted every chance he could get and took quail, rabbit, and perhaps other animals, cooked them and dried them in the sun for gnawing when he was hungry.

He braced himself for Joe's solution to his hunger and slipped his canteen from his saddle horn. If he chewed fast and swallowed with water, maybe he wouldn't notice the sand and the dirt or the gamy taste of wild rabbit.

In the meantime, he thought, Joe Eagle was a good man to ride the river with any old time.

Chapter 11

The trip into the town of Shawnee Mission on the buckboard was a jouncy five miles. Joe Eagle handled the reins while Dane sat next to him trying to figure expenditures and other logistical problems on a notepad. Their horses were tied to the wagon with rope and were wise enough to flank the wheels that kicked up dust and rocks.

Joe pulled up behind Christianson's Mercantile & General Store. He set the brake when he was parallel to the loading dock. He wrapped the reins around the brake handle and stepped down as Dane left his seat and touched down on the opposite side. Both men lifted saddles from the bed of the buckboard and spread the saddle blankets over their horses' backs.

"I hope you can get those two Mexicans to make the drive with us, Joe," Dane said as he swung his saddle up and settled it on the blanket.

"Me do," Joe said.

"Take your time. I've got to go to the bank and see about getting another cook and chuck wagon."

"You get two chuck wagons?" Joe asked.

"Yeah, I have an idea on how we're going to drive that many cattle up to Nebraska."

"Good luck," Joe said.

Dane left his horse tied to the wagon and climbed the steps up to the ramp. He went in through the back double doors, through a large storeroom, and into the store proper.

There were three men and a half dozen women walking through the aisles with wicker baskets, selecting foodstuffs and other items from the shelves and counters.

Fred Christianson walked from behind the counter and met Dane as he passed.

He wore a small torn apron, a faded work shirt, and lace-up shoes. He was a lean, skeletal man with mutton-chop sideburns and hair turning gray that was kept in place by a green cap.

"Well, well, Mr. Kramer, what brings you to town so early of a morning? And into my store?"

"Got a list of things we need out at the ranch," Dane said. He handed the storekeeper a sheet of paper with numbers and names of items he needed.

"Looks as if we can fill these. Wagon out back?"

"Yes, Fred. I'll be back in the afternoon to pay my bill."

"That will be fine, Mr. Kramer."

"Know where I can find a camp cook?"

Christianson bowed his head slightly and scratched a spot behind his left ear.

"Come to think of it, I do," he said. "Do you know Len Crowell? Has a small ranch northeast of the settlement."

"Yes, I do know Len," Dane said. "He had a small spread he started about five years ago. Was trying to crossbreed Herefords and black Angus, last I heard."

"That's him. Don't know if he was able to mix the two breeds, but he thought he had a sale up in Abilene, Kansas. Small herd, but good price per head."

"And what happened?" Dane asked.

"Apaches jumped him on the Brazos and then a twister wiped out his herd and scattered what wasn't killed outright."

"He can start over, I reckon," Dane said.

Christianson shook his head. "Bank had a mortgage on his property. Foreclosed a week ago. Len's got a month to clear out and he's selling everything he owns, the whole kit and caboodle, I hear."

"So, he has a chuck wagon, you say?"

"Yep. He was in here yesterday askin' if I wanted to buy it. Got him a cook too, a man what was on the drive with him over the winter."

"White man?"

"Chinese, I think. Wong Loo, or Wong Ling, something like that."

"You didn't buy his wagon?"

"Nope. No use for it. He built it last summer, so it's like new. Storms didn't hurt it none."

"I'll ride out and talk to Len."

"Ain't but a few miles to his spread. Or what used to be his spread."

"Throckmorton held the mortgage?"

"A thousand dollars, I heard, and there's something else that's funny about that drive Len made."

"Oh, what's that?" Dane asked.

"Len thinks there was Apaches on the Brazos, but he thought there were white men a-leadin' them."

"Hmm. That's strange," Dane said.

"He thinks he recognized a couple of the white men, Mr. Kramer. Said he's pretty sure he'd seen them both at the Prairie Dog Saloon."

"He know who they were?"

"He thinks one of 'em's named Concho," Christianson said. "Other'n might have been Lemuel Norton. Both of 'em have been in here to buy liquor and tobacco."

"Can he prove it?" Dane asked.

"He don't want to, near as I can figure. He's plumb scared to death of those two gunslingers. I told him he was smart to just keep it under his hat."

"Any connection between this Concho and Norton?"

"Not that I know of. But I've seen Concho go into the bank now and again. His last name's Larabee and he's one tough citizen, I hear."

"I guess I never ran into him or Norton," Dane said.

"Consider yourself lucky. I hear things in this store, I truly do. And what I heard about those two is not good. Constable runs off about them every now and then but can't prove anything."

"Like what?"

"Robbery. Strong-arm stuff. Bar fights."

"Thanks, Fred. I'll see you later today. I want to talk to Len about his cook and chuck wagon before he finds a buyer."

"Good luck," Christianson said.

Dane walked out to the dock and descended the steps to his wagon. He untied his horse and lifted himself into the saddle.

He headed for the bank to see Throckmorton.

Throckmorton was in his office when Miss Watson ushered him in after announcing him to her boss.

"Ah, Mr. Kramer," Throckmorton said without rising from his chair. "What brings you into town?"

"I'm paying on my mortgage, Mr. Throckmorton."

"How much?"

"Three hundred. That leaves another thousand and three hundred due in September."

"I don't recollect rightly. Sit down, sit down."

Dane pulled some folded bills from his pocket and laid them on Throckmorton's desk.

Throckmorton reached over and picked up the bills. He counted them and his lips moved as he murmured the denominations to himself. "Yes, that's three hundred all right."

"I want a receipt," Dane said.

"Of course, of course. I'll have Miss Watson give you one before you leave."

"I'd be obliged," Dane said.

"Now, will you be able to meet your obligation by September?"

"Yes, I believe so."

"And how will you do that, Mr. Kramer? I've carried you before a time or two."

"I think you know damned well how I intend to pay off my debt to you, Mr. Throckmorton. I think you hired Randy Bowman to spy on me."

"I don't know what you're talking about, Kramer."

Dane noticed there was no "mister" this time when Throckmorton used his name.

"It's not important," he said. "What's done is done. But I'll give you fair warning, Throckmorton. If you interfere with my cattle drive in any way, if you send Indians after me or gunmen, I'll find out. And when I do, I'll come back all right and pay you in hot lead."

"Is that a threat, Kramer?"

"Take it any way you like, Throckmorton. Warning or threat."

"You're mighty uppity for a sodbuster, Kramer."

"I ain't no sodbuster, Throckmorton. I'm a cattleman and if you had any brains, you'd realize that cattle is the real wealth of this world."

"That's where you're mistaken, Kramer. Land is the basis of all wealth."

"Well, the two go together in this country. Someday we'll rival Texas with the beef we raise in these parts."

"You're a dreamer, Kramer. Cattle must be tended. They must be fed and driven to market. Then they must be butchered and packed and sold to restaurants in the East. You're just one small part of a very long chain. And the chain is anchored in the lands. That's where real wealth resides."

"I'll have that receipt now," Dane said.

Throckmorton tapped a small bell on his desk. The door opened and Miss Watson peered in.

"Yes, Mr. Throckmorton?" she said.

"Please give Mr. Kramer a receipt for three hundred dollars and see that his payment is entered in the ledger."

"Yes, sir," she said. "If you'll come with me, Mr. Kramer, I'll write out a receipt."

Dane looked up before he left Throckmorton's office. He saw the sign, which he had never noticed before. But Throckmorton had been eyeing it during their talk.

LAND IS THE BASIS OF ALL WEALTH, it read.

He turned before he left the office.

"Land may be the basis of all wealth, Throckmorton, but in my book, cattle is king. And one day, we'll run all over you and your damned bank."

Throckmorton snorted but did not retort.

Dane slammed the door on him and walked to Miss Watson's desk.

"How can you work for a man like that?" he asked.

"Mr. Kramer, please."

"He's a greedy tyrant," Dane said.

She sat down and took a book of receipts with carbon paper from her desk drawer. She wrote hurriedly, bearing down on the pen so that the carbon would leave its impressions.

"There you are, Mr. Kramer," she said as she handed him his receipt. "I hope you find our services satisfactory."

"You must go home at night and throw plates at the wall, Miss Watson," he said.

Linda Watson did not reply, but she bit her lip and bowed her head.

Dane got the impression that she was holding a lot of anger inside and might be afraid of losing her job.

He walked out of the bank with the folded receipt consigned to a shirt pocket.

When he looked over at Christianson's store, he saw Randy sweeping the dirt in front of the store. Randy looked up and saw him.

Then the young man turned away and showed Dane his back.

How far, Dane wondered, *does Throck-*

morton's hand reach? No telling.

He mounted up and rode out of the little village, headed for Len Crowell's spread. He was filled with a sadness that a tyrant like Throckmorton would take away a man's livelihood without any consideration or understanding. He had seen others divested of their lands because they were short of money or had fallen on bad times.

Throckmorton, he decided, was a big fat spider sitting on a web that stretched in a wide circle around his bank. The minute there was something stuck to one of the strands, he pounced.

It was an ugly image, but he knew it was an accurate one.

He knew that from that moment on, he had to be on guard.

Throckmorton was just waiting to pounce.

CHAPTER 12

Leonard Crowell carried a pile of wool blankets out of the house and dropped them into a small wagon that stood next to the water pump. He looked up to see a rider pass under the archway he had built to indicate the entrance to his ranch. The rustic Lazy L seemed to droop in sadness as he saw the rider look up at what used to be the emblem of his ranch.

Nearby was Chang Wu Ling, the Chinese cook he had hired out of Muskogee before he made the fall drive the year before.

"Somebody come," Wu said as he finished oiling a wheel on the chuck wagon.

"I see him."

"Bank man?"

"No, I don't think so," Len said. "Horse looks familiar." Len leaned against the sideboard of his wagon and waited. The horse was a sorrel gelding with one white stocking on his left foreleg and was approaching at a fox-trot, which showed good breeding or diligent training.

"I know that horse," Len murmured with a sudden flash of recognition lighting up his mind. "That's Reno, one of Dane Kramer's favorites."

Wu said nothing. He put down the oil can and stood by the wagon wheel wiping his hands on his duck trousers to remove the oil sheen on his bony fingers.

A light breeze stirred the wrought-iron weather vane atop the roof of the house. Instead of a rooster sitting on the arrow, there was a silhouette of a crow and the device squeaked as it turned in a slow circular arc. Wu looked up at it. Beneath one of the crow's feet dangled the letter L. It was made out of tin and glittered in the sun as the vane turned to catch every whiff of wind. Len had made it represent his name, Crow L. And now it was a relic he would never see or need again.

"I should oil crow," he said.

Len chuckled. Wu was a hard worker and did a lot more than cook. Len was saddened that he would have to send Wu packing without any pay for his last year of service. There was just nothing left of a dream he'd harbored for several years since his father and mother had staked a claim on the land

and he had bought adjoining acreage for twenty-five cents an acre. Now both of them were dead and all he had left were a few head of cattle that he no longer owned.

The rider came up and slowed Reno to a walk.

"Howdy, Len," Dane said. "I just heard about your troubles from Fred at the general store."

"Yep, I'm packin' up. Light down, Dane, and join the funeral procession."

Dane swung out of the saddle and walked toward his friend. The two men shook hands.

"Sorry to hear that you're wiped out," Dane said.

"You can thank Throckmorton for that. The man wouldn't listen to reason. I told him I could get caught up if he let me stay and rebuild my herd."

Dane looked out and saw a few head of cattle grazing on the new grass. It made him sick to think of how many head Len had lost in that tragic drive. His house looked deserted, like a remnant of a ghost town. Empty and silent. He looked over the things in the wagon and felt his stomach wrench at the pathetically few belongings Len had packed.

Len wore faded denim overalls over what

Dane would have called a pea green shirt that had seen better days, and a straw hat that covered thinning brown hair. His eyes were brown and close-set, bordering a straight nose that was slightly hooked at the tip. He had a three-day beard and looked haggard as the sunlight flickered over his sallow features.

"Where you headed, Len?" Dane asked.

"I don't know. Thought I might go over to Missouri and see if I could find work, maybe some cheap land down in Arkansas where I could get a fresh start. Lydia left me, you know."

"No, I didn't know," Dane said. "When?"

"Last week after we got the foreclosure papers from Throckmorton."

"Damn."

"Went on back to Ohio, I reckon. Said she couldn't take this bleak life no more."

Len looked over to the side of the house. There was a garden there, with neat rows all lined up in a rectangle of composted earth. Green things were beginning to poke up through the loamy earth.

"That was her garden," Len said. "Rabbits can have it now."

"I'm sorry," Dane said. "You got more than your share of troubles, Len."

"I reckon there's more to come. Somewhere."

Wu walked over and Len introduced him to Dane. The two shook hands.

"What brings you out here, Dane? Not just to offer me condolences, I reckon."

"No, Len. Matter of fact, I wanted to talk to you about buying your check wagon and to see if Wu might want to come to work for me, to gather a drive up to Omaha. Three thousand head to start and pickin' up another nine hundred in Kansas City on the way."

Len blew a low whistle.

"Long ways," he said.

"I could use another hand too, if you're interested."

Wu's eyes lit up and his mouth twisted into a semigrin. Len worried his tongue around inside his mouth for a moment.

"What's your offer, Dane?" Len asked.

"Thirty a month and found for each of you. Plus a bonus when we get paid in Omaha."

"How much of a bonus?"

"A half month's pay for each man who finishes the drive."

Len hesitated only for a fraction of a second.

"Count me in," he said.

113

Dane turned to Wu. "How about you? Would you like to cook for my hands?"

"Sure," Wu said. "I a pretty good cook, you betcha."

Dane laughed. "All right, it's settled, then. Len, you know where my ranch is. Just set up in the bunkhouse, get Wu settled, and we'll go to work tomorrow."

"I got food in wagon," Wu said. "Beans, flour, coffee, salt, sugar."

"I'll pay you for it," Dane said.

"Pay Mr. Len, you betcha."

"I ain't takin' no pay for what's in the wagon, but if you want to buy it, I'm listening."

"Thirty dollars," Dane said.

"I figure it's worth fifty," Len said.

Dane reached into his pants pocket and drew out some bills. He counted out five ten-dollar bills and handed them to Len.

"Thanks, Dane. Now I don't feel so dad-gummed poor."

"You may not have a lot of money, Len, but a man like you is never poor. You'll get back on your feet again."

"I tell you one thing, Dane. I'd never sell my soul to that devil Throckmorton again. No matter what."

"Len, I'll tell you something," Dane said. "With this drive I expect to pay off my debt to Throckmorton's bank and never darken his door again."

"He got a mortgage on your place?"

"He has and he's breathing down my neck about it. Come September, I'll be free and clear."

Len's face brightened.

"Good for you," he said. "There ain't an ounce of kindness in Throckmorton's kit, that's for danged sure."

"You betcha," Wu said, and Dane wondered if he knew much about Len's and his financial dealings with Throckmorton's bank. He doubted it.

"See you at the Circle K," Dane said as he climbed back into the saddle.

"We'll be there, Dane. You ride easy."

"So long," Dane said, and turned Reno to head back into town.

He didn't look back, but he could feel Wu's and Len's eyes on him. He was glad that Len had accepted his offer and that he had bought another chuck wagon and hired on an additional cook. He was beginning to feel better about the upcoming drive. He was still figuring the logistics of the route, but now that he had two more men, he was sure he could make it work.

He was loading up the wagon behind the store when Joe Eagle rode up. With him were two Mexicans whom Dane did not know.

"Carlos, him not come," Joe said to Dane as the three of them dismounted.

"I am Rufio Chavez," the taller of the two men said as he held out his hand. He was wearing a .45 Colt on his belt and Dane noticed that both men had rifles attached to their saddles. "And this is my friend Alfredo Alicante."

Alfredo stepped forward to also shake Dane's hand.

He looked the two men over. They both had hard chiseled faces and dark skin with just a touch of vermilion in their cheekbones, a sign of their Indian heritage. They both had shiny black hair that dripped to their shoulders. Chavez had a yellow-speckled bandanna wrapped around his head and showing beneath his battered hat. Alicante wore a similar one under his hat, except that it was red with speckled floral designs.

Dane looked at their hands and saw the calluses and filled-in cracks. These were working men, not barroom drifters. Both wore pistols. Both were wiry and muscular.

"Know anything about cattle?" Dane asked them.

"We are vaqueros," Chavez said. "Now we

raise the horses."

"But the horse business, she is poor," Alicante said.

"The pay is thirty a month and found," Dane said. "You get paid at the end of the drive in Omaha. That's five hundred miles from here."

"We know," Alicante said. "We ride from Mexico. We drive the longhorns to Abilene in Texas."

"Good men," Joe said. "Work hard. Me know."

"Married?" Dane asked both men.

They both shook their heads.

"You speak very good English."

"We listen. We learn," Chavez said.

"You okay with the pay?"

"Yes, those are fine wages," Alicante said. "Like Texas."

Dane and Chavez both laughed.

Joe's face was a bronze blank.

"You boys can help me finish loading up this wagon and then we'll all ride out to the Circle K. There's plenty of work to do before we start the drive. You need anything special while we're in town? Tobacco, whiskey?"

Both men grinned and shook their heads.

"Then, let's get this wagon loaded and head for home."

The four of them made short work of the loading. Dane paid Christianson for the supplies and told him about Len and Wu.

"I'm glad you hired them on, Dane," Christianson said. "Len was nearly a broken man when he lost his ranch. And his wife."

"You didn't tell me about Lydia," Dane said.

"There was too much bad news as it was. I knew Len would tell you. Women. There's no explaining them."

"Women want security," Dane said. "And they want a husband who comes home every night. The wife of a cattle rancher must either be made of iron or get used to playing solitaire."

"That's why I've been married for a spell, I reckon. Nigh onto twelve years now."

"You and your wife are both lucky, then," Dane said.

"How about you, Mr. Kramer? You ever goin' to get married?"

"Maybe. Someday. If I find the right woman."

"That's the fly in the ointment," Christianson said. "You never know if it's the right one until you've been married a good long time."

"That's why I'm going to wait," Dane said. "I'll know the right one when she

118

comes along."

Dane left the store and drove the buckboard back to the Circle K, flanked by Chavez and Alicante.

All he needed now was a few more men and for the grass to grow. He had the cattle and the contract.

The only unknowns now were the weather and a couple of hard men he did not know, Larabee and Norton.

He was almost certain he would meet up with them one day.

He looked up at the sky as he drove and saw the thin streamers of clouds against an almost painfully blue sky. The recent rain should help grow the grass, and the sun would pull the shoots up high with its warm smile. He took tobacco from his pouch and crammed it into his mouth.

He was feeling better by the minute.

But, he knew, this was the time to be on guard for anything strange or unusual. He had no idea what was on Throckmorton's mind, but if two gunmen were working for him, that could not bode well for him or the drive. Randy had been a lesson for him. He had never caught on to him until it was too late.

He would not make the same mistake again, he vowed, as he chewed his tobacco and tasted the juices welling up in his mouth.

As they approached the Circle K, he could smell his cattle, and the horses perked up too.

He slackened up on the reins and let the horse in harness have his head. He slapped the reins across its rump and the horse broke into a fast trot.

Joe Eagle smiled and the two Mexicans spurred their horses and waved their hats.

"Adelante," Chavez yelled.

And Dane knew what the word meant, and it made a warm spot in his chest.

"Forward."

CHAPTER 13

Newly branded cattle crowded around the hay ricks that were scattered over the ninety acres called Sunnyland. They nudged and shoved each other to get at the loose hay that stuck out between the slats. More cattle streamed in and sought grass on lean pickings. But when they caught the scent of alfalfa, they trotted toward the ricks and started to muscle into the cattle already fighting among themselves for fodder.

As soon as the drovers saw the cattle moving onto the North Ninety, they turned back to where other men were laying on trail brands while others were riding through the herd and cutting out those cattle that were to be driven to Omaha. They separated the cows with calves and the seed bulls and moved them to other pastures.

Paddy had set up a competition among the cowhands, both for the branding and the cutting. He separated the men into teams and told them they were to compete with one another. At the end of each day he would tally up the number of cows with fresh trail brands from each group, and the same with the cutters, counting the number of cattle they were able to bring to the branding fires and drive to Sunnyland.

As a reward, each man in the winning group got a new silver dollar and a pint of whiskey.

"That makes every man work harder and we get the jobs done faster," Paddy told Dane.

"Just be sure you don't run out of silver dollars," Dane warned.

"Oh, I been exchanging paper for silver a whole lot of days," Paddy said. "Takin' it out of the camp funds."

"What in hell are the camp funds?" Dane asked.

"You know, the money you give me for nails and paint and lumber and such. Always some left over because I know how to bargain. I believe the term the accountants use is 'petty cash.' "

"First I've heard of it."

"What you don't know, Dane boy, sure as hell can't hurt you none."

"You're a slick one, Paddy."

"Oh, I have me ways," he said.

Paddy also gave a schedule to the two cooks, with Wu and his chuck wagon on the Circle K range, while Barney cooked for those who stayed in the bunkhouse overnight. Any ranch hand could find grub at either place, and the wagons stayed put. He wisely did not hold a competition for which cook the hands preferred since he was aware of how sensitive both Barney and Wu could be about the grub they prepared. But he watched and listened and declared to himself that between the two cookies it was a draw.

Paddy drew Dane away from the other cowhands, out of earshot, to discuss a couple of other matters.

Cattle were streaming into Sunnyland and out to the Two Grand spread, with riders guiding the cattle on both routes. The branding was continuing at a brisk pace, with two men checking the trail brands to see if they were adequate.

"Something funny's goin' on around here, I think," Paddy said. "Somethin' you ought to know about."

"What's that?" Dane asked.

"I got a feelin' yesterday that we was bein' watched. I don't know, it's the kind of feelin' you got in school when somebody behind you was starin' at you. And when you turned around, sure enough, somebody was."

"I know what you're talking about, Paddy. So, what did you see when you turned around out here?"

"You know that bog over there, the one with the cattails and the blackbirds?"

Dane glanced over to the edge of the pasture and saw the waving cattails and the redwings flitting among the reeds. "Yeah, what about it?"

"Well, when I looked over there, I thought I saw a glint of light, like when the sun hits a glass pane or one of them thingamajigs what tinkles when the wind blows."

"A wind chime?" Dane said.

"Yeah, one of them. It was just a single shot of bright light, but then I thought maybe somebody's standing amongst them cattails a-watchin' us with a field glass."

"Did you go over there?"

"Nope. I got a creepy, crawly feeling up my neck and then a cow got its head stuck in one of the ricks and was bawlin' like crazy, so I had to help Cal and Steve turn the cow's head so's I could pull on its horns and free it up."

"I can walk over there now and take a look around."

"Would you? I didn't see nobody, but it

could be somebody's mighty interested in what we're a-doin' here."

"I'll check it out," Dane said. "Go on back to work."

"One other thing, Dane," Paddy said as he watched some of the riders chasing cattle on to the Two Grand.

"Go ahead," Dane said.

"You got two cooks and two chuck wagons now. You figgerin' on breakin' up the drive into two separate divisions?"

Dane took out his tobacco pouch and pinched off a wad and stuck it in his mouth. He chewed and he spat out the juice. "This is just between you and me right now, Paddy. Understand?"

Paddy nodded. Dane spat again.

"Yes, I am going to split the herd in half. Well, almost. You'll take the larger herd up the Missouri and keep right on going past Kansas City. I'll ramrod the trailing herd, pick up the nine hundred head in K.C., and then join you in Omaha."

"Aye, begorra," exclaimed Paddy. "It'll be like ridin' naked for me without you bein' along."

"I'm going to take Len Crowell with me as trail boss, Paddy. He's experienced and I'll be along if he runs into trouble."

Paddy worked a piece of bare ground with

the toe of his boot. Dane expectorated another stream of tobacco juice onto the shoots of grass that were now several inches high.

"Might work," he said. "We got good hands now, enough maybe for two herds."

"You'll have about two thousand head to drive, Paddy. I'll take the other thousand and by the time I get to Omaha, I'll have nearly two thousand head after I pick up those waiting in the feedlot in Kansas."

"A heap of responsibility, Dane. More on your shoulders than mine."

"We can do it. I think it's the best way. I won't be but a few days behind you and we can always send riders back and forth if either of us gets into trouble."

"You worked out how far behind us you'll be, Dane? I mean, how far would a rider have to travel to get a message to you, or back to me?"

"You'll have a day's start on me, Paddy. I figure we'll never be more than ten miles apart, unless you get slowed or I get slowed."

"That sounds about right to me," Paddy said.

"Fingers crossed," Dane said.

Paddy laughed and shook the dirt off his boot. "All right. When do we divide up the hands and tell everybody what we're a-goin' to do?"

"Probably either the night before we set out or the next morning. I'm still going over my list to see who goes where."

"We're goin' pretty lean at that," Paddy said.

"That's where ingenuity comes in," Dane said.

"Inja what?"

"Ingenuity. Makin' do with what you got. I know the men will earn their pay on this drive. We don't want to lose any cattle and we don't want any trouble with the herd. So you, and me too, are going to have to make sure the men riding flank and drag, as well as those riding point, know what their jobs are and stick to 'em all the way."

"I'll make sure my men do what they're supposed to do," Paddy said.

"Then, we don't have anything to worry about, do we?"

"I reckon not," Paddy said, but Dane knew that his foreman was not entirely convinced.

They didn't have the number of men they really needed to handle two drives, much less one with three thousand head. It was going to be hard work all the way to Omaha and they might even get a deserter or two.

He hoped not, but it was something that sometimes happened on long cattle drives. Men missed their wives and girlfriends, they got thirsty for hard liquor, and they got homesick. They were only human, after all.

The real test of a leader was how he handled men. His job was to inspire them and instill pride and confidence in them so that they would stay on the job. Paddy had done that on the ranch. He would have to do it on the trail. A leader had to be prepared to help out and work alongside his hands while maintaining some distance and control. He hoped that he and Len could be an example to the men who worked under them and make sure they toed the line all the way upriver.

He and Paddy parted company. Dane walked over toward the marsh, at an angle so that he appeared to be going to another place on the edge of the pasture. Out of the corner of his eye, he watched the birds fly up and down among the cattails. He looked for any odd glint of light. And he listened.

When he got close, he walked around the edge of the marsh looking at the muddy soft ground for boot or horse tracks. On the opposite side, he saw where the mud was roiled as if some animal had wallowed there. Perhaps quail, he thought.

No boot tracks.

No horse tracks.

He walked a few yards in back of the boggy marsh and climbed a small knoll.

There, he saw two puzzling impressions in the grassy slope and on the top. The grass was flattened as if two bodies had lain there. Beside one of the bodies, the larger one, he saw two impressions on either side, as if a man had lain there and dug his elbows into the ground. Perhaps someone who had a pair of binoculars and was watching the gather.

Dane lay down on the larger impression and dug his elbows in. He pretended he had something in his hands and he peered through the cattails.

When he did that, he had a full view of the hay ricks, the path the riders took when they drove the branded cattle onto Sunnyland, and the path they rode when they drove cattle onto Two Grand.

"Now, why would someone care what we were doing here?" he asked of himself as he rose to his feet. He worried the wad of tobacco around in his mouth and walked a few yards away and spat.

Then he walked in a series of semicircles well behind where he had found the impressions. He looked down at the ground and saw two sets of boot tracks coming and going to that spot. Two men, he reasoned, spying on them. But who? And why?"

He kept widening his search and then saw a pair of old pecan trees with some of the bark rubbed off. Before he had bought his land, a sodbuster had set up a tent and tried to grow an orchard. There were a few pecan and peach trees and the remnants of a vineyard.

There were lots of horse tracks around the two trees and he saw specks of corn and oats ground into the dirt. Whoever had come here to spy on his men had brought feed bags for their horses. So they had stayed a fairly long time, he figured. Why two men? And not just one?

He followed the tracks and saw that they had come from town and headed back that same way. Dane walked back to the little knoll and looked down at the two outlines of men lying on their stomachs. One was longer, taller than the other. One was thinner than the taller one.

He let his mind roam over what he was seeing.

Two men, he thought. No, a man and a boy.

Then it struck him. The smaller impression might have been made by a young slender man. There was only one who came to mind.

Randy Bowman.

And, he wondered, why had Randy Bowman been there with the man who had the field glass? There was only one answer to that question. Randy knew all the men who worked on the Circle K. He could have been there for only one reason, to point out to the older and larger man who each man was.

Including himself.

Dane spat the tasteless cud of the tobacco into the marsh.

Throckmorton was behind this, he was sure. The banker had sent a man to watch them and Randy to point out who was who.

The larger man was probably an assassin. Someone Dane did not know. But someone who now knew who he was and what he looked like.

That could only mean one thing, Dane realized. He was a marked man.

Throckmorton meant to kill him so that he could not pay off his mortgage on the ranch. It was a chilling thought.

Dane walked back to his horse, the back of his neck prickling just as Paddy's had been when he had seen that glimmer of light in the bulrushes.

Someone had been watching him. Someone who meant to kill him, either here on the ranch or out on the prairie during the drive.

And this, this horror, he would tell no one. This was his cross to bear and his alone.

But from then on, Dane would be on guard. He would watch his back and be prepared.

He looked all around when he mounted Reno and saw nothing but grass and cattle, men at work.

It was just about time to start the drive north. Another day, two at the most, he decided.

Every day and every night, the grass grew higher and thicker.

CHAPTER 14

Concho Larabee sat in Throckmorton's office, an unlit cheroot in his mouth. Throckmorton counted a stack of greenbacks. He plucked each bill from one pile and placed each one on another pile. He did this twice while Concho chewed on the cheroot and watched the banker as if mesmerized.

"I got ten men, Earl, and I'm takin' the kid."

"Kid?"

"Randy Bowman. He's a good spotter and he might be useful."

"He's still wet behind the ears," Throckmorton said.

"We'll dry 'em out for him right quick. He's got good eyes, he follows orders, and he tells me he can shoot pretty straight."

"That's up to you, then. Pay him out of your own pocket."

"I'll pay for the first ten days, Earl. After that, you pay him, say, twenty bucks a month."

"You think it'll take you more than a month to turn that herd back and put Kramer six feet under?"

"I figger the herd won't move more'n ten or twelve miles a day and I was goin' to wait until they've crossed the border into Kansas."

"Do you know what track Kramer's taking?"

"North to Kansas, then east to Kansas City is all I know. Kramer didn't give me no map."

"That's not funny, Concho."

"You hired me on, Earl. Let me do it my way. There's plenty of open prairie and he's got to foller creeks and rivers. With that many head he ain't goin' to move real fast."

Throckmorton reached into the cash box and took out another bill and added it to the counted stack.

Concho stroked his chin and stared at the pile of greenbacks.

"Here's money you might need to spend before you leave and extra for expenses on the way. I'll pay you and your men when you get that herd back here and show me proof that Kramer is out of the way."

"Fine with me," Concho said. He reached across the desk and took the bills from

Throckmorton's hand. He folded them in half and slid them into a front pocket of his denim trousers. He patted them flat and crossed his legs.

"Do you know when Kramer's pulling out?" Throckmorton asked.

"I reckon tomorrow or next day. He's got cattle on what Randy says is the Two Grand Pasture, two thousand acres, and they're crammed in there like sardines. We can't get too close no more, 'cause Kramer found out where we was a-watchin' him on what Randy calls Sunnyland."

"Kramer's not stupid, Concho. You should have been more careful."

"Hell, we was well hid, but I saw him walk over to that slough and tramp around lookin' for our tracks. He found where we had stashed our horses and spent a lot of time lookin' at where me'n Randy was a-lyin' whilst we watched what them cowpokes was doin'. At least now I know what Kramer looks like and I got his foreman, Paddy O'Riley, tagged. I figger I'll have to take him down first. Cut off the head of the snake."

"Sounds to me as if you've got your scheme pretty well planned," Throckmorton said.

"Yep, I reckon I do. Won't be hard to foller that herd, and when they bed down at night, me and my men can ride on ahead and pick the spot for our ambush."

"You can't mess up, Concho." Throckmorton looked at the sign up his door. "And you will be well rewarded."

Concho stood up and moved the cheroot to the other side of his mouth, pushing it with his tongue. The cigar irritated Throckmorton. To him, it showed a lack of respect on Concho's part.

"And so will you, Earl," Concho said. "See you in a month or so."

"Good luck," Throckmorton said.

"I got my luck right here," Concho said, and patted the butt of his pistol.

Then he left Throckmorton's office and nodded to Miss Watson as he stalked past her and walked to the front doors of the bank.

Randy was loading up a sulky with bags of groceries when Concho approached the general store on foot. He waited until the young man was finished and the buggy pulled away from the store. Then he walked over and grabbed Randy by the collar before he could reenter the store.

"Hey," Randy said, surprised. He looked at Concho when he turned around, and his jaw dropped an inch.

"You want to go with us, kid? There's cash in it for you."

"Where?" Randy asked, still somewhat bewildered by his abrupt encounter with Concho.

"You know. Me and some other men are goin' after that herd of cattle from the Circle K."

"You're goin' to steal it?"

"You better not use that word 'steal' a whole hell of a lot, kid."

"No, sir, I won't. You want me to help you?"

"I want you to be my spotter. You'll get fair wages, and maybe learn a thing or two. Won't be easy. You'll have to grab grub outen your saddlebags and do some night ridin'. I'm going to count on you to keep track of two men."

"Two men?"

"That foremens, Paddy, and Dane Kramer."

"Why?"

"Don't be askin' too many questions, kid. Now, do you want to go with us or not?"

"Sure," Randy said.

"Okay. Now you go in there and tell Christianson you're quittin' and draw your pay. Don't tell him nothin' else, hear?"

"Yes, sir," Randy said.

"Then I want you to saddle up and ride out to the Circle K and watch out for when they start the drive. Then you wear out leather getting back to me at the Prairie Dog. I'll be waitin'. Me and my men will be saddled up and ready to ride."

"I'll do it, Mr. Larabee," Randy said.

"And you might as well get used to callin' me Concho. We're going to be saddle pards."

Randy's face brightened.

"I'll do everything you want me to do, uh, Concho," he said.

"I figger that herd's goin' to be movin' late today or tomorrow. You find out and let me know. I'll have trail grub for you when you get back."

"I got some jerky and hardtack still in my saddlebags, Concho, from when we was spyin' on Mr. Kramer and Paddy and all."

Concho grinned and threw the chewed cheroot onto the ground. He slapped Randy on the back.

"Now get crackin', kid," he said.

Randy hesitated. "Concho?"

"Yeah?"

"Since you want me to call you Concho, would you mind callin' me by my given name? Randy."

"Not at all, Randy," Concho said, and

waved the young man away.

He walked toward the Prairie Dog Saloon, where he had called a meeting of the men he had assembled.

It was getting close, real close, to that large herd hitting the trail north. By now, all his men should be packing their gear and loading their saddlebags with trail grub he'd had Lem Norton buy over a period of days from Christianson so as not to arouse too much suspicion about his intentions.

When Randy returned with the news that Kramer's herd was moving, he and his men would be ready.

Concho licked his lips.

He couldn't wait to do the job Throckmorton had hired him to do.

He relished the thought of killing a man and stealing a large herd of cattle.

What more could a man ask for?

CHAPTER 15

All of the Circle K hands, the drovers and wranglers, the two cooks, and the ranch foreman, Paddy O'Riley, were all assembled on the Two Grand range when Dane made his announcement.

"Men," he said, "we break trail before sunrise tomorrow morning. I'm counting on each one of you to give your best on the long drive to Omaha. It's nearly five hundred miles, but there should be good grass and plenty of water along the way."

Some of the men applauded and soon were joined by all the others as Dane paused.

"Paddy will be trail boss of the first herd, around two thousand head. I will be leaving the next day, with Len Crowell acting as trail boss."

There was some laughter. Some nervous titters in the more than twenty men assembled.

Dane held up both hands to silence the outburst.

"We'll be right behind you. Oh, we may stray a little if the first herd gobbles up too much grass, but we won't be far behind."

"I'm ready to leave right now," one man called, out and the others laughed.

"Hold your horses," Dane said. "We have plenty of time, so we don't want to rush this. The main thing is not to lose any cattle and to keep the weight on as much as we can. You will all get grub along the way and pay when we hit the stockyards in Omaha. Paddy will tell you which bunch you're in. I'll see those on Paddy's drive in the morning when you leave."

Men began to raise their hands, some begging to be in the lead herd, others wanting to go with Dane and Len. They crowded around Paddy while Dane walked to his horse with Crowell.

"I should be able to pick my own men if I'm trail boss," Len said.

"You should, but that's not the way it works. We're the leftovers. If you don't like any of the men riding with us, you let me know and I'll see to it that you don't have to deal with them."

"I guess that'll work," Len said.

"Anything will work if you make it work,"

Dane said.

That day, he and Len went over the maps and when Paddy joined them, they looked for alternative routes they might take if they ran into troublesome landowners, hostile Indians, or rustlers. They all sat at the table in the ranch house while Thor listened from his chair.

"So, we got the Chinaman as cookie," Paddy said at one point.

"That's right," Dane said. "Any objections?"

"Ain't none of us tasted his cooking," Paddy said.

"Just tell him what you want to eat and he'll fix it for you," Len said.

"Can he make bear claws?" Paddy asked.

"Better'n any you ever tasted," Len assured him.

"Let's not get into a squabble over the grub right now, men," Dane said.

In affirmation, Thor thumped his cane on the floor. The men at the table ignored him.

"I wish I could be in two places at once, Paddy," Dane said, "but I can't. If you run into anything you can't handle, send a rider back and I'll come a-runnin'."

"Fine with me," Paddy said.

Then he leaned back in his chair and regarded Dane with an odd look.

"Onliest thing I'm worried about, Dane, is you. You never said anything when you got through lookin' around that bog the other day. But I walked over later and saw your tracks and read what you saw."

"So?" Dane said.

"So someone was a-watchin' us and you never said a word."

"No, I didn't. No reason to."

"Know who it was a-spyin' on us?" Paddy asked.

"I've got a pretty good idea. Why?"

"It was that kid, wasn't it? Randy."

"Maybe. One of 'em might have been."

"That little sneak," Paddy said. "Now, why in hell . . ."

"Paddy, don't you fret over that. You got enough on your plate you don't need to be reachin' toward the middle of the table."

"I just don't like to be spied on," Paddy grumbled, somewhat mollified.

"It's Throckmorton, ain't it?" Len said, and the room went dead silent.

Dane leaned over and patted Crowell on the shoulder to reassure him.

"Throckmorton's got money tied up in our herd," Dane said. "He might be lickin' his chops a little early, but you don't need to worry about him."

"I know what he done to me," Len said.

"Well, he's not going to do it to me," Dane said. "Don't worry. I'm going to keep my eyes open, and the men riding point, those ridin' flank, and the ones on drag will all be eagle-eyed just in case."

Len and Paddy exchanged looks, but neither man brought up the subject again.

The next morning, while it was still dark, Dane and Len rode to the Two Grand to see Paddy and his hands off. The evening before, he knew, Paddy had divided the men up and told them which drive they'd take, so the ones who were riding with Len and Dane were still asleep in the bunkhouse.

Dane looked over the men. He held a lantern burning coal oil in his hands and stared at each orange face.

"I don't see Joe Eagle here, Paddy," Dane said. "I thought you might pick him."

"I wanted him, but I thought you might need him more than me. You said somethin' about an eagle eye, and Joe's one what has it."

"Good. I was hoping Joe would ride with us."

"Well, you got him. These are good men in my bunch."

"You can start anytime you're ready," Dane told Paddy.

Paddy ordered his men to saddle up.

"I got me a lead cow all picked out and I'll ride up and get her started," he told Dane. "See you in Omaha, if not before."

Dane watched Paddy's foreman mount up and ride to the front of the herd. He disappeared in the darkness.

He and Len watched as the men took up their positions at the rear and flanks. In the distance, they heard a faint shout from Paddy.

"Forward, ho," floated back to them on the night.

Then, very slowly, the herd began to move. The cattle jostled and shouldered the ones next to them. One or two bolted and the flanker ran them back in. Gradually, the ranks of the cattle began to thin and move faster as the lead cattle broke trail.

To Dane, it was a glorious sight to see all those cattle moving. He listened to their moans and bellows and began to feel good about the start of the long drive to Omaha.

Len seemed enraptured too as the cattle streamed past them, their horns glinting in the moonlight, their white faces like foam combers upon a rolling sea. It was a magnificent sight and brought a longing in both men to be among the drovers.

Dane felt as if he were onshore watching a great ship leave the dock and sail into the blackened sea. The lantern flickered in his hand and he held it high to light the cattle nearest them begin to pick up the pace as if they could not wait to get to a new range.

"I can't wait until we leave tomorrow," Len said.

"It's tough to just stand here when you see all these cattle on the move," Dane said.

They heard hoofbeats. Both men turned around.

Joe Eagle emerged out of the darkness and rode up to them. He swung out of the saddle before his horse had stopped.

"Mornin', Joe," Dane said.

"Hunh," Joe grunted.

"We'll do this tomorrow."

"Me know. Good cows. Go far."

"Yeah," Dane said.

The three men stayed until the dawn broke on the horizon and the last switching tail vanished into the distance. It was suddenly quiet. Then they heard the cattle in their herd lowing in the distance. It was a mournful, sad sound.

"They know, don't they?" Len said, his voice just above a whisper.

"Animals communicate in ways we can't understand," Dane said. "They know."

"Know heap," Joe said. "Cow smart. Horse smart. Dog smart. Make talk, arf,

arf, moo, moo, whinny."

Len laughed. Dane did not. He knew that Joe Eagle believed that all things were alive and that animals talked to each other. He said that they could see inside a man's mind and tell what a human was thinking. He believed that everything was alive: water, rocks, trees, clouds, sky, the stars, the moon, the sun.

Len shook his head but said nothing. When Joe walked back to his horse to ride back to the bunkhouse, Len watched him go.

"That's some Injun," he said.

"He's a half-breed, Len. And he can talk better than that. The way he talks lets him keep separate from the rest of us."

"He got something against white men?"

"Not any more'n I do, Len. He just keeps to himself. If people think that he only knows a few words in the white man's language, he learns more by just listening."

"Kinda spooky, ain't it?"

"No more spooky than my pa. Sometimes he looks like he ain't got good sense, but my pa hears every word said in that house and he's a good judge of men. Like Joe Eagle. If a man ain't right, Joe can tell, and if he thinks I need to know he'll tell me."

"Sounds like a good man to have around,"

147

Len said.

"That's why I have him around."

The two men climbed into their saddles. They rode toward the rent in the horizon that had turned to a soft cream. Their horses began to cast shadows, and there was a breeze that cooled their faces.

Dane's blood was churning. It had been a thrill to see two thousand head of cattle he had helped raise start off on a long trail.

As his pa had often said to him:

"The journey's the reward, son."

Dane thought that was true. It was not the goal that swelled a man's heart. It was the getting there.

CHAPTER 16

Randy awoke to the sound of thunder.

He scrambled out of his bedroll on the abandoned property next to the Two Grand range with the expectation of lightning and rain. Instead, he knew he heard only the sound of thousands of cloven hooves and horses pounding the ground as the herd broke trail.

He quickly rolled up his bedroll, secured it behind the cantle of his saddle, and hauled himself up on his horse.

In the distance, he saw shadows and the silhouettes of horsemen taller than the rolling sea of dark cattle. He rubbed his eyes and blinked to clear them of the granules sticking to his eyelids.

"Oh boy," he breathed.

He saw the flashing horns and listened to the moans and grunts of the cattle as they picked up speed. He saw the rise and fall of their curly-haired backs and the ghostly pallor of their white faces, and something tugged inside him. He thought, for a fleeting moment, that he could have been part of that migration, and he saw himself on a horse chasing after the cattle and halting the breakaways with a surefooted cutting horse or an agile cow pony. A feeling of deep longing engulfed him when he saw the cattle leaving their home range and venturing into the unknown, toward new grass and flowing rivers and little towns along the way and then the big city, where men would laugh and drink and recount grand and grandiose tales of treacherous fordings on raging rivers and nightmare stampedes at midnight.

The feeling passed, but Randy felt very alone at that moment. He had no friends on the Circle K, and he was working with men who could not be trusted, men who indulged in suspicious activities. He was working with a greedy little martinet who had ice water in his veins and devilment in his mind.

He waited until all the cattle had deserted the Two Grand and the rumble of their hooves subsided before he headed for town. The eastern sky was opening up with a soft mellow light, and in the west, the sky was changing from black to blue and erasing the stars. Only the silvery glow of Venus still shone and flashed against the fading darkness and the faint jewels of the Milky Way.

Randy rode slowly into the sleeping settlement of Shawnee Mission. A few lights burned orange in some of the houses, and the rest looked drab and deserted. The saloon was closed, as he knew it would be, so he tied up at the hotel next door and entered the lobby.

A sleepy desk clerk finally came to the bell and regarded Randy as if he were an unwelcome intruder, an orphan off the street begging for a handout.

"Can you tell me the number of Mr. Larabee's room?"

The clerk, an old man with white whiskers and a shiny bald head that glistened in the salmon glow of the oil lamp, looked over the top of his pince-nez and frowned. "You a friend of his, sonny?"

"Well, I, uh, kind of. I got an important message for him."

"You can write your message and I'll put it in his box. He ain't awake yet."

"Uh, no, he wants me to tell him somethin' real important."

"He's in room seven, down the hall. You better not wake up nobody but him, though." The clerk looked up at the big clock on the wall of the cubicle. "Do you know what time it is?"

"No, sir, I don't, but I got to see Mr. Larabee right away."

"Number seven," the clerk said, and walked through a door and left the desk area deserted.

Randy walked down the hall on the thin carpet. There was no light and he had to stare at the numbers on tiptoe when he passed each door.

He tapped lightly on number seven.

No answer.

He knocked again, more loudly.

He heard a rustling when he put his ear close to the door.

Again, Randy knocked, this time louder and longer.

"Who in hell is it?" came Concho's voice through the door.

"It's me, Randy Bowman," the young man said in a loud whisper.

"Who?"

"Randy." This time he said his name aloud. He heard feet hit the floor and then the pad of those same feet approaching the door. He stepped back.

"Damn, it's still night out, kid. What you doin' here this time of mornin'?"

"Concho, they're movin'. The herd has done taken off."

"Get your sorry ass in here, kid."

Randy stepped inside and Concho pulled the door shut.

It was then that Randy noticed that Concho had a pistol in his hand. It had been in his hand all the time, just out of sight behind his leg. His bare leg. He was wearing only undershorts and a plain wool shirt. He was barefooted.

Concho walked to the table and pulled out a chair.

"Set down," he gruffed.

"Yes, sir," Randy said, and sat down.

Concho walked to the bureau and picked up a sack of tobacco, a packet of cigarette papers, and a small box of matches. He sat down opposite Randy and began to roll himself a cigarette. "Tell me all about it. How long ago and who all was with Kramer? How many hands?"

"I couldn't make out who all was ridin' with the herd. Too dark. But there was a passel of cows headin' north."

"Randy, get me that map over on my nightstand."

Randy walked back to the rumpled bed. The room was Spartan, with a bureau, wardrobe cabinet, a table, and three chairs. He took the map to Concho and sat down. He was trembling and hoped that Larabee

153

wouldn't notice. Most of the shakes were inside him. He licked his dry lips and watched as Concho laid out the map and began to scan it.

"Likely, they'll head up to the Canadian and cross it or head east. So we got time. Randy, go knock on door number six and roust Lem out of his bed. Tell him I said to round up all my men and have 'em here in a half hour. Can you remember all that?"

"Yes, sir. I got it."

"Now, scat," Concho said, and he shooed Randy toward the door.

A half hour later, Concho's room began to fill with sleepy-eyed men. Most were unshaven and had shadows on their faces. All were grumpy at that early hour, but Concho had ordered in a large pot of fresh coffee and several tin cups. The men went to the table and poured coffee. Most of them sat on the floor, or the bed. Randy sat next to the wardrobe while Lem took a chair at the table with Concho.

"Men, this is it," Concho said. "Kramer's movin' his herd north. We got time to get ahead of him and look for a prime chunk of country to waylay him and turn them cows back to the Circle K."

"When do we leave?" asked Lyle Fisk, a lean whip of a man with carefully trimmed

154

sideburns and a hawk nose, beady brown eyes.

"Within the hour. We'll do some campin' before this job is done. But I want everything set by the time that herd crosses the border into Kansas."

"Everything's set," Lem said. "Just have to throw our saddles on our horses and pack our saddlebags and bedrolls."

"Everybody got plenty of ammunition for both rifles and pistols?" Concho asked.

The men grunted and nodded in assent.

"We won't follow the herd directly," Concho said, "but some of you will be outriders who will keep the cattle in sight. Anybody here know what Dane Kramer looks like?"

"I do," Mitch Markham said. "I rode for his brand oncet 'bout a year ago."

"You'll be ridin' with one of the others to track the herd. I want to know where Kramer is, whether or not he's ridin' point or drag or just bein' a flanker."

"Shouldn't be hard," Markham said. "He chaws on tobacco and has to spit ever' so often."

The men in the room chuckled or laughed.

"Likely, Kramer will foller one of them rivers into Kansas. In a week, we might know which one." Concho rolled a cigarette.

155

A couple of the men stuck quirlies in their mouths and struck matches to light them.

"He'll play hob crossin' the Canadian," a man named Skip Hewes said. "If it rains he could be stalled there for a couple of days."

"That's why we're goin' to keep close watch on that herd," Concho said. He turned to Randy.

"Did you hear the clank of a cowbell when that herd started movin' out?"

Randy shook his head. "Nope," he said. "I know what you mean. I listened but I didn't hear one."

"Okay," Concho said. "Kramer ain't sure of his lead cow yet. When he is, he'll bell it and we ought to be able to hear it if we get within a couple hunnerd yards from the head of the column."

"Yeah, you can hear one of them cowbells from a long ways off on a good day," Dan Foster said. He was one of the older men and his hair was streaked with gray so that when his hat was off, his head resembled a badger. He smoked a ready-made cigarette and wore a faded gray bandanna around his scrawny neck.

"Logan," Concho said, fixing his steely gaze on Logan Heckler, a grizzled man in his early forties with a dark beard, "you and Markham will scout the lead cow in that herd and I'll spell you after your first report. We'll take turns scoutin' the herd so's we don't make no mistakes."

"Sounds like a fair plan," Lem said. "Easy trackin' and there's plenty of places up in Kansas where we might jump the drovers and relieve them of all them cattle."

Some of the men laughed.

Concho scowled.

"Don't think it's going to be real easy," he said. "Kansas is flatter'n a damned pancake. A man can see for miles."

"See what?" Will Davis cracked. "Jackrabbits?"

Some of the men laughed.

"I see you've been there, Will," Concho said, and blew a stream of gray-blue smoke from his mouth.

"I got out of Kansas fast as I could," Davis said, and there was more laughter.

"Well, I see you're all in a good mood and ready to ride," Concho said. "Let's saddle up and grab our grub and set out. Finish your coffee and we'll all meet at the livery. The kid there is goin' with us."

There were a few groans, but Concho ignored them.

Randy shrank against the wall and did not look at any of the men.

The men gulped the rest of the coffee in

their cups and filed out of the room. Finally there was only Concho, Lem, and Randy.

"On your feet, kid," Concho said. "I hope you got plenty of cartridges for that hog leg you're wearin', and got a rifle stuck to your saddle."

"Yes, sir, I have two extry boxes of cartridges for each of my guns."

"Ever killed anybody?" Concho asked.

Randy stood up and shook his head.

Lem gave the young man a contemptuous look.

"Hell, he ain't never swallered a frog neither," Lem said.

"Well, maybe on this ride he can do both," Concho said.

Randy's knees began to shake and he was sure they were knocking together. But he knew enough to keep his mouth shut. If he said anything, both men would probably make fun of him.

"Let's head out, then," Concho said as he picked up his hat and his rifle, which were inside the wardrobe cabinet.

The three walked into the lobby of the hotel. Concho stopped at the desk and laid a bill on the counter.

"Jeff, you can have the maid clean up my room and take away the coffee and cups."

The clerk looked at the double sawbuck.

"Yes, sir, Mr. Larabee," Jeff Osteen said.

"I'll be gone for a couple of weeks. Maybe a month."

"That'll be fine, Mr. Larabee. I'll hold your room for as long as you like."

"He'll want the presidential suite when he gets back," Lem said.

Concho shot him a dirty look.

Then the three of them walked out of the hotel and into the burning dawn. They headed for the livery stable as the sun crept up the street and chased away the shadows of the buildings. It was a fine morning and they even heard birds chirping in the few trees that grew along the street.

Concho twirled his rifle like a baton and started to whistle "Billy Boy."

Randy was beginning to admire Concho, while he was taking a strong dislike to Lem.

One thing he knew.

He sure didn't want to kill nobody.

Nor eat a damned frog.

CHAPTER 17

That first day of the drive was pure hell for Paddy O'Riley.

The cattle were unruly, to put it mildly, and the drovers ran their horses to a lather running wayward cattle back into the herd. The homeward urge was strong in those cattle bringing up the middle and the rear. Several bolted and turned back toward the home range, so the drovers had to corral them with agile horses, and sometimes it took two or three riders to stem the tide of runaways.

Paddy rode point and kept his eye on the leaders in the herd. The next morning, after making a distance of some eight or nine miles, he got the bell from the chuck wagon and attached it to a collar he put on the lead cow's neck. Now, with the cattle following his lead, the herd could hear the bell and know where the leader was. It was an old trick, but it worked.

When Paddy turned the herd to bed down for the night on a long stretch of grassy plain, he was plumb worn out.

"We just barely broke the gravity of Shawnee Mission," he told Steve Atkins, who had assisted him on point.

"They'll settle down tomorrow," Steve said. "We're gettin' 'em trail broke, I think."

"I think them cows can still smell the home range," Paddy said. "Another day or two, they'll sniff new ground and grass and maybe get the idea that they're goin' someplace where the grazin's better."

"I guess you have to think like a cow," Steve said.

"It helps," Paddy replied.

The nighthawks circled the herd all night, singing to them and chasing a few head trying to escape the herd, but not a head was lost, and by morning, Paddy was satisfied that his drovers were top-notch. They all listened to the yodeling of coyotes during the night, but they had a full moon and could spot any furry marauders before they got after the bedded-down cattle.

Wu made a large campfire that first night with kindling carried in the supply wagon, and some of the drovers gathered enough wood from along a creek to keep the blaze going all night. Men grabbed plates of chow, ate quickly, then returned to their duties as nighthawks tending the herd. Alfredo Alicante finished hobbling the horses in the remuda that he quartered near the supply wagon. He gave them each a dip of corn and oats before joining the men at the campfire.

Paddy sat there, scraping up the last morsels of beef and beans on his plate.

"How're the horses, Fredo?" he asked.

"Jumpy," he said. "The horses are not accustomed to be around so many cattle."

"They'll get used to it after they've been under saddle in the days to come."

Wu filled Alicante's pewter plate and handed him a tin cup full of hot coffee. The Mexican sat on the bare ground like the others and gobbled his food. Paddy watched him. He knew a hungry man when he saw one, and Alfredo, he knew, had put in a good day's work leading all the horses in the wake of the cattle.

"We want to have an early start in the morning," Paddy told the men around the campfire. "Dane's going to be comin' up behind us and we got to make more miles tomorrow."

"He'll do fifteen mile a day, I'm thinkin'," Cal Ferris said. "With only a thousand head, he could catch up to us."

"I wouldn't mind that," Paddy said. He looked up at the stars and the round moon that flickered its eerie glow. "We can't expect all the goin' to be as easy as it was today."

Wu came over and stood next to Paddy.

"I will make the sandwiches," he said. "In two weeks, you must kill cows for me to butcher."

"I know," Paddy said. "We allowed extry head for that."

"Good," Wu said, and bowed slightly before he went back to the wagon to make sandwiches for the drovers to take with them before the herd moved out again around dawn.

Harvey Tolliver had just finished laying out his bedroll and was taking off his boots to lie down and get some sleep when Paddy called over to him.

"Harve, got a wee minute?" Paddy said.

"Sure, boss," Tolliver said. He pulled his boots back on and walked over to the fire.

"You relieve Bill at midnight, don't you?" Paddy said.

"Bill or Whit. We're doubled up on the night herd."

"You got a spyglass or field glass?"

Tolliver shook his head. "Nope," he said. He was a tall, gangly man with light flaxen hair that blew into his face when his hat was off. His hat was off now and he kept brushing away the rampant strands of hair. Half of his teeth were missing and, with his twice-broken nose, he looked like a half-wit.

"I got me a spyglass in those saddlebags over yonder by the wheel of Wu's chuck wagon. 'Fore you go to sleep, you get it. Don't double up, but widen your ridin' circle. Okay?"

"Sure, boss, but why?"

"You're going to be lookin' for any distant campfire, listenin' for any hoofbeats out on the prairie. You look and you listen good, hear?"

"Sure, boss, but why? There ain't nothin' out there but jackrabbits and coyotes."

Paddy spat into the fire. The fire hissed and the spittle evaporated. "Might be some folks a-watchin' where we go."

"Rustlers?" Tolliver asked.

"Could be."

The others at the fire turned their heads and listened more intently.

Wu peeked out through the back flap of the chuck wagon, then backed out of sight just like a curious prairie dog.

"Well, a rustler ain't goin' to light no fire," Tolliver said.

"If they's a bunch of 'em laggin' ahind us,

164

they might. It can get mighty cold out here at night."

Tolliver scratched the side of his head.

"Yeah, yeah, they might," he said. "If they be a long ways off and think we're not goin' to pay them no mind."

"Or if you hear some riders checkin' anywheres on our tail or maybe tryin' to steal our horses, you come tell me. I'm sleepin' right behind the cook wagon."

"Sure, boss," Tolliver said. "But I'd rather be ridin' with someone. I don't see too good in the dark."

"You got big ears, Harve. Seein' at night is mostly listenin'."

Tolliver's face wrinkled up in perplexity, but after thinking if over for a few seconds, he nodded. "Yeah, I got good ears," he said.

"Big ears, Harve," Steve piped in.

Alicante laughed softly and then drank a swallow of coffee.

"Left saddlebag," Paddy said to Harvey when he walked over and picked up the bags next to the wheel. "Looks like a black tube or box. It's one o' them collapsin' thing-amajigs."

Tolliver pulled out the spyglass and turned it one way, then another.

"Pull on the end of it," Paddy said.

Harvey tugged at the wrong end, then

tried the other end. To his surprise the tube elongated and he marveled at its new size.

"Now you look up at the sky and twist that ring on the end to make it come into focus."

Tolliver put the eyepiece to his eye and tilted the tube upward. All he saw was a blur of lights in the sky. He twisted the ring and saw the lights converge and give him a clear image.

"I got it," he exclaimed.

Cheers from the campfire.

Tolliver walked back to where Paddy was sitting and tried the spyglass on others seated there. He twisted the ring to bring their faces into focus.

"It's a marvel," he said.

"You use that and move it real slow when you're lookin'," Paddy said. "You see a fire or riders, you come and get me."

"I'll do 'er, boss," he said.

He walked off then, looking at everything within view. He stumbled a few times and finally retracted the telescope and went to his bedroll and took off his boots. He slept with the instrument close at hand.

Paddy stayed by the fire until his eyes began to droop. He listened to the lowing of the cattle after he crawled into his bedroll and heard the cowhands on night watch singing off-key songs to keep the cows bedded down. He fell asleep with the smell of cattle, coffee, beef, and beans in his nostrils.

Wu made beef sandwiches with mustard and ketchup, stacked them in wooden boxes lined with butcher paper.

Finally the fire died down and red and orange sparks flew up in the air whenever the breeze tugged at the burning wood. The camp was quiet and the cowhands' songs floated over the cattle and lulled them to sleep.

The long drive had begun and by morning, another herd would be wending its way north, following a parallel path to the same destination.

And above it all, the North Star was the guiding light for all travelers, near and far, friend or foe.

CHAPTER 18

Ora Lee touched Dane on the shoulder and gently shook him awake.

"Len Crowell is here," she said to him. "He's having coffee with your pa."

Dane blinked his eyes and sat up in his bed.

"What time is it?" he asked.

"By my clock it's four thirty," she said. "Dark as pitch outside."

"Tell Pa and Len I'll be right there."

Ora Lee left the bedroom and Dane could hear her pattering footsteps down the hall. Then he heard low voices. He rubbed his eyes, swung out of bed, and touched the cold floor with his bare feet.

He walked to the sideboard and poured water from a porcelain pitcher into a metal bowl. He splashed water onto his face and rubbed some in his hair, smoothed it out. He looked in the small oval mirror hanging from the wall and pulled the skin down from under both eyes.

"Not too red," he said to himself.

He dressed quickly and strapped on his gun belt. He carried a Colt .45 single-action revolver in a plain black leather holster. The pistol had five cartridges in the chamber. The firing pin rested on an empty cylinder. His belt held two dozen cartridges in its leather loops.

He pulled on his boots, retrieved his hat and bandanna from the wardrobe, and walked out to the front room.

Dane sat down at the table with Len. A moment later, Ora Lee appeared and poured coffee into his empty cup.

"I got ham and eggs for you," she said.

"No. Too much goin' on, Ora Lee. I'll skip breakfast this morning."

"Suit yourself. I knew you wouldn't eat anyway. So I'll eat it myself."

Dane chuckled.

He sipped his coffee. He could tell that Len was waiting to talk to him, holding a whole spate of conversation inside like a kid who had just caught his first crawdad. Wisely, Len waited.

Thor sat in his chair trying not to doze off. He smelled of talcum powder and mustard plaster. Dane had heard him coughing the night before and then the

169

soothing voice of Ora Lee as she doctored him with home medications, honey and sorghum, the chest pack.

"All right, Len," Dane said after his third sip of coffee. "Men all up and rarin' to go?"

"Yep. Bunkhouse is plumb empty. Your horse, Reno, is saddled and the saddlebags packed with grub, your canteens are both full, and all you got to bring is your bedroll and rifle. We're all set."

"Barney all packed up?"

"Chuck wagon's loaded to the gills," Len said.

"Remuda?"

"Rufio's got 'em all on a long leash. One other thing."

"Yeah?"

"You know that Mex that Joe Eagle said wouldn't come on the drive?"

"Carlos something," Dane said.

"Well, sir, he showed up last night and I hired him on. Of course, you can fire him. Name's Carlos Montoya."

"Why'd he change his mind — do you know?"

"Well, he said he sold some horses to a man named Concho and then he saw Concho and some other hard cases head out yesterday mornin'."

"Head out where?"

"Carlos heard them talkin' about trackin' a big herd of cattle and rustlin' them. Made Carlos mad because he knew his friends were on that drive. He said there were about a dozen men, all armed to the teeth, and they lit a shuck for the north."

"Damn," Dane said.

Thor roused from his torpor and let out a long wheeze.

"Throckmorton," Thor said. "You can bet your britches he's behind all that."

"Yeah, Pa, I think you're right."

"Carlos is ready to fight those hombres, he said. He said they are all killers and he don't want to lose his friends."

"You did right to hire him on, Len. We can use another hand anyway. Paddy and I are both on the light side as far as hands go."

"Good," Len said.

"Well, you go on and make sure everything's ready to start those cattle. I'll be along directly."

"Sure thing, Dane." Len got up from the table and left through the front door.

Dane turned to speak to his father.

"You all right, Pa?" he asked.

"I been better."

"I'll be gone a good three months, I reckon."

171

"Wisht I was a-goin' with you."

"You got something you wanted to tell me about Throckmorton before I go?"

"I been thinkin' on it. Ain't somethin' I'm right proud of."

"Families shouldn't have secrets from each other," Dane said.

"Well, families do have secrets. Plenty of them. I don't know. Maybe I ought to tell you. Case I ain't here when you get back from Omaha."

"Oh, you'll be here, Pa, ornery as ever."

Thor laughed and convulsed into a coughing fit.

When his chest cleared, he looked up at Dane with bleary eyes. "A long time ago, when I was a young sprout, I was a drummer. I met a woman at a county fair. I didn't know she was married. Didn't know she was unhappy and planning to leave her husband. But she did leave him and went with me down south. Later, she started drinkin' real heavy and then she committed suicide."

"What has this to do with Throckmorton?" Dane asked.

"Her name was Earlene Throckmorton and she was Earl's mother. She abandoned him. Later, he tracked her down and then found out she was livin' with me. When she killed herself, Earl blamed me. But the

172

trouble in her life went back a long way. Long before I met her."

Dane was aghast. He slumped over and reached out to grab his father's hand. "Pa, you can't let this get to you. It's a long time ago."

"Yeah, but the past has a way of catchin' up to you. When you borrowed money from Throckmorton I wanted to tell you about him and his ma, but I couldn't get up the courage. And I knew you needed the money to build this ranch."

"Throckmorton's an ass," Dane said.

"But he carries a big old heavy grudge against me. And that means he's got a grudge against you, Dane."

Dane squeezed his father's hand. "Don't you worry none, Pa. Looks like I got a grudge against him too. And it don't go back very far."

"He means to kill you, son, sure as shootin'. He wants you dead. He wants your cattle and your ranch. And if he gets all that done, he'll come after me."

"I would never let any of that happen, Pa."

"Well, I ain't got much time left no-how. When I married Olga, I thought it was for life. Then she died and I met your mother, Scarlet. Two of the best women I ever knowed. But I had a soft spot in my heart for Earlene too. Talk about secrets. She had a whole passel of them and never let on."

"I'm glad you had a good life with at least two good women, Pa. I knew about Olga, of course, and I loved my mother. But they both died young and that's why I never took to no woman. I didn't want the grief."

"Usually the women outlive their men, Dane. I was just unlucky. From the first to the last."

Dane patted his father's hand, drank the rest of his coffee, and stood up. "You get well, Pa. We'll talk some more when I get back."

"Good-bye, son. Watch your back."

"I will," Dane said.

He walked to the corner where his rifle leaned against the wall. He picked up his bedroll and slung the rifle over his shoulder.

Ora Lee came out into the front room.

"Good-bye, Mr. Dane," she said.

"Ora Lee, I wish you'd drop the mister before my name. I always think you're confusing me with my pa."

She laughed and raised a hand in farewell.

"Yes, sir," she said, and then bent over to check on Thor, who waved her away.

"Don't block my chance to see my son walk out the door," he said.

Dane left. His horse, Reno, was at the

hitch rail. It was quiet and dark. Very quiet. Very dark.

He tied on his bedroll and slid his rifle in its scabbard. He mounted up and took one last look at the house. He was filled with a sudden sadness at leaving his father for so long a time.

He caught up with Len and Carlos Montoya, introduced himself to the Mexican.

"Glad you decided to join us, Carlos," Dane said.

"You got big trouble, Mr. Kramer."

"Call me Dane, will you? I know we have to keep a sharp lookout for Concho and his gang."

"Concho, he is very bad man."

Dane sensed that Carlos had more to say about Concho. He waited, but Carlos did not offer him any more information.

"What do you know about Concho and those men with him?" Dane asked.

"I know who Concho is and what he does," Carlos said.

"I'm listenin'."

Then Carlos opened up. "He is from Nebraska," he said, "but he come to New Mexico. I live there with my brother, Eladio. We find wild horses and break them. We drink in the cantina. Concho, he like a girl. Eladio, he like the same girl. Concho, he

175

shoot Eladio at the cantina. Eladio, he have no chance. Concho tell sheriff it was the self-defense. Ha! It was murder."

"Were you there? You saw it happen?"

"I was there. I see it all. Eladio, he do not want no trouble. He try to get away. Concho, he shoot him dead. I cry. I could do nothing."

"That's a sad story, Carlos. I'm sorry."

"There's more to it than that, Dane," Len said. "Do you know why they call Larabee 'Concho'?"

"No, I don't. Do you?"

"Tell him, Carlos," Len said.

"This Concho, he kill many men in New Mexico. He work for cattlemen and they pay him to kill other rancheros. When he kill them, to collect his money, he put the little shells of the snail on their eyes. So he get the name Concho."

Dane drew in a breath. "A man like that doesn't deserve to live, Carlos. But you don't mean to kill him, do you? For revenge?"

"I do not want him to kill my friends Alfredo and Rufio. They do not know this man. They do not know they are in danger."

"Would you kill Concho if you had the chance?"

Carlos's chest swelled with breath. His

face hardened. "Yes, I would kill him. I hate him for killing my brother."

"Well, if the man shows up and tries to rustle our cattle, we'll sure as hell turn every rifle on him that we can."

"I'd like to kill him myself," Len said. "And then go back and kill Throckmorton for hiring him to do his dirty work."

"I've never hated anybody," Dane said, "but I'm startin' to think it wouldn't be too hard with men like Concho and Throckmorton taking land and money and people as if life didn't matter to them."

"Bad men," Carlos said.

In the distance, they heard the lowing of the cattle, the restless mooing and grumbling of a herd being bunched up. There was the tang of their offal on the air and the heavy scent of cattle hides, horseflesh, and the sweat of working men.

"I reckon we got two horse wranglers now, Len," Dane said.

"And another gun," Len said.

Dane's stomach roiled, not from hunger, but from a growing fear. Maybe he had taken on too much, and he might have made a mistake by splitting the herd up into two sections. If Concho and his men had ridden out of town the day before, it would not take them long to find the first herd.

How long, he wondered, would it take Concho to realize that Paddy's herd was only part of the total number of cattle he was driving to Omaha? And if his job was to rustle all the cattle and prevent him from paying off his mortgage at the bank, would he be satisfied with only two thousand head?

The questions came in a rush and Dane had no answers for himself.

But behind all the speculation about the rustling of his cattle, there was another, more ominous question.

Was Concho out to murder him and make the way clear for Throckmorton to steal his ranch without hindrance?

That was a distinct possibility.

Dane touched the stock of his rifle and then his hand drifted to the butt of his pistol.

He had to be ready if Concho came after him.

No, he thought, no if.

When Concho came after him, as he surely would.

He saw the humps of his cattle in the murky distance, the moon shining on their curly hides and tingeing their horns with silvery dust. It was a fine morning and he saw his men riding around the herd, heard the whicker of the horses and the chirps and whistles of birds roused by all the activity on the Two Grand range.

His stomach unknotted and he put all thoughts of Concho and Throckmorton out of his mind. There was work to do and a thousand head of cattle to move off the ranch and begin their trek to Omaha.

Somewhere along the way, he was almost certain, he would find out what Concho was up to, and if it came to a fight, he was ready.

But, he wondered, was he also ready to die?

That was probably the ultimate test of a man's courage, in war and in peace.

It was a thought he would carry with him as he rode off in the early darkness with new country ahead and murderous men lying in wait. Like a pack of wolves.

He pulled out his pouch and tucked tobacco into his mouth.

"Time to go to work," Dane said to Len.

Len nodded and spurred his horse into a trot.

Carlos and Dane caught up with him and then they were among their own kind, the cowhands who were the very salt of the earth.

CHAPTER 19

Concho took the lead with Randy riding alongside him in the early darkness of the morning. Concho set his course by the North Star, but at Randy's urging, he angled to the east. An hour or so after leaving the livery, they both heard the rumble of the supply wagon and the chuck wagon. It was still too dark to see, but Concho chose a parallel course that put them within earshot of the herd but out of sight of both the herd and the outriders.

He signaled for Lem to join him on point. Lem rode up alongside.

"I hear 'em," he said in a low voice.

Concho looked up at the starry sky.

" 'Pears to me they're headin' on a path that will take them between Stillwater and Tulsa," Concho said

"Likely," Lem said. "You know the country."

"Been a while, but I'm thinkin' them

cattle got to have grass and water."

"How many miles do you think they'll make today?" Lem asked.

"We're at a fast walk and we're catchin' up to the head of the herd. I'd say they won't get far this first day. Say eight or nine miles."

"Hell, that'll take them months to get all the way up into Nebraska."

"They'll pick up the pace tomorrow or next day," Concho said. "Likely, they got to train the herd, make them cows forget their home range."

"I reckon," Lem said, his voice quavering from the bounce of his saddle.

Randy didn't much like riding in darkness. But when he thought of all the hard men following them in single file, he felt almost like a soldier. He was part of something, something that made him feel important. He was glad to be riding with the leader, Concho, and not just one of those anonymous men who followed after them like sheep. He did feel important, and to listen to grown men talk made him feel as if he were older than he was. He had always wished for an older brother, someone he could look up to and who would make him feel important. For now, Concho was that older brother.

When the sun rose, they could see the dust cloud raised by the cattle and horses. The dust was filled with swirling ribbons and tendrils of gold and peach, the small grains shining in the sunrise like tiny jeweled insects. To Randy, it was a magnificent sight. It meant that a mighty herd of cattle was on the move and men were guiding them into unknown country. He would have liked to be part of that group of drovers, a man among men, but he knew he was far from living up to their standards. Unlike the hard-bitten men he rode with now, the cowhands were a breed apart. They were men who worked for a living and did not drink or carouse on a daily basis. They were men who took pride in chasing down a cow, roping a steer, and burning a brand into its hide. They were the kind of men he could learn from and Dane was the kind of man he might have grown to be if he had taken a different path. But he knew he was young and foolish and when Throckmorton had recruited him to spy on Kramer and the Circle K, that had made him feel important and wanted. And now Concho had wanted him to ride in the front of the column with him.

Oh, he knew why, but that didn't make any difference. Concho wanted him to identify all the men on the drive and point out, especially Dane Kramer. But he was being paid for it, maybe not cowhand's wages, but enough to make him feel that Concho and Throckmorton needed him. Maybe, when his job was finished, he could go somewhere and hire on as a cowhand and forget his past as a spotter for a band of outlaws. That was what he wished as he watched the sun rise and could smell the cattle in the drifting dust, see the land spread out before him all green and gentle, the dew still glistening on the grass like tiny crystal beads.

"Lem," Concho said, after a time, "tell Mitch and the others to widen way to the left of us and go on ahead. Tell 'em I said to wait for us somewhere between Stillwater and Tulsa. But don't let nobody get within sight of the herd."

"You ain't goin' to jump nobody until we cross over into Kansas, right?"

"That's right. Kramer's going to run his cattle until just before dusk, then bed 'em down. I doubt if they'll make it as far as Stillwater, but they might. Me and the kid are going to ride in for a closer look just so's I know where Kramer is ridin'."

"You want me to go with Mitch and them?" Lem asked.

"No, you ride with me and the kid. Might need you."

"Sure, boss," Lem said, and slowed his horse so that he would drop behind.

When the others caught up to him, he spoke to Mitch and Lyle, the first two riders in the column. He told them what Concho had said and they nodded and swung wide to the left as Mitch passed along Concho's orders to the rest of them.

Concho slowed his horse so that Lem could catch up. He watched as his men took a path well off to his left. He watched them until they disappeared and then breathed a sigh of relief.

"Now we don't have to worry about them until nightfall. And it's less likely any of those drovers will spot us."

"I think the cattle are slowin' down, Concho," Lem said. "Listen to them wagons."

"Kramer's probably lettin' the cows do some grazin'. Then he'll start 'em out again and eat up some miles."

The morning wore on and the three men slowed their horses to a walk. The dust cloud thinned as the cattle snatched up grass and moved on at a slower pace. They crossed a creek and figured that the cattle would slow even more while they drank at the stream.

There, the horses drank from the creek as well. Lem and Concho built smokes and lit their quirlies while Randy looked at the leaves of the trees and watched them giggle and twist in the morning breeze. The air was fresh and scented with wildflowers and far-off fields of corn and wheat that were just beginning to emerge from the earth. He felt good and relaxed as the occasional strand of smoke scratched at his nostrils. The aroma of grown men, he thought. And he could smell their horses too and the leather of their saddles and bridles.

The two men finished their smokes and they all crossed the creek. The horses' hooves splashed water and Randy could see tiny rainbows in the spray. They left dark splotches of water on the banks and then they were in grass and the muffled sound of the horses' hooves was soothing to him as he rode with Lem and Concho.

Finally, when the sun was at its noon height, Concho looked to his right and saw no more dust blowing in the breeze.

"Noon stop, I reckon," he said.

"Could be," Lem agreed.

"Lem, you keep on our track until you see that herd raise dust again. The kid and I are goin' to mosey over closer for a look-see."

"Okay," Lem said. "You be careful, Concho."

"We'll take it real slow. Just goin' to watch awhile and see what's what."

"Do some scoutin'," Lem cracked with a slow grin. He spurred his horse and rode off.

Concho turned to Randy. "Ready to do some spottin', kid?"

"Sure, Concho. I wish you'd call me by my real name, though. I hate 'kid.' "

"All right, Randy. Come along. We're going to sneak up on that herd and then I'll put the glass on 'em and hand you the binoculars whilst you point out who's who and who's where."

"I'll do it, Concho," Randy said.

"Mind you, we may have to ground-tie our horses and crawl on our bellies for a ways."

"That's okay with me, Concho."

The two rode over until they saw the brown sea of cattle. There was a rider moving along the left flank of the herd, and every so often he would stop and scan the horizon with a long black object.

"That's the outrider a'lookin' for us," Concho whispered to Randy. "He's got a spyglass and he could spot a wart on your nose from where he's at."

"I don't have no wart on my nose," Randy said in a whisper.

"Hunch down in the saddle," Concho ordered as he did the same. "Wait until he rides on. Likely he won't look back."

Randy hunkered down over his saddle horn, which pressed into his chest so hard it became painful.

The outrider rode on. The herd moved slowly forward.

Still, Concho waited.

He waited until he saw the chuck wagon rumble up into view, followed by the supply wagon. Then he saw the remuda, the horses all on a long rope, following the wrangler single file.

He raised the binoculars to his eyes as he sat up straight in the saddle. He swept the glass over the wagons and the wrangler.

"Here, you take a look, Randy boy. Tell me who's a-drivin' that chuck wagon and the man on the supply wagon, then look at the wrangler with the horses. See if you know any of 'em."

Randy sat up straight. Concho passed the binoculars over to him and Randy held them up to his eyes without slipping the strap around his neck. He took his time and looked at each wagon, then settled on the wrangler leading the horses.

187

"Well?" Concho asked when Randy handed the field glass back to him.

"Looks like a Chinaman settin' on the chuck wagon seat. Don't know him. Never seen him before."

"That's what I thought. It's a Chink and I seen him before. He worked for Len Crowell, a damned sodbuster. How about the man on the supply wagon?"

"I think that's Jim Recknor. Looks like him."

"And what about the horse wrangler?"

"Don't recognize him at all. But he could be one of those Mexicans Joe Eagle is always talkin' about."

Concho put the glass back to his eyes and looked long at the wrangler. "He's a Mex all right. I think he's one of them what works with Montoya raisin' horses. Don't know his name, but he's one of that greasy bunch."

"Kramer never had no Mexes workin' for him that I know of," Randy said.

"Likely he scraped the bottom of the barrel with them three," Concho said. He let the binoculars dangle from his neck. "Let's ride up ahead and see who's on point and maybe you can tell me who's ridin' drag ahead of them wagons and the remuda. If we see a flanker, you see if you know who it is."

"Are you lookin' for anybody in particular, Concho?" Randy asked.

"Yeah, the trail boss and Dane Kramer. And maybe that half-breed, Joe Eagle."

"I know them three," Randy said.

They rode on, keeping their distance from the herd, hunkering low in their saddles. Then Concho reined up and they halted.

"Now look to the tail end of the herd and see if you know who's ridin' drag, Randy boy."

Randy didn't like the word *boy* tacked onto his name any more than he liked *kid,* but he said nothing. He took the glass from Concho and held it to his eyes. He adjusted the focus and brought the rider roaming the tail end of the herd into sharp view.

"That looks like Donny Peterson," Randy mumbled as if he were talking to himself. "Yep, that's Donny all right. He's ridin' back and forth at the rear of the herd."

"Keep the glass for a spell," Concho said. "I see a flanker up ahead. See if you know who that is."

They rode on a little farther until Concho stopped again.

"Fix your eyes on that flanker," he said.

Randy looked through the binoculars at a man riding along the left flank of the herd.

The man's horse danced as it drove back any straying cow, and it was hard to see his face under the brim of his hat, which shaded his eyes.

"I don't know who that is, for sure, Concho," Randy said. "Looks like Chub Toomey, but it could be Orville Hanratty. He resembles Toomey somewhat."

"Not Kramer, though," Concho said.

"Nope. That's not Dane. That's either Chub or Orville."

"All right, now let's see who's ridin' point. My hunch is you'll see both Kramer and O'Riley up there. Watch out for that one with the spyglass, though. Stay low in the saddle."

They rode on until they had passed the lead cattle in the herd. The outrider with the spyglass had ridden to the other side, apparently.

Concho halted. "I can just barely make out the riders in the front. You take a look, Randy boy, and tell me who you see." He handed the glass to Randy.

Randy adjusted the field glass until the riders came into focus.

"There's Paddy," he said, "ridin' way up front, and there's another man with him."

"Kramer?"

"Wait a minute. No, that ain't Dane

neither. I don't know who it is."

"Gimme that glass," Concho said, traces of both anger and impatience in his voice.

He looked through the binoculars for a long moment while Randy watched the herd and the point men come closer.

"Well, I'll be damned," Concho said as he let the binoculars dangle from his neck. "I'll be double damned."

"What is it?" Randy asked.

"The other man with O'Riley is Lester Pierson. Worked for Crowell. We run them off'n his ranch about a month ago."

"You sure?"

"As sure as anything. That's Pierson ridin' right alongside that Irish potato eater."

"I don't think Dane is with the herd," Randy said after a moment or two of silence between the two of them.

"I don't think so either," Concho said, "and now that I look over that herd, I don't think there's three thousand head in it. More like half that number. Maybe more."

"What does that mean?" Randy asked.

Concho turned his horse away from the oncoming herd. Randy followed him.

"It means we been snookered, that's what. Kramer has done broke up the herd. He ain't with this one, so he must be followin' behind with the rest of his damned cattle."

"So, what are you going to do, Concho?"

Concho scratched his chin and tilted his hat back on his head.

"I don't rightly know, kid," he said. "I got to think on it."

Randy asked no more questions as they rode on, well ahead of the herd. Soon, he knew, they would catch up to Lem. Then Concho might talk to him about the situation and maybe they would discuss what to do.

For now, Randy felt a strange sense of relief that Dane Kramer was not with the first herd. He had outfoxed Concho and Throckmorton. So he must have known that Throckmorton would try and stop him from selling his herd in Omaha and paying off his mortgage.

Pretty smart of Dane, Randy thought.

He tried to quell the sense of pride in Dane that was rising inside him. He had no reason to be loyal to a man he had spied on and betrayed, but he did have a strong sense of admiration for Dane that he could not deny.

He just hoped Concho could not read his thoughts right then.

CHAPTER 20

Joe Eagle rode out to meet Dane. It was still pitch-dark, but the Cherokee breed had an uncanny sixth sense, or so it seemed to Dane.

"Joe," Dane said, "do you read human minds like you do animal minds?"

"Me know much," Joe said. He looked at Montoya and rode close enough so that the two men could shake hands.

"Happy you here, Carlos," Joe said. "You ride with us?"

"Yes, I ride with you, *hermano,*" Montoya said. "Maybe we blow out the lamp of that Concho, eh?"

"Now, now," Dane said, "let's not put the cart before the horse. We've got a long drive ahead of us and we don't want to look for trouble."

"Concho bad man," Joe said.

Wisely, no one else made any comment, and the four men rode into the tail end of

193

the herd, which was still bedded down.

"Everything all set, Joe?" Dane asked as he swung out of the saddle and walked to the fire the hands had started a short time before his arrival. Several were there warming their cold hands over the blazing flames.

"All set," Joe said, from the saddle.

Len looked over the herd and led his horse over to the supply wagon, where he tied the reins to the left front wheel. Maynard Cuzzins was tying three small barrels together and then securing both ends of the rope to the sidewalls of the wagon.

"Howdy, Len," Cuzzins said. "I got two extry wheels and a pile of spokes, like you said."

"And all the tools?"

"Every last one and some extry too, case we need to do some fixin' on the trail."

"Firewood and kindling?"

"Enough to burn a coupla nights. I 'spect I'll gather more along the way when we run out."

"First night or two, it's important that we have cook fires."

"I know. I done talked to Barney. He said he'd be right frugal with the wood."

Len frowned. Frugal was a word cookies seldom used. He wished Wu Ling was on their drive, not Barney Gooch.

"Well, you have a good ride, Maynard," Len said, and walked back to the fire where some of the men were waiting for his orders.

"When do you want me to kick up the lead cattle, Dane?" Len asked.

"Let's wait for the streak of dawn in the east, Len," Dane said. "No use headin' 'em out in the dark when they don't know where they're goin'."

"That's what I figgered," Len said. "We had a hell of a time last night gettin' all of 'em to bed down. I think they wanted to follow Paddy's herd."

Dane laughed.

"Cows are funny," he said. "They see their brothers head out and think they're missin' somethin'."

"Ain't that the truth?" piped in Chad Ransom, one of Dane's most experienced hands. He was a Texan from the Rio Grande Valley and stood a head taller than any of the others. "Why, I cut an old cow out of the herd oncet and a dozen follered me all the way to the woodshed. They stood around while I knocked that cow down and butchered her."

Everyone at the fire laughed.

"Where is Rufio?" Montoya asked. "I want to tell him I am here."

"He's probably over by the tank yonder

with the horses," Len said. "Just go on past the chuck wagon and you'll find him."

Montoya left and the men were silent for a few moments.

"I think we've got a good man there, Dane," Len said.

"We can use him. As long as he's not a hothead."

"Him no hothead," Joe Eagle said.

"I'll take your word for it, Joe," Dane said. He plucked tobacco from his pouch just as Barney showed up at the edge of the fire's glow carrying a big pot of steaming coffee and several tin cups dangling on a length of twine tied to his belt.

"You clank like a rusty cart, Barney," Dane said as he put the pouch away without putting tobacco in his mouth.

"Figgered you all might want some hot coffee afore you start out," Barney said. "I'll pick up the cups and pot before we leave."

"Thanks," Dane said.

One of the men grabbed up the twine and started stripping off cups. Another handed them out to all who were there. Barney poured the coffee in each man's cup.

"No shiverin', now, fellas," Barney said. "I don't want you spillin' good coffee on the ground."

Len was the only one who didn't laugh,

but he was reforming his opinion of Gooch. He missed Chang Wu Ling, but he might get along with Barney after all.

The men blew on their cups, shredding the warm vapors that arose above the rims. They drank slowly and watched the dark and star-studded sky, shifting their weight on first one foot, then the other.

Dane could see that they were all eager to set out and so was he. But he was determined to wait until sunup. He didn't want any hitches when he started the drive and he knew the herd would be jumpy, with some cattle breaking away to test the men on horseback. He didn't want any horses gored by a nervous and frisky whiteface that wanted to return to its home pasture. So many things could go wrong at the start of a drive and along the trail that he wanted it to go smooth. That would build confidence in his men and teach the cattle to behave or get a rope or quirt across their snouts.

Carlos and Rufio embraced when they met next to the water tank. The horses drank and pawed the ground, bobbed their heads, and whickered softly.

The two men spoke in rapid Spanish. Carlos told Rufio what had happened in town when Concho and his men had bought horses from him and then headed north

197

before dawn.

"You must take care, Rufio," Carlos said. "That Concho is very dangerous."

"And he is the man who killed your brother."

"He has killed many men, Rufio."

"You will kill him, then?"

"If I see him, I will kill him."

"Do you think he will try to steal the cattle?"

"Yes. I heard him talking to his men. They have many guns and they are going to attack us and they will kill some of us."

"We have many men too, and Len told us we must be ready to fight off the rustlers of cattle."

"The men with Concho, they are used to killing people."

"We can all shoot the rifle or the pistol. We are good shots."

"They will sneak up in the dead of night and try to kill us," Carlos said.

"I will sleep with the one eye open," Rufio said.

Carlos slapped him on the back. "I will be right beside you, amigo, with one of my eyes open."

"Then we will have two good eyes open."

The two men laughed and then Carlos helped Rufio run a rope through the rings of the halters so that all the horses were tied together. Rufio led them over to where his saddled horse was tied to a post.

"I will get my horse," Carlos said.

"I welcome your presence, my friend," Rufio said.

Carlos walked back to the campfire and drank coffee while they all waited for the dawn.

Dane cleared his throat and held up a hand.

"Men," he said, "I want you all to pass the word before we start out. Leonard Crowell here is the trail boss. He is going to choose our route and see that we all work together and carry out our duties. As for me, I'm just along for the ride and to do all the paperwork in Kansas City and Omaha. We're going on a hell of a journey and our beef cattle are the best in the country. As soon as it gets light, we'll get this herd going and head north. Good luck to all of you."

The men all cheered Dane and he felt his face grow hot and redden.

Then Len spoke up.

"I'm grateful to Dane for giving me this opportunity. As some of you know, I lost my own herd on my last drive. I'm determined that this one will be successful. You and all of the other hands have your assignments. If you have any gripes, please come to me so that I can settle them. It's a long drive, but we should have good weather and the cattle are all healthy and robust. Let's show the country we pass through that we are cattlemen and know what to do. I'm proud to be your trail boss."

More cheers from the men around the campfire. And the word quickly spread, although most of the hands already knew that Crowell was to be the trail boss.

Dane kept looking at the sky and when he saw the soft blue of the coming day begin to creep up over the horizon, he nodded to Len, who ordered the men to their stations. They all drained their cups and walked to their horses. Len and Dane rode to the front of the herd.

The eastern horizon began to open up and the stars disappeared as the sky lightened.

"You pick out a lead cow yet?" Dane asked as they rode along the left flank of the stirring herd.

"Yep," he said. "I think she misses the herd that left yesterday. I've got a man up there holding her in check. She wants to run off the range."

Dane laughed.

"Good," he said. "If she continues to lead,

you can bell her and we'll hear that sweet sound all the way to Omaha."

"I'll have it done when we bed down for the night."

By the time they reached the head of the herd, most of the cattle were on their feet. They moaned and groaned as if they were eager to set out. Len rode up to the lead cow and chased her away from the herd and pointed her north. His horse, a trained cutter, zigzagged back and forth on her tail as she bellowed. The cows behind her started after her. Dane took the right flank to get out of Len's way and kept the cattle bunched.

As he rode along, he watched as all the cattle picked up the pace and followed blindly in the wake of the lead cow. When he looked back, he saw bobbing white faces and horns. He felt a deep satisfaction when the more than one thousand head began to break trail. The flankers turned the bolters back into the herd. He heard the wagons begin to roll, and behind them, the whinny of the horses in the remuda told him that they were on the move as well.

The cattle followed the track of the first herd for a long while, and when the sun came up, he watched as Len turned the lead cow toward a slightly different track on his left flank. The cattle followed as the drovers shouted and yelled both encouragement and warnings.

As the sun cleared the horizon and drenched the land in a fiery glow, the dew on the grass sparkled like tiny gems and evaporated. In the distance, he saw the lights of Shawnee Mission come on and smoke rise from the chimneys. They passed isolated homes that were still dark, but on the farms, there were lamps and lanterns lit, and men milked cows and slopped their hogs while women gathered eggs from the henhouses.

Soon they left the town and the ranch behind and the cattle settled into a steady, brisk walk on new grass, some of them snatching up clumps of gama grass they trudged on, one long caravan behind a leader they could not see.

Dane felt a strong feeling of satisfaction swell within his chest. There was a thrill to seeing the herd moving smoothly. The cattle seemed almost eager to be on the trail. He was sure they could smell the spoor of those cattle which had left the day before and this was probably what drove them on with little prodding from the drovers.

Joe Eagle rode up behind him and they rode alongside each other.

"What do you think, Joe?" Dane asked.

"Cows move good."

"Any trouble back there?"

"No, all good, Dane," Joe said. "Cow leads. Herd follow."

They both watched Len continue to turn the lead cow well away from the track of the cattle that had left the range the day before. Soon they were well away from the other trail.

"Him good boss," Joe said.

"He knows what he's doing all right."

"Cows follow him. That good. Heap good."

"Joe, by the time we get to Omaha, you're going to be ready to give a speech."

Joe chuckled and shook his head. "Joe Eagle no give speech. Have smoke. Drink firewater."

"You can't drink firewater, Joe."

"Smell firewater," Joe said with a quick laugh.

"That's better. I'll drink for you."

"You not worry about Concho?"

"I won't worry about him until I see his ugly face."

"Maybe not see face. Maybe see only bullet."

"A man should not worry about what might happen, Joe. To worry is to be afraid."

"That true," Joe said.

"To worry is to have fear," Dane said, "and fear brings failure."

Joe made a grunting sound of agreement.

As the sun rose higher in the sky and the land blossomed with light, Joe drifted back on the flank and Dane rode alone, holding the lead cows to the track Len had set.

He breathed deeply of the fresh air and felt the cool breeze on his face.

A man could not ask for much more, he thought. These were his cattle and they were heading for high grass on miles of open prairie. There would be rivers and streams to cross, and his men were all primed to face any dangers that might lie ahead.

Concho be damned, he thought.

And Throckmorton too.

One day, he thought, his ranch would swallow up the bank and spit it out like so much tripe. Land was no good if you didn't work it and make it pay. Cattle were the real wealth of the country, and this fine morning he felt very rich

He plucked tobacco from his pouch and tucked the wad into his mouth. The juices quelled his hunger and when he spat, he felt like a king. He was doing what he was born to do.

The drive was off to a great start. He

wanted to let out a yell, but there was no reason to show his exuberance. He could feel it in his bones and in the horse he was riding.

"You feel it, don't you, Reno?" he said to his horse as he patted him on the withers.

Reno snorted and tossed his head.

And he stepped out like a champion when Dane gave him his head, lightened up on the reins.

Soon the herd rode through wild clover, and the smell was sweet in Dane's nostrils. Wildflowers poked their petals up in the midst of the green, and their scent mingled with the grasses.

The scent made him slightly homesick and he thought about his father as he chewed the tobacco in his mouth.

"Hold on, Pa," he said to himself. "I'll be back home before you know it."

But with each mile, he felt his home fade in the distance, as if all had been an illusion.

And there were a thousand miles to go before he would see his father again.

CHAPTER 21

Concho's anger crescendoed into a towering rage by the time he rejoined the rest of his men. Randy could almost feel the heat radiating from Concho when they rode up and saw the men standing next to their horses as the animals grazed.

"That son of a bitch Kramer done dealt from the bottom of the deck," Concho said to his men.

"What you talkin' about, Concho?" Skip Hewes asked.

"Bastard broke up his herd. He ain't with the one we scouted."

"You mean he's makin' two drives?" Logan asked.

"Either that or he's goin' to be short on delivery in Omaha," Concho said.

He dismounted and started kicking grass and gouging grooves into the earth with the toes of his boots.

His men all stared at him as if had gone

plumb mad all of a sudden.

"So, what are we goin' to do, Concho?" Mitch asked. "Rustle two separate herds?"

"Shut up, Mitch," Concho snapped. "I got to think."

The men went silent. Randy slowly dismounted and stood apart from the others. He didn't want to be anywhere near Concho in case he started swinging with his fists all balled up like a pair of hammers.

No one spoke for several moments.

Finally Concho squatted on the ground and picked up a stick that was lying nearby. He drew a circle in the dirt. The others watched him and then squatted around him.

"Here's what we got," Concho said. "Likely, Kramer sent one herd on ahead. "Remember, Lem, I told you I didn't trust that Mex we got them horses from?"

"Yeah, I remember, Concho," Lemuel said. "What's that got to do with Kramer sending out only part of his herd?"

"I think Montoya heard me or you or somebody say somethin' before we left town. He probably hightailed it out to the Circle K and shot his mouth off. So Kramer says he'll outfox me and send only part of his herd north."

Concho drew a line across his circle.

"Here's one herd," he said. "Now, we

might could rustle this bunch once it crosses into Kansas and hold 'em until Kramer shows up with the rest of his herd."

Lem scratched his head, knocking his hat off slightly to the side.

"What good would that do?" he asked.

"Kramer might think that first herd got slowed up and stalled and run his cattle right in with them what we cotched."

"So?" Mitch said.

"So we kill two birds with one stone, maybe," Concho said.

"You count how many hands are with this herd?" Skip asked.

"Not to a man, no," Concho said. "But they got at least a dozen men."

"All with rifles and six-guns," Will Davis said dryly.

Concho looked at Davis with hard eyes. His lips clamped together. They flattened in a straight line in the center of his jaw.

Then he let out a breath through tight lips. "Yeah, they got guns. And so do we. Question is, can we outsmart Paddy O'Riley and take him out before we have to draw down on the others? Might be we can cut off the head of that snake and just get them others to throw down their guns and do what we say."

"A whole lot of ifs and maybes in there,

Concho," Lyle Fisk said.

Concho drew a line across the other line and then drew a small circle just above it.

"Let's say this is the herd O'Riley's ramrodding," he said, pointing the stick at the little circle. "We rustle that herd and scatter it out so it's like a wall clear acrost where Kramer's headin'. So he comes up, sees all the cattle spread out like they're on their home range, and rides right in, drivin' his herd right through the middle. We can pick him off and cut down any of his waddies that bring rifles to their shoulders. Likely, by the time Kramer figgers it all out, it'll be too damned late."

"Might work," Skip said. "We could use the cattle in that first herd for cover and shoot over their backs. Some of us could be on horseback and come runnin' up when the shootin' starts and cut the flankers and the man ridin' drag before they could gather up all their wits."

Concho smiled at Skip.

"You're gettin' the idea," he said. "Anybody here got a better idea?"

Lem spoke up. "Once you start shootin', say when Kramer comes up, that first herd ain't goin' to sit still. They'll spook sure as hell and stampede all over creation. Be hell roundin' 'em all back up."

There was a silence. Concho rubbed fingers across his forehead. "You got a point, Lem. We might just stampede the herd with Kramer too."

"Which wouldn't be a real bad thing," Lyle said, a nervous quaver to his voice.

"We might have to gun down a lot of them cowhands," Skip said.

"Hell, some of 'em'll probably run back to home once they see Kramer go down," Mitch said.

"We can't count on that," Concho said.

"What if we jumped them cowpokes at night when some of 'em are sleepin' in their bedrolls?" Logan Heckler asked. "Might stampede the cattle, but it would sure cut down the number of guns we'd have to face."

"Don't use no guns," Mitch said. "Slip up on 'em when they're asleep and slit their throats." His mouth twisted in a savage leer.

"Not a bad idea," Lemuel said. "No noise. No guns. Bye-bye, cowhands."

Some of the men laughed.

Mitch licked his lips and flashed another bloodthirsty grin.

"It's something to think about," Concho said.

"Why in hell do we have to wait until they drive that herd into Kansas?" Skip asked.

"We're a long way from Kansas and they might have other tricks up their sleeves besides splittin' the herd in half."

Concho stood up, his anger boiling up again.

"Throckmorton wants us out of Oklahoma, that's why," he said. "He don't want no connection to him, so we got to rustle them cows up in Kansas."

"Well," Skip said, "who's to know? We could take 'em here, run 'em up to Kansas, and come back when we get the rest of Kramer's herd."

Two or three of the men seemed to agree. They grunted and nodded.

"We'll do it Throckmorton's way," Concho said. "Besides, if we let O'Riley think he's not goin' to be jumped, he'll let his guard down and when we do hit him, he'll have a big surprise."

"You're the boss," Skip said.

"And don't you forget it, Skip," Concho said. He walked to his horse.

"Where do we go now, Concho?" Lem asked.

"We'll ride up to the Verdigris. That's a river O'Riley's got to cross. We'll count men there and see how he handles the ford. Won't be too far after that before he'll be in Kansas and we can jump him."

"Sounds like a fair plan," Lem said.

"It'll give me more time to think. I didn't expect Kramer to hold back part of his herd. What he done was put a big old kink in my rope and I don't like it none."

"Seems to me we got a lot of possibilities. Might be easier dealin' with one herd first, then waylay the next one when Kramer crosses the border."

"Yeah, Kramer might have done us a favor."

Randy had listened to all the talk and now he wondered just what Concho would do.

Of one thing he was certain, and the thought sent shivers up his backbone.

A lot of men were going to die.

And some of them were men he knew.

Suddenly he felt his knees turn to jelly as he stood up and started to walk to his horse.

"You come with me, Randy boy," Concho said.

Randy winced.

"I ain't no boy," he said.

"Wait'll you get some blood on your hands, kid. Then you can call yourself a man."

Randy closed his eyes for a second.

"There will be blood on the trail, boy," Concho said. "You can count on it."

CHAPTER 22

Paddy sent Whit Hawkins west along the deep fork of the Canadian River and Bill Coombs east along the same river.

"Find us a ford," he said. "A shallow crossin'. I don't want no cattle drowneded."

Whit rode off with Bill to the bank of the river and then they split up.

The cattle grazed south of the river, but they could smell water and were kicking up a fuss. Three men held the lead cow in check and turned the others back, chasing those that jumped out of the herd and tried to head for water.

"We can't hold 'em much longer," Steve yelled at Paddy.

"Do your dadgummed job, Steve," Paddy yelled back. "River's too deep here."

Steve ran a steer down before it reached the riverbank and gave his horse its head. The cutter matched every twist and turn of the steer and diverted it from its course until it ran bellowing in protest back into the herd.

"Hell, Paddy, how come we can't let 'em drink before we take 'em acrost?" Harvey asked. He was out of breath because he had just chased three cows back, halfway down the wide column of cattle.

"Harve," Paddy said, "you're supposed to be out scoutin' with that spyglass."

"Paddy, that glass is wearin' a hole in my eye. I ain't seen nothin'. Fact is, you can take your telescope, wet it down, and shove it up your ass."

"You got a smart mouth, Harve. Gimme the glass. I'll find somebody else to scout."

Harvey reached into his saddlebag and pulled out the collapsed telescope. He handed it to Paddy.

"From here on, Harve," Paddy said, "you ride drag."

"Damn it, Paddy, I'm a drover. I don't fancy lookin' at cattle butts and eatin' dust all damned day."

"Do as I say, or draw your pay," Paddy said. He was reaching the limit of his patience with Harvey. It was true he had not seen any of the outlaw band he suspected was following them, but it was plain that Harvey longed for human companionship and didn't take to riding circles around the herd all by himself.

"I'll ride drag," Harve said. "At least I won't have to see your ugly face all damned day."

Paddy resisted the urge to retort. He understood that there were tensions among the men. They were worried about being bushwhacked, or attacked by Indians. They'd had a run-in with a farmer a couple of days ago who demanded payment for the cattle who had dumped manure in his pond. He had pointed a shotgun at Paddy, but Paddy told him he was sorry and his men would fix his fence before they moved on. The cattle didn't always follow the leader. Sometimes they smelled new grass or hay or some other fodder and changed course. At other times, some farmer's dogs would run out and chase them or bite at their hind legs. If they couldn't drive the dogs away, they shot over their heads, and if that didn't send them scampering back to their porches or kennels, they killed the dogs.

It was all part of the drive, but it made men uneasy when they were forced to confront some unseen obstacle.

Some of the worst times occurred when townspeople or children got word of the approaching herd and rushed out to see what all the fuss was about. Sometimes people would line up as if they were witnessing a parade, and sometimes the little boys, maybe playing hooky from school, would tease the cattle or the cowhands and there was nothing they could do about it but keep riding. They certainly weren't going to fire their rifles over the heads of gawking on-lookers or shoot cattle-teasing children.

Harvey, even though he was riding well away from the herd, was not immune to incidents such as had happened, but such events were doubly irritating because he often had to ride away all alone with nobody to talk to or help him shoo away dogs or truant children.

Paddy knew the herd was getting restless. He knew they could smell water and wanted to drink from the river.

But he also knew that if he let them line up on the Canadian, some of them would wander into the current and be swept away or drowned. He didn't have enough men to keep them all in check if they started to spread out over a mile or so, like kids in a candy store, all wanting to drink at once.

Cows, he knew, got jealous or envious of others of their kind. If one cow was eating from a particularly lush patch of grass, other cattle would move in on them and push them away or lock horns over feeding privileges.

Cattle, he reflected, were often like human children. They needed a firm hand to make them obey the rules of the trail.

Downstream, Bill cut a slender limb from a willow and stripped it of bark and leaves. Upstream, Whit did the same. They would use these makeshift poles to test the depth and footing in the river when they came to a likely spot.

Bill looked at the muddy water and knew that there had probably been a rainstorm upriver. There were chunks of grass and pieces of wood, tree limbs, a bush or two, racing and tumbling with the current. He rode for a mile, then another before he came to a bend and what looked like a sandbar somewhere just past the middle.

His horse did not want to step into the water, despite his verbal coaxing.

Bill rammed his roweled spurs into the horse's flanks and it took one step toward the water, then backed away.

"All right, you mule-headed son of a buck," he exclaimed, and whacked the horse's rump with the willow pole while he eased up on the bit in the horse's mouth.

His horse leaped into the water and it was shallow next to the bank.

He kept digging in the spurs and urging the horse toward the elongated sandbar. He poked the pole into the water at intervals. When it touched bottom, he pushed on it. He looked down at the horse's front hooves when they came up and just saw swirls of mud. The bottom seemed sound and never reached the horse's belly until they had crossed the bar. Then his horse stepped into a hole and sank nearly to its withers.

The horse floundered and his forelegs lashed out in a frantic attempt to swim. Water splashed and the horse's hind legs found good footing and it surged forward into shallower water. He rode clear to the opposite bank, testing the bottom with his pole. The horse lunged from the river and clambered up on the low bank. It shook itself and droplets of water scattered in all directions, sunlit and fragile as tiny glass globes.

Bill waited until his horse had calmed down, then turned its head and pointed him back toward the river. This time, he took a slightly different path and there was no deep hole all the way across. The horse scampered over the lower tip of the sandbar, then splashed its way to the bank while Bill just dragged his pole along the bottom.

On the bank, he dismounted and ground-tied his horse to a small cottonwood. He threw the willow pole into the river and watched it float downstream. Then he started looking for rocks. He gathered them in different sizes. He set the largest and flattest next to the bank, then a smaller one atop it until he had built a stone cairn that could be seen when he returned with Paddy.

Satisfied, he untied his horse and mounted up.

Whit met him at the point where they had parted company and they rode back to the herd together.

"Deep all the way up for two mile," Whit said. "Did you find a ford?"

"Yep. Don't know how wide it is, but cattle can cross there if we line 'em up right."

"I hate big rivers," Whit said as they rode along together.

"Cattle love 'em," Bill said with a chuckle. "And if we didn't have 'em, there'd be no towns, no trade, no game to hunt."

"You got a point. But they scare hell out of me and this one is full of deadwood and scraps of grass and clumps of mud. No tellin' what lives under that water. Maybe gators or snakes."

Bill laughed.

"No gators," he said. "And I didn't see no

219

snakes."

"That's just it, Bill. You don't see 'em until they bite you."

"Hell, I ain't seen a water moccersin since I left Louisiana and I don't think rattlers swim in these rivers."

Whit went into a mock shivering fit.

"I don't even want to think about rattlers," he said.

"Then, don't," Bill said, and flashed him a wide grin.

Paddy rode out to meet them.

"Well?" he said to both men.

"Bill said he found us a ford downriver," Whit said. "I didn't see no safe place to cross upriver."

"I marked the spot with some rocks," Bill said. "You're going to have to run 'em over maybe two at a time, three or four at the most."

"That's like askin' me to drink whiskey from an eye dropper," Paddy said. "Once I turn that lead cow loose and drive her across, the rest of the herd will jump in like a bunch of Sooner wagons at the startin' gate. It'll be a damned avalanche of cattle wadin' across."

"Or swimmin'," Whit said.

Paddy shot him a scouring look of displeasure. "No more jokes. This is serious work.

You boys take your flanks and make sure none of the herd breaks out and tries to cross in this deep fork of the river."

The two men rode off.

Paddy called out to Steve, who was holding the lead cow at bay as she lowered her head and pawed the ground, making noise in her chest and throat.

"Head 'em out, Steve," Paddy said, "but keep 'em away from the river until you see a stack of stones. I'll lead the way."

"Okay, boss," Steve replied.

Paddy rode toward the river and then cut south. He looked behind him and saw the herd began to move. Steve and Cal Ferris turned the leaders so that they were on a more or less parallel course to the Canadian.

Paddy began to breathe normally.

"Now," he said, "if nothin' happens to spook the herd, we'll make the crossin'."

He patted his horse's neck as it craned its head to look at the surging river winding its way to some unknown destination.

He slowed his horse and kept looking back. Steve and Cal were doing their jobs. The cattle were rolling big brown eyes at the river, but were following the riders and the lead cow.

The real test would come, he knew, when he drove the herd into the river at the ford

Bill had found for them. If the following herd didn't scatter and think they were smarter than their leaders, they would cross all right. If they did scatter, they'd have a mess on their hands. The river was strong enough to wash a cow downstream if any strayed into deep water.

Paddy said a silent prayer and rode on, looking for the stone cairn.

Chapter 23

When Concho saw the first herd being held off from crossing the Canadian River, he made up his mind and came to a decision.

Lem sat his horse alongside Concho, staring at the stalled herd, which he could not see very well. His horse pawed the ground and whickered. It kept turning its head to look back at the other horses, which were dipping their noses in the creek, blowing bubbles with their rubbery noses, and slurping water into their thick-lipped mouths.

The men following him had been grumbling for several days. They were not used to being idle on the trail of a large cattle herd. They could be idle in town because there was whiskey to be had, and women as well. They could pass the hours playing cards or shooting craps. But the trail was a lonesome existence. They had been told that they were on a mission that would line their pockets with hard coin.

Concho let the binoculars fall to his chest and turned to Lemuel, who had ridden to this spot with him. They were on a brush- and tree-covered hillock that gave them both cover and a clear view of both cattle and drovers, along with the chuck wagon and supply wagon.

The other men in his surly band were all lounging about fifty yards away by a small creek, lying or sitting under the shade of some poplar trees.

"Randy," Concho called, "come on over here for a sec, will you?"

Randy arose from the creek bank. He had a piece of hardtack in his hands that was half-eaten. He left his canteen lying where he had been sitting and ran to Concho's side.

He looked up at the outlaw, a questioning look on his features, eyebrows wrinkled like a pair of humped caterpillars.

"Yes, sir," he said.

Concho removed his hat and slipped the binoculars over his head and handed them down to the young man.

"Who's that man ridin' toward the tail end of the herd?" Concho asked.

Randy fitted the glass to his eyes and scanned the herd until he saw the man riding slowly along the near flank. He recognized him instantly. It was a man they hadn't seen before, but Randy knew who he was.

"That's Tolliver," he said. "Harvey Tolliver. I wonder why we're just now seein' him."

"Ha," Concho snorted. "Because he's the jasper I been seein' damned near ever' day ridin' circuit on the herd and starin' out over the country with a damned spyglass. Lookin' for us, most likely."

"A spyglass?" Randy said as he handed the binoculars back up to Concho.

"Yep, one of them long telescopes what can make a man's eyes see damned near into next week."

"I didn't see no spyglass," Randy said.

"No, you don't," Concho said. "A few minutes ago, I saw that Tolliver hand it over to Paddy up at the head of the herd. And then the trail boss sent two men up to the river. They ain't come back yet."

"Paddy's probably lookin' for a ford acrost the Canadian," Lem said. "One went west, the other'n to the east."

"Well, that don't make no difference right now," Concho said. "I done made up my mind."

Randy stood there, wondering if Concho was through with him. Neither man on horseback looked at him, and he started to chew on the hardtack, trying not to make any noise.

"You have?" Lem asked.

"We ain't goin' to wait until Paddy gets that herd up to the Verdigris. This is a better place."

"To do what?" Lem asked.

Concho let out a long breath and then sucked more air into his nostrils. "From here to Kansas, we're goin' to start pickin' Paddy's men off. One by one."

"What?" Lem said.

"You heard me. No use waitin'. By the time he gets to Kansas, he won't have so many drovers if we pick 'em off along the way. By the time he crosses into Kansas, we can just jump him and take 'em all out and turn that herd back toward the mission."

"That's a hell of an idea, Concho," Lem said.

"And the first one I'm going to drop is that Tolliver. He'll be at the tail end of the herd, likely, and it'll take the rest of them a while to find him. Then they'll bury him and start losin' sleep at night."

"Where'd you get that idea, Concho?"

"Back when I rode with Quantrill, we was guerillas. We'd see a column of Yankees and start pickin' 'em off from the rear of the column. Caused a hell of a lot of confusion, I can tell you. We rode in and rode out nobody catched us."

"Guerillas, huh?" Lem scratched the side of his head just above his right ear.

"Yeah, guerillas. Like ghosts, we was. Night riders. We'd hit a town, shoot everybody what came at us with rifles or shotguns, then light a shuck before half of 'em was full awake."

"What if they see us? Then what?"

"They'll see maybe some fire and smoke. Hear the rifle. But by that time, we'll be someplace else."

"Might work."

"It'll work. I declare, you're about as sharp as a cow's tit sometimes. I could pick off Tolliver from here and by the time he hit the ground, we'd all be miles away."

"Ain't no need for you to scorn me, Concho. I was just wonderin' out loud."

"Yeah, well, you got to use that cotton in your head you call a brain. It'll work. Trust me."

Lemuel didn't reply. A long time ago his pappy had told him to watch out for the man who said "trust me." *"When a man says that, boy, it means you can't trust him as far as you could throw a sack full of iron anvils."*

Concho looked down at Randy. Randy

227

froze with the hardtack stuck to his mouth.

"You can go on back to where you was, Randy," Concho said. "Ain't nothin' goin' to happen just now."

Randy took the bread from his mouth and walked back to the creek. He was bursting with information for the others, but he knew he'd better not take any thunder from Concho. He would keep what was said a few minutes ago to himself.

"When you goin' to take down that drover?" Lem asked.

"We'll wait until Paddy takes the herd to the ford. Once them cattle start movin', I'll drop him."

"Hell, it's a good five hunnert yards to where that herd is grazin'," Lem said.

"I'll get closer, but I bet I could put out his lamp from here."

Lem's eyebrows arched, but he didn't say anything. He had never shot a deer that was more than forty or fifty yards from the muzzle of his rifle. And the men he'd shot had been a hell of a lot closer. Less than ten feet, most of them. Some so close the muzzle blast set their shirts on fire.

"You stay here, Lem, and keep an eye on the cattle. When they start movin' you call me."

"Sure, Concho. But my horse is mighty thirsty."

"Just wait here," Concho said.

He turned his horse and rode over to the creek.

There, he told the men of his new plan.

"So, every day we pick off another drover, clear to the Kansas border. I guarantee you'll all get a chance to draw blood."

"I'd rather spill it than draw it," cracked Skip.

"Skip, one of these days your damned mouth is going to get you into a heap of trouble," Concho said.

"It already has," Skip said.

Some of the men laughed.

Randy felt a tenseness building inside him, in his muscles and tendons. These men were talking about killing other men and none of them batted an eye. They gave him the inward shivers, even under a hot sun.

"Just one a day, Concho?" Will asked.

"Enough to make them worry about where the next bullet's comin' from," Concho said.

"What if they don't have no more drovers to get 'em across the border into Kansas?" Lyle asked. He chewed on a blade of grass he had plucked from the creek bank, sucking out the juices from its root.

"We'll make sure we leave that Mick bastard a skeleton crew."

The men all wore blank looks on their faces.

"Get it?" Concho said. "A damned skeleton crew."

Skip was the first to laugh and he was joined by all the others. Some of them whacked each other on their backs. Even Randy tittered a quiet little laugh of his own.

"When?" Logan said.

"Soon," Concho said. "They got to ford the Canadian, and once that herd starts movin', I'll sneak up ahind it and shoot the man on drag out of his saddle."

"Then what?" Logan asked.

"Then we all scatter like leaves in the wind and tomorrow Skip will get the second shot."

They all looked at Skip. He sat up and raised a fisted hand.

"Hooray for me," he said.

"And if you miss, Skip," Concho said, "you'll get a slug in the back from my Colt .45."

"I don't miss," Skip said.

"You missed breakfast once or twice," Lyle said, and the men laughed again.

"All right," Concho said. He dismounted and let his horse drink from the creek.

"Nothing to do now but wait. But when you hear my rifle shot, be ready to move. We'll find a place to cross the river and be waitin' on the other side."

"It's about time we got to do somethin'," Will said. "I been itchin' to get me a cowpoke and see him holler and kick like a stuck pig."

"Should be fun," Concho said.

Randy cringed inwardly. They were talking about men he had known, men he had spoken to, and men whose horses he had groomed and shoed. He was beginning to feel sick.

One of the men, Mitch, noticed that Randy's face had gone bloodless. The kid looked sick, he thought.

"What about Randy here?" Mitch asked. "Does he get to bushwhack one of them drovers? Maybe the Mex wrangler?"

Concho looked at Randy, then back at Mitch.

"If he wants to, the kid can shoot old Paddy when we rustle that herd. I can put him real close. What do you say, Randy?"

All were silent as they looked at Randy. He looked as if he were about to vomit.

"I ain't never shot nobody," he said. His voice came out of his mouth in a thin, high squeak.

The men laughed and Randy felt himself shrinking with shame.

"Never mind," Concho said. "Randy's been a big help to me and if he bears a grudge against any of them waddies, he'll get his chance to sling some lead."

That seemed to satisfy the men, and they began to fill their canteens or build smokes.

Concho sat down and looked at the sun-shot waters of the creek as it laced between the green banks. There were sparkles and diamonds in the tiny wavelets, and up-stream, birds chirped and dived at their shadows, twittering and darting up and down, chasing each other, and alighting to sip from the stream.

It was a beautiful day that afternoon.

But the pall of death hung in the air and Randy wondered if the men were as keyed up as he was. If they were, it was for different reasons.

He was afraid. Deep down inside him he was afraid.

And he dreaded the sound of that first shot from Concho's rifle.

It would mean the end of something and the beginning of a whole lot of other things.

He wished he could run away and never see Concho or any of these men again.

He wished he had the courage to do just that.

But he knew he didn't. He was trapped. He had ventured into a deep dark cave and he couldn't get out.

Poor Tolliver, he thought.

He was in a cave too, and he didn't know it.

Only Tolliver would never get out alive.

And, maybe, neither would he.

CHAPTER 24

Dane watched as Joe Eagle rode well ahead of the herd and finally disappeared from view. He was riding point for Len, nearly a quarter mile from the lead cow with its clanking bell. The cattle were on good grass and foraging along the trail as they headed toward Sweetwater.

His face was wan and haggard from lack of sleep, and the furrows in his forehead seemed deeper and more wrinkled. He had patrolled the far outskirts of the place where the herd had bedded down for the night, riding with slowness and caution, listening to every sound, from the mournful songs of the whip-poor-wills to the wild yips of coyotes and the yap of farm dogs and the hoot of barn owls.

He knew Concho and his men were somewhere out on the prairie. But they were invisible. He did not know where they had gone, except he knew they had left town.

Were they following Paddy with the first herd? More than likely. But he couldn't chance any of those outlaws sneaking up at night and cutting out part of the herd or shooting his men as they tended the cattle or slept in their bedrolls.

And where now, he wondered, was Joe Eagle? For the past two days, Joe had just disappeared, ridden away without telling either him or Crowell where he was going. Was he also looking for Concho? Unlike Dane, Joe was sleeping at night. Dane was out like some owl-hooter, hunched over in the saddle to present as little silhouette as possible, looking, listening, riding wide circles over uneven ground, careful not to let Reno step in a gopher hole or stumble into a prairie dog town and break a leg.

Dane rubbed his eyes. He knew they were red from lack of sleep. The land ahead shimmered under visible waves of heat, and he saw puddles of water shining like small lakes. Mirages, of course, but they seemed real, and sometimes he could see what looked like a man on horseback in the middle of the phantom mirror, a rider that evaporated after a few seconds and left an empty view of land stretching to the distant horizon.

He looked back, just to erase the dancing

images of watery roads and tilting ponds. The herd was far behind him, still moving, the cattle snatching grass or chewing on their cuds as they plodded blindly behind the leader. He thought he caught a glimpse of Crowell on his horse, riding just ahead of the brown waves of cattle in a long, wide line behind him.

He put a chaw of tobacco into his mouth, hoping it would help keep him both alert and awake.

Moments went by that seemed like hours, and then he saw a rider in a distant mirage. At first he thought it was only an illusion, but this time the rider did not disintegrate into mist before his eyes. He kept coming on until Dane realized that it was Joe Eagle returning from wherever he had been.

Joe raised a hand in greeting.

Dane lifted his hand and touched spurs to Reno's flank, propelling the horse forward at a trot.

They met this side of the blinding mirage. Joe reined up and so did Dane.

"Where you been, Joe?" Dane asked.

"Me track. Look for Concho."

"And did you find him?"

"Find track. Many tracks. Two, three days old. Horse tracks."

"You think that's Concho and his men?"

Joe turned his horse and rode a few feet. Dane followed.

"You come," he said. "Me show tracks."

He rode alongside Joe for another half hour. Then Joe turned his horse to the left and they both rode out onto empty prairie.

Finally Joe reined up and halted his horse. He pointed to the ground.

"There track," he said.

Dane looked down. He saw the tracks of several horses. Joe dismounted and Dane did the same.

Joe knelt by the tracks and pointed to those that were most clear.

"See sides of tracks. Wind blow edges. Two days, three. They ride slow."

Dane looked at the tracks closely. He could see where grains of dirt had fallen into the flat impressions made by the horseshoes. The sides were crumbling and the earth was dry. He nodded.

"Come," Joe said, and climbed back into the saddle.

To Dane's surprise, he reversed direction and rode across the path the herd was taking. He rode on for another fifteen or twenty minutes and then raised an arm to point.

Dane looked at the ground ahead. It was churned up and there were places where grass had been cut by teeth, leaving small clumps of dirt in little piles. And there were loose blades of grass lying helter-skelter in several places. They rode on and Dane saw the unmistakable hieroglyphs of cloven hooves. These, he knew, were the tracks of the herd Paddy was taking north.

Dane looked back to the spot where they had seen the horse tracks.

"Concho is following Paddy's herd," he said to Joe.

Joe nodded. "Him watch. Him yonder." Joe pointed to the north. Dane knew what he meant.

"That means Paddy might be jumped by Concho and his men," Dane said.

"Concho bad. Him hunt. Ten men. Maybe this many." Joe held up ten fingers, closed both hands, and then held up two more fingers.

"A dozen?"

"Maybe."

"We're at least a day behind Paddy. Maybe fifteen or twenty miles, Joe. Think we ought to try and catch up with him?"

"Concho and men sleep yonder. Flat places where beds leave track. Concho not hurry. Come, Dane. Me show you other track."

Dane followed Joe as he rode on a course that took them midway between where the first herd had passed and where they had seen the horse tracks.

Joe kept looking down at the ground and then he pointed.

"Here horse track," he said.

Dane saw the tracks. He followed along behind Joe as he pointed to the ground. The tracks were distinct, but also bore signs of aging over a two- or three-day period.

"One of Concho's men, Joe?"

Joe shook his head and halted his horse. "Horse belong Tolliver. Harvey him scout. Him guard for Paddy."

"How do you know that?" Dane asked.

"Horse stop. Horse circle herd. Horse far from herd. Know tracks. Know horse."

Of course, Dane thought. Joe would know the tracks of most, if not all, of the horses on his ranch and in Paddy's remuda. Joe was a tracker. As a Cherokee youngster, he had been taught to track. He sometimes spent hours as a boy lying on his belly and watching a small section of grass. He would see which bugs came and went, what worms crossed in front of his eyes. He would watch the grass when it was covered with dew and how the blades reacted under the warming sun.

Joe had told all this to Dane one night when both were nighthawks keeping coyotes and wild dogs away from the newborn calves. Dane had been fascinated. In the days following that night of childhood revelation, Joe had spoken more than once about the tracks of animals and people. He said he could form pictures in his mind of how large a man was, how much he weighed, and whether or not he was injured in foot or leg, and he could do the same with horses, cattle, rabbits, coyotes, quail, squirrels, and any other animals.

"Tolliver, him look for Concho. No see. No find."

"You can tell all that just from the tracks you've shown me today?" Dane asked.

Joe nodded.

"Tracks tell story," he said. "Joe see what men do from tracks on ground."

"I believe you."

"Concho far away. Concho hunt Paddy."

"Well, I told Paddy to send a rider back to find me if he runs into any trouble."

"Maybe big trouble," Joe said.

"Where? When?" Dane asked.

"Joe not know. Maybe at river."

"What river?"

"Big river. Deep river, maybe. Cattle stop. Paddy look for crossing. Concho pounce like big cat."

Dane felt a sudden chill. Up ahead was

the deep fork of the Canadian. Paddy would have to hold the herd back for a time while he and his men found a ford. He had talked about it with Paddy the week before he left the Circle K. He to, knew how treacherous such a river could be.

Maybe Concho knew that too.

Dane asked himself a question: "How can I think like Concho? What is his plan? Does he mean to rustle the whole herd or just part of it? Will he shoot Paddy and then throw down on the drovers and make them drive the herd back to the Circle K?"

There were so many questions that he could not answer.

He knew Joe could not answer them either.

"What do, Dane?" Joe asked after Dane had been silent for several seconds.

Dane felt helpless at that moment. He waited several seconds before he answered.

"Sometimes, Joe," he said, "a man has to ride a trail that leads him into a dangerous place. He knows the place is there, but he can't do anything about it until he rides up on it. Then, if there's a mountain to climb, he climbs it. If there's a bad river to cross, he crosses it. I can do nothing with tracks. I have to see the men who made those tracks and if they steal my cattle, I have to shoot them or hang them from a cottonwood tree."

Joe nodded and grunted in agreement.

"So we go on until we run into Concho and his men."

"Be big fight," Joe said.

"I just hope he doesn't jump Paddy and steal all my cattle in that first herd."

Joe made a fist and patted his chest just over the place where his heart was.

"I pray to Great Spirit," he said. "Pray my rifle find Concho. Make rifle speak to Concho. Concho die. Great Spirit smile."

"I didn't know you were religious, Joe," Dane said.

Joe shook his head.

"Not religious," he said. "Believe in Great Spirit."

"To a white man that sounds like religion."

"No. White man have God. Cherokee have Spirit. Not same."

"You may be right, Joe."

They waited there in the sunlight until they saw the lead cattle in the herd come into view. Crowell waved to them. They waved back and then started their horses.

The sun was arcing down the slope of the western sky, and their shadows were stretching toward the east. There was nothing to see but prairie and green grass.

And, of course, they saw the dancing mirrors of mirages in the distance and the ghosts of menacing men appear and disappear like wraiths in the daylight.

CHAPTER 25

Concho watched through his binoculars as the herd started moving toward the river. The drovers hollered and waved their hats to bunch them up into a tighter column. The wagons stood at rest behind the herd, but he saw Tolliver, riding drag, pack the rear of the herd just by letting his cutting horse range back and forth on the rear.

With him were Lem and Randy. The other men were up ahead, scouting a ford that would let them swim their horses across or wade them in a more benevolent current. One of them would wait on this side to guide them to the ford when they were finished with their business.

Concho drew his rifle from its scabbard. It was a Winchester '73 lever-action .44/40.

Sunlight glanced off the polished bluing of the barrel and the cherry-wood stock. Concho had it custom-made in Santa Fe soon after he had bought it. The stock had been replaced and his first name etched into the metal on one side of the receiver.

"You know, Lem," he said, "I got this rifle sighted in at twenty-five yards."

"So you goin' to ride that close to shoot that Tolliver?"

"No. Don't have to. You sight a rifle like this in at twenty-five yards and it's sighted in at a hundred yards."

"I never knew that," Lem said.

"Well, it's a fact."

"So, can you measure out a hunnert yards with your eyes, Concho?"

"Pretty much. I practiced shootin' at several yardages and got so I could measure distance pretty damned well."

"Want me to back you up?"

"Only if you see me miss, Lem."

Concho turned to look at Randy. "You stay here, Randy boy. Just watch and see if any of them drovers spot my smoke and start ridin' this way. Got that?"

"Yes, sir," Randy said.

"You holler if any of 'em even look like they mean to chase us."

"I'll yell real loud," Randy said.

They all sat there on their horses and watched the slow-moving herd. Then they saw the chuck wagon move and turn to round the right flank. Next, the supply wagon followed the same course. The Mexican wrangler followed the wagons with the horses. They all moved faster than the herd.

"They don't have to eat no dust thataway," Lem observed.

"That's just perfect for me," Concho said.

"What're you going to do, Concho?" Lem asked.

"You and me are going to ride up way behind the rear of the herd and when we get close enough, we'll stop and I'll lay my sights on Tolliver."

"You don't think he'll see us?"

"By the time we get close enough for him to see us, it will be too late for him."

"Okay."

"Look at him," Concho said. "He's got his eyes on those cows and ain't lookin' no place else."

"Sounds like you got it figgered all right," Lem said.

"Tell you somethin', Lem. Listen real close."

"Go ahead," Lem said.

"When I go to kill a man, I do it all up here." Concho pointed to his head. "I play it all out in my mind. Every move. Every move I'm gonna make. Every move the man I'm going to jump might make. That way, when I get to it, I don't make no mistakes.

I've already played it all out in my head."

"Hmm," Lem murmured.

"I done played this one out already. Just look at the way that herd's a-movin' and watch them wagons and the drovers on the flanks.

"Yeah, I see 'em."

"As the herd gets closer to the river, they're all leavin' poor old Tolliver way in the rear. In a little while, most of the herd will be alongside the Canadian, or crossin' downstream. Then Tolliver will be all by his lonesome and nobody up front is even goin' to see him fall out of his saddle."

"You're pretty smart, Concho. I'll give you that."

"Damned right I'm smart. Smarter than any of them drovers or the trail boss, that poor Mick."

Lem said nothing as they continued to watch.

Randy wanted to drink from his canteen. His throat and mouth were dry and he could feel his lips cracking from a lack of moisture. Yet he dared not move. They were a long way from the herd and shielded by trees, but every time Tolliver turned his horse toward them, he jumped inside his skin.

Finally Concho gave the order.

"Let's move. Randy, you stay put. Keep your eyes open."

"I will," Randy croaked.

He watched as Lem and Concho rode in a straight line until they were almost out of sight. Then he saw their bobbing heads as they rode toward the herd in another straight line.

When his heart was firmly lodged in his throat, he saw Concho ride toward the rear of the herd. Lem was right behind him.

He looked for the wagons and the horses, but they were now out of sight.

He saw only one drover waving his hat at the herd, and then he too rounded the corner of the herd and Randy didn't see him any longer.

Concho and Lem closed the gap and then Randy saw them both stop.

He watched as Concho brought his rifle up to his shoulder. He saw the barrel move from side to side. Concho was hunched slightly, peering down the barrel.

Randy's gaze shifted to Tolliver.

It was just the way Concho had said it would be. Harvey was concentrating on the rear of the herd, whopping the rumps of cattle to keep them moving and bunched up. He had his hands full and had no idea that a rifle was pointed at him.

Then Tolliver, perhaps feeling that he was being watched, turned his horse and looked back to where Concho and Lem were sitting their horses right out in the open.

Randy wanted to scream a warning.

Instead, he held his breath.

The rifle cracked. It sounded like a bullwhip. He saw the orange flame spew from the barrel, and then a white puff of smoke billowed from the muzzle and floated back on Concho and Lem.

Randy shifted his eyes to look at Tolliver.

Tolliver grabbed his chest. Clawed at it as if it had filled suddenly with sharp thorns.

Blood spurted from a hole in the center of Tolliver's breastbone. He tumbled sideways out of the saddle. When he hit the ground, his hat crumpled and came off, rolled a few inches, then wobbled to rest.

The cows at the rear turned their heads at the noise of the man falling. Tolliver's horse skittered away, its reins dragging along the grassy ground. Then it stopped, stared at the body of its rider, its ears twitching and turning in a hundred-and-eighty-degree plane, twin cones atop a bobbing head.

Concho rammed his rifle back in its scabbard. He and Lem spurred their horses, slapped them with their reins, and made a beeline for where Randy was waiting. Concho motioned for him to move north.

Randy turned his horse and started out, leaving the hillock and the shielding trees. His heart was still in his throat and his chest felt as if it were wearing a heavy iron plate.

Tolliver was dead. Randy knew that.

In the distance he heard muffled shouts, but he did not look.

Soon Concho and Lem caught up with him.

"Let's ride, kid," Concho said to him, and galloped away.

Randy kept up with Lem and Concho, but just barely. They were really moving fast. He felt light-headed and dizzy.

It seemed to Randy that he was in a dream, that what had just happened wasn't real.

Yet he could still see Tolliver raking his hands over his chest that was spurting blood and falling to the ground.

The bile rose in Randy's throat and he leaned away from his horse and vomited. But the sickness was still in him. His stomach still roiled with the half-digested hardtack and jerky.

He stayed in the saddle, but Concho and Lem were blurred as his eyes filled with tears and his stomach boiled over again until he heaved the rest of its contents in a yellowish-brown stream that splattered his horse's hooves and left a streak on the grass.

His throat constricted and burned.

His mind screamed silent insults at Concho.

Damn you, he thought. *Damn you, Concho, to hell.*

Then they were at the river and Randy wiped his sleeve across his mouth, gulped air to hold down the rancid ooze that threatened to erupt once again.

Mitch was waiting for them.

"Heard your shot, Concho," he said. "Get him?"

"What do you think, Mitch?" Concho gruffed. "Damned right I got him."

"Thought so," Mitch said, and turned his horse toward the fording place.

Randy slumped in the saddle. He didn't want to cross the river. He wanted to turn his horse and ride straight back to Shawnee Mission.

He never wanted to see Concho again.

But he couldn't run.

He knew Concho would drop him the same way he had dropped Tolliver.

The man was a killer and now Randy hated him as he had never hated another.

He hated Concho, yes.

And, finally, he hated himself.

CHAPTER 26

The cattle at the rear of the first herd lunged and scrambled to get away from the dead man and his skittery horse. They fanned out and broke from the herd to seek safer quarters.

Up at the river, Chub Toomey heard the crack of the rifle and rode out to look back down at the shrinking line of cattle.

He saw the cattle scatter and knew something was wrong.

He called over to Steve Atkins, who was turning the herd toward the crossing place.

"Steve," he yelled, "get somebody to ride to the rear of the herd. Cattle are streamin' all over. I don't see Harve nowhere."

Steve reined his horse into a tight turn and hollered to Cal Ferris, "Watch 'em, Cal. I'm goin' back to see what's goin' on with Harve."

Cal nodded and touched a finger to the brim of his hat. He watched as Steve galloped away, right on the heels of Chub. He rode over to where the cattle were turning and made sure that none of them jumped out and headed for the river where it was deep and running swift.

"What in hell's goin' on back there?" Paddy yelled from the other side of the bank. Whit Hawkins was sitting his horse in midstream beyond the sandbank in case any cattle broke and headed his way. He had already turned three or four back by waving his hat at them and cursing a blue streak.

"Damned if I know, Paddy," Whit said. "Some kind of ruckus at the tail end of the herd, I think."

"I thought I heard a shot," Paddy said. "Like a rifle shot."

"Me too," Whit said.

Cattle sloshed across the ford and clambered up on the opposite bank where drovers kept them moving out of the way. As the leaders widened the distance, Bill and Lester began to bunch them up so that they didn't wander too far from the remainder of the herd.

Paddy was pleased with the way the cattle were taking to the water. They had good footing and the water wasn't too deep where they crossed. Some tried to stay on the sandbar, out of fear, he supposed, but Whit was shooing them on the rest of the way.

Now, though, there was some kind of fuss at the tail end of the herd, or so it seemed. He knew that Harve was riding drag and he was an experienced hand with a good cutting horse. The drive should have gone smoothly at that point. He wondered if one of the hands had shot at something and spooked the herd. He hoped that was all it was. And if someone had been fool enough to shoot at a jackrabbit or rattlesnake, that man was in for a good ass-chewing. He had given strict orders not to fire their weapons unless they were attacked by Indians or rustlers. There were no farms right close, so he didn't think some farmer was responsible.

He heard distant shouts and couldn't make out who was yelling or what they were saying.

"Can you make any of that out, Whit?" Paddy asked.

Whit shook his head. "Maybe one of the boys is yellin' at the cows what strayed from the herd."

"Could be," Paddy said.

But he doubted it. It sounded to him as if one or two of the hands were in trouble, or they were just trying to scare cattle back into the herd.

He waited and listened.

"Son of a bitch," Whit exclaimed. He was staring upriver. "Here comes Steve, a-ridin' hell-for-leather."

Paddy saw Steve. He was riding straight toward the ford, whipping his horse at a gallop, the brim of his hat flattened from the wind his horse had created.

He reined up just on the other side of the turning herd.

"You better come quick, Paddy," Steve yelled across the river. "We got puredee hell to pay."

"What's wrong?" Paddy yelled.

"Somebody shot Harve. He's plumb dead. Come quick."

Paddy wasted no time. He spurred his horse into the river and splashed across. "Watch 'em, Whit. I'll be back soon as I can."

"Don't worry, Paddy," Whit said. "Most of 'em have done crossed."

Paddy rode around the herd and joined up with Steve.

"Take me there," he said.

Steve wheeled his horse and clapped spurs into its flanks. The horse exploded into a run with Paddy right on its heels.

The two men did not speak. When they reached the tail end of the herd, there was

255

no need for words there either. Cal stood over the body of Harve Tolliver, his hat off, holding the reins of his horse.

"Good God," Paddy said.

"He's deader'n a doornail," Cal said. "Shot square in the chest."

Paddy saw Tolliver's horse standing several yards away, its head drooping, its tail switching. It stood hip-shot, with one rear foot cocked toe down as if to brace its leg.

He saw the small hole in Tolliver's chest, the blood spatter on his striped shirt, the pool of blood under his body. The blood was already turning black and coagulating.

Tears welled up in Paddy's eyes.

"My damned fault," he wailed. "I sent Harve back here. I sent him to his death, sure as if I'd pulled the trigger meself."

"Paddy, come on," Steve said. "You didn't have any more to do with this than I did. You weren't even here. And neither was I."

"Damn, damn, damn," Paddy said, and crossed himself as if he had just entered a Catholic church.

"I feel bad about Harve too," Steve said. "And so does Toomey. Don't you, Chub?"

Chub's eyes were wet too. He nodded and looked away from Tolliver's body. He looked out over the prairie. He looked along the horizon, then set his gaze in one spot.

"There's a crick over yonder," Chub said. "I saw it shinin' when we rode by here. And look, there's a little hill there with trees. Men could have been watchin' us, just waitin' for when Harve was alone. And then, bang."

Paddy drew himself up and wiped his eyes. "Chub, why don't you ride over there and see if you see any horse tracks?"

Chub mounted up and headed toward the small hillock.

"Steve, it looks to me like Harve was shot by somebody up ahind him," Paddy said. "Not from way over there. Why don't you walk back and see if you see any horse tracks that oughtn't to be there?"

"Well, shoot, I reckon I can do that," Steve said.

Paddy raised his arm and pointed to a line leading directly from the tail end of the herd to the southern horizon. "Just walk along that general line. Look real hard."

Steve walked away.

Paddy turned toward the river.

"Lester," he shouted as loud as he could. "Lester, bring that supply wagon back down here."

He didn't know if Lester Pierson heard him, but he thought he saw the tail end of the supply wagon just sitting there. He waited and watched to see if the wagon would turn and come toward him. A few minutes later, the wagon did turn and he saw Lester swing the team to head his way.

Paddy picked up Tolliver's crumpled hat and put it over his face. Harve's eyes were frosted over and staring up at the sky, frozen from the moment of death. Paddy began to weep again, sniffling and bellowing low in his chest.

The wagon rumbled up and Paddy wiped his eyes with his bare hand.

"What's goin' on, boss?" Lester said as he hauled in on the reins, stopped the wagon, and set the brake.

"Are you blind, Lester? Looky there on the ground."

"Who is it?" Lester asked.

"Harvey Tolliver."

"Is he hurt?"

"He's dead, you dumb bastard. Now get down off that wagon and grab a shovel. Go through Harve's pockets and get his personals, money, change, whatever's in 'em."

Lester swore under his breath. He climbed down from the wagon seat and walked back to rummage through the wagon bed. He picked up a shovel and walked over to Tolliver. "God, he is dead, ain't he?"

"Go through his pockets," Paddy said.

Lester knelt down and laid the shovel beside Tolliver. Gingerly, he patted Tolliver's pockets, then slid his hand in. He pulled a small pocketknife out of one of them, two quarters from another. There was a bandanna stuffed in a back pocket and a worn empty wallet in the other. His shirt pockets contained a sack of makings in each and papers in one, matches in another. He laid the items out.

"Bundle 'em all up in his bandanna and tie a knot in it, then hand it to me," Paddy said. "Then find a soft bare spot and start diggin' a hole six foot long and two foot wide. I'll get the boys to spell you when they get back."

Lester did as he was asked and handed the bundle to Paddy. Then he walked around with the shovel. He rammed the blade into the soil where no grass grew and finally found a large enough bare spot so that he could begin to dig Tolliver's grave.

The sound of the shovel striking dirt and gravel made Paddy wince as he shielded his eyes with one hand and looked for Chub. Chub was not in sight, but he saw Steve wandering around a spot some hundred yards away. Steve squatted down and examined something on the ground. Then he walked on a line that seemed to lead to the small hill. Halfway there, he turned and started back toward Paddy.

"What did you find, Steve?" Paddy asked when Steve drew near.

"Looks like you were right. There are tracks of two horses about a hunnert yards straight back, and when I follered them a ways, they came and went from that little hill over yonder. That one where you sent Chub."

"So maybe they was watchin' us from there and when it come time, they rode up behind and shot Harve."

"Looks that way. Them two horses walked out there and then, on the way back, they went lickety-split back to where they come from."

"Well, let's see what Chub's got to say about that when he gets back. Meantime, you spell Lester on that shovel, Steve."

"Sure thing, Paddy," Steve said. He walked over and spoke to Lester, then took the shovel from him. He cut a rectangle and started shoveling dirt as if he were on a road crew.

Clang, clang, scrape, scrape, clump, clunk, as the shovel did its work. To Paddy it was an annoying sound, but a necessary one. They had a drive to make and he had to take steps to see that his men were protected or could protect themselves. In the open prairie they were all naked targets for any bushwhacker with a rifle.

He saw Chub riding back and he let out a breath that he hadn't realized he had been holding so long in his chest.

Chub rode up and swung himself out of the saddle. "Yep," he said as he walked up to Paddy, pulling his horse along behind him, "they was a passel of them over at that crick. Some stood on that hill and could see the whole herd for quite a spell."

"How many?" Paddy asked.

"Hard to tell. I saw where they pissed and ground out their quirlies when they was done smokin'. And places where they lay down and bent the grass, left marks in the dirt."

"Good job, Chub."

Chub looked over to where Steve and Lester stood. Steve was wielding the shovel and Lester was breaking up clods with his boot heels.

"You gonna bury Harve here?" Chub asked.

"Have to, I reckon. We got to keep the herd movin'."

"Them men what was over yonder all rode off toward the Canadian. I followed their tracks a ways and that's where they was

261

headed."

"Likely, they've already crossed," Paddy mused. "We can expect to see them again."

"What're you gonna do, Paddy?"

"One thing, Chub. I want you to ride back to the chuck wagon and tell Wu to give you trail grub."

"What for?"

"I want you to ride straight back and find Dane and tell him what happened here today."

"You want him to come and help us?"

"I ain't givin' him no orders. Let him decide what he wants to do. But you tell him we got rustlers a-trackin' us, and there's goin' to be more killin's, sure as I'm standin' here grievin' for Harve."

"How far back is Dane?"

"Maybe ten miles, maybe twenty. Just find him and tell him I sent you. You can tell him to look for that stone cairn where it's safe to take the herd across."

"You want me to stay with Dane?"

"Do whatever he says. Now light a shuck, Chub, while there's still daylight to burn."

Chub mounted his horse and took off at a gallop.

Paddy walked over to look at the grave.

"How deep you want it, Paddy?" Steve asked.

262

"Two foot at least. Then we got to get back to the herd."

"That ain't deep enough," Lester said. "Coyotes'll have him dug up before mornin'."

"Put some rocks on the mound when you finish up," Paddy said. "And get back to the river when you're finished. Quick as you can."

"Ain't we gonna say no words over him?" Lester asked.

"Say all the words you want when you put him in the ground, Lester," Paddy said. "He sure as hell ain't gonna hear you."

Paddy walked to his horse and rode toward the river.

He hated death. He hated funerals. He hated to lose a man and he felt guilty about Harvey.

But there was no use in blaming himself. Harvey could have been shot while he was scouting with the telescope. What happened just happened, that's all.

Now it was his job to see that nothing like that ever happened again.

CHAPTER 27

Concho and his men found a deserted and crumbling cabin a few miles from the river. The house had been constructed of native stone and inferior logs. The fields around it showed signs of having been plowed some years before, but nothing was growing there, not even prairie grass.

Once they had made the inside of the abandoned cabin halfway inhabitable, Concho sent two riders, Will and Skip, back to check on Paddy and the herd.

"Will, you see what them boys did with Tolliver, and, Skip, you see about the herd, if they got all the cattle across the river and where they're headed."

Randy found a stick and started to whittle on it with his pocketknife while the men produced a bottle of whiskey that they passed around in celebration.

Concho bragged about his kill, and his men congratulated him. They all seemed eager to draw blood themselves.

The talk made Randy sick to his stomach. Here was a man who had sneaked up on a defenseless cowhand and shot him dead. Harvey never had a chance. It was a cowardly murder in Randy's mind, not something to brag about. Tolliver had never done Concho, or any of the other men in his band, any harm. Yet Concho had taken his life without batting an eye.

Randy continued to whittle on the stick. His strokes were savage now and the shavings piled up on the bare floor of the derelict cabin.

He was tired of hearing Lem say that Tolliver ". . . fell like a sack of taters."

"Damned if he did," Randy said to himself. "He dropped like a defenseless man shot in the chest."

There was a brick fireplace that had begun to crumble, filled with bricks from the chimney that were turning to rubble from wind and water. The place stank of rat droppings. One of the men had chased a rattler out when he first stepped in. But most of the roof was still overhead, made with froed shingles and patched with pieces of tin from large lard cans that had been flattened and cut to fit. It was not a pleasant place, but it was shelter from the winds that came in the night and blew cold across the prairie.

A couple of hours later, the two men Concho had sent out returned with their stories.

Randy set aside his whittling to listen to their reports.

Will spoke first.

"Cattle's all crossed the river," he said. "There's a fresh mound on the flat with rocks piled all along the top."

"Fresh dirt?" Concho asked.

"Yep, that's Tolliver's grave all right. Only hump of soil I seen along the path them cattle took."

"Maybe we ought to go back and read from the Good Book for poor old Tolliver," Lyle cracked.

"You shut your flap," Concho snapped. Then he turned to Skip. "You get a good look at the herd, Skip?" he asked.

"Old Paddy had the cattle all lined up along the Canadian fillin' their bellies with water. The hands took 'em away in small bunches and got the herd movin' again. Kind of on a northeast path, I'd say."

"I reckon they'll head for the border," Mitch said.

"More rivers to cross," Concho said, musing aloud.

"What do we do next, Concho?" Logan inquired.

"We get some shut-eye," he said, and took another swig from the whiskey bottle before he passed it on to Lyle.

"No, I mean tomorrow and maybe the next day."

"First thing I'm gonna do is sic Randy on that lead cow, the one clanging that copper bell. You can do that, can't you, Randy?"

Randy, startled, looked at Concho, wondering if he was serious.

"What?" Randy said.

"You can shoot a cow, can't you?"

"I never shot one, but I reckon I could."

"Then, that's your job tomorrow. Or next day. Paddy will have to find himself another leader of that herd. It'll give him fits."

Randy's stomach churned, both with fear and the thought that he was going to have to prove himself by killing a cow.

"What about us?" Lyle asked. "We goin' to shoot cows?"

"Tomorrow, somewhere along the trail, we'll pick another man to take down," Concho said. "We'll drop one a day, so that by the time Paddy crosses into Kansas, he won't have much control over the herd. He won't have enough hands to take him clear up into Nebraska. When we finally rustle the entire herd, we won't have to wade through a lot of rifle fire."

267

"Sounds good to me," Mitch said.

Lyle grinned and took a drink.

"I can't wait," he said as he passed the bottle to Mitch and dragged a sleeve across his mouth.

Randy lay back on his bedroll and closed his eyes. But he couldn't plug up his ears. He listened to the men talk about killing as if they were going to regular jobs in town or building fences.

And tomorrow he was going to have to kill a cow.

It all seemed senseless and cruel to him as he dropped off to sleep.

CHAPTER 28

Dane felt a strong hand on his shoulder. His upper body shook and he was wrested out of the dream. He lay in his bedroll under the supply wagon where he had spent the night. He opened his eyes and saw Len Crowell's face a few inches from his.

"Rider comin' from the north," Len said. "Hear him?"

Dane arose on one elbow and listened.

He heard galloping hoofbeats way off in the distance.

"I got two boys on it, but you'd better come see. I'm just about ready to get the herd movin' anyway."

"Be right with you, Len," Dane said as he climbed out of his bedroll and threw the blanket off his boots. Out here, a man slept with his boots on. Every man had to be ready to tackle a stampede or trouble of any kind.

It was still dark, but the sky was lightening some when Dane walked with Len in the direction of the hoofbeats.

"You can hear sounds a long way off at night," Len said.

"I know." Dane rubbed the sands of sleep from his eyes. "He's getting closer."

"Be here right soon," Len said.

Out of the darkness rode a man whipping his horse's flanks with the trailing ends of his reins.

A few yards away, Gooch was stirring the morning campfire with an iron poker. Dane smelled the steamy aroma of Arbuckles' coffee, with its faint tang of peppermint. He stepped outside the glow of the fire so that he could see in the darkness. Gooch sent showers of orange-red sparks into the air as he knocked a faggot against one of the rocks in the ring around the pit.

"Coffee's 'bout ready, Cap," he said to Dane.

"Set out an extra cup, Barney," he said. "We might have company in a couple of shakes of a lamb's tail."

"Eh?" Gooch said, but Dane and Len had already stepped into the darkness beyond the fire.

"Here he comes," Len said as the rider came dashing up on them.

"Ho the camp," the rider yelled.

"Why, that's Chub Toomey," Dane exclaimed. "Hey, Chub," he called out, "where's the fire?"

Chub jerked on the reins and his horse skidded to a stop a few feet from Len and Dane.

"There's a fire all right," he said as he leaped from the saddle almost before his horse had fully stopped. "We got trouble, Dane. Big trouble."

Chub was short on breath and his words came out like puffs of wind-borne syllables spewed from a burning chest.

"Slow down, catch your breath, Chub," Dane said. "How long you been ridin'?"

"Half of yesterday and all blamed night," Chub said. "Feelin' my way in the dark and followin' the polestar till I seen your cook fire. Then I laid the leather to old Whistler here and he 'bout left me in the dust."

The horse was winded too and snorting steam and dew through its nostrils, its chest heaving. A yellow rope of sweat girded its lower neck and there was froth at the corners of its mouth.

"Paddy send you?" Dane asked.

"Whew. Let me get my breath if there's any left."

Dane and Len looked at Chub. His face and clothing were covered in a sheen of sweat. He looked plumb tuckered to both men.

"Yeah, Paddy sent me. Harve Tolliver was kilt yesterday. Shot in the chest. We buried him."

"Know who shot him?" Dane asked.

Chub shook his head.

"Bushwhacked," he said. "He was by hisself, ridin' drag. Nobody saw who shot him."

"Where did this happen?" Len asked.

"Up on the deep fork of the Canadian. We was makin' the crossin'. Some of us heard the shot. Next thing, we saw Harve just a-lyin' dead."

"Did you get the herd across the river?" Dane asked.

"Far as I know. Warn't many left to cross when I lit out to find you."

"Did Paddy want me to come and help him?" Dane looked up at the sky. It was still very dark, but the night was on its last legs, he figured.

"I ast him that. He said it was up to you. He just wanted you to know that Harve got kilt."

Dane looked at Len. "I'd better ride on ahead, if that's all right with you. I'll take Joe Eagle with me."

"You're the boss," Crowell said.

"Chub can stay here and help you with

272

the herd. That all right with you, Chub?"

"Sure, Dane. I don't fancy ridin' back all them miles."

"We're probably just a shade under twenty miles," Dane said. "I could be there before sundown if I leave pretty quick."

"Better get started, then," Len said.

"See if you can find Joe Eagle," Dane said. Then, "Wait a minute. Here he comes now."

He saw Joe walk past the campfire and head their way. The entire camp was up by then. Men saddled their horses as the night herders continued their rounds. The herd was still bedded down, except for a few head that were up and grazing.

Dane told Joe what Chub had told him and said he wanted to join Paddy.

"You might have to do some trackin', Joe," Dane said.

"Me go," Joe said, and turned away to go after his horse and pack up his bedroll, rifle, and saddlebags.

"I'll get your horse, Dane. Reno?"

"Yeah, Reno. I'll pack up my gear. Tell Barney to pack some grub for Joe and me."

"Will do," Len said, and walked over to the campfire.

"He didn't suffer none, I don't think," Chub said.

"Get yourself some coffee, Chub," Dane

said. "Barney'll get you breakfast pretty quick."

"I appreciate this, Dane."

"Hell, I'm glad you came and told me what happened."

"What're you gonna do, Dane? There's a passel of men. Seen their tracks over by a crick. Hell, they could pick us off one by one."

"I'm not going to let that happen if I can help it. Joe's a good tracker. Do you know where Concho and his men went?"

"Tracks showed headin' for the river, upstream of the ford. I figger they're long gone by now."

Dane patted Chub on the back. "Grain your horse and get yourself some coffee and grub."

Dane walked back to the supply wagon and rolled up his bedroll. He strapped on his pistol and lugged his rifle and saddlebags over to the fire.

"I'll have some of that shit you call coffee, Barney," Dane said to Gooch.

"It's Arbuckles' finest," Barney said. "I saved the peppermint stick for you if you want it."

"You suck on it, Barney. Might help rid you of your foul breath."

"Now, now, me bucko, don't you be raggin' the cook this early in the mornin'. He might quit on you."

"Barney, if you ever quit cookin' for this outfit, all my men would die of starvation."

"Ain't that the truth?" Barney said. He poured coffee from a large blue pot and handed the tin cup to Dane.

Dane felt the steam graze his face as he blew on the coffee. He took a sip and scalded his tongue. "Ouch," he exclaimed.

"You might want to fan it with your tongue 'fore you take another swaller," Barney said, a mischievous smile on his face.

"I ought to pour it down your gullet, you old coot," Dane said.

Barney laughed.

"You'd have to hog-tie me and conk me out to do that," Gooch said.

"It would be a pleasure," Dane said.

Len brought Reno up. Dane handed him his bedroll.

"Joe'll be here in a minute," Len said. "Barney, you got grub to give the boss and Joe?"

"I got two sacks, one for each," Barney said. He walked to the sideboard and held them up.

"Good man," Len said.

"Don't compliment him too much, Len," Dane said. "His head is so swolled up he

275

can hardly keep his hat on."

Barney laughed good-naturedly. Len smiled. He tied Dane's bedroll behind the cantle.

"I can slap those saddlebags on for you too, Dane," he said.

"Obliged," Dane said, and handed the saddlebags to Len. Barney gave him a sack of food. Len stuffed that in one of the saddlebags.

"Rifle?" Len said.

"I'll take care of the Winchester," Dane said.

Joe came up, leading his horse. He let the reins fall and the horse stood hipshot. Barney handed him one of the flour sacks.

"Grub for the trail, Joe," he said.

Joe grunted.

"Want some coffee, Joe?" Dane asked.

"Coffee good, yes," he said.

Barney poured him a cup and one for Len as well.

"I don't know how good it is," Dane said. "I think Barney grinds up mesquite beans covered in cow shit."

"I always wash the mesquite beans first," Barney joked. "One of these days, I'm gonna make coffee with chili beans to see if you notice the difference, Dane."

"I probably wouldn't. Your coffee's so

damned hot a man can't taste it."

The sky was losing its blackness. There was no daylight yet, but Dane knew it was coming. He finished his coffee and handed his empty cup to Barney. By then, the other hands, most of them sleepy-eyed, were gathering around the fire and Gooch was pouring hot coffee into their cups. Some of them rolled quirlies and lit them.

"Cattle are restless this mornin'," Maynard said. "They was coyotes on the prowl last night."

"Maybe they smell the river twenty miles away," Dane said.

"If'n they do, they'd make good bloodhounds."

The men laughed.

"Well, boys," Dane said, "Joe and I are lighting a shuck to meet up with Paddy O'Riley. Chub can fill you in on what happened and why he's here."

Joe threw down his cup and mounted up. Dane got aboard Reno. The two men rode out, past the head of the herd and into the birthing dawn as the sky began to pale and turn a dusky blue.

They waved good-bye and got answering waves from the hands around the campfire.

Dane felt as if he were leaving home. He was glad Joe was with him. He would have someone to talk to on the long ride to the river and beyond.

"Len tell you what happened to Harve Tolliver, Joe?"

"Him tell."

"Concho left tracks. Think you can find him and his men?"

"Can find, sure. Tracks stay long time."

"Of course, I don't know what we'll do when we do find them."

"Shoot," Joe said. "Kill."

"We'll be outnumbered."

Joe snorted. "Hunt. Like turkey. Pick off one, then another."

"Yeah, we'd have to sneak up on 'em."

They talked no more as the sun painted the sky in the east. Painted it a bright and radiant crimson, painted it with fire. The stars and the galaxy of the Milky Way disappeared and the sky turned the color of a robin's egg, a quiet pastel blue.

"That red sky bothers me, Joe," Dane said.

"Red sky. Big storm come."

"Yep. That's the old sayin', 'red sky in the morning, sailor take warning.' "

"Much rain. Big wind," Joe said. "Tomorrow."

"Yeah, maybe tomorrow. The sky looks clear, except for those long clouds in the east."

Joe said nothing and the two men rode on as the land lit up like a stage set, soaking up all the shadows and glistening on the beads of dew that clung to the prairie grasses.

Joe studied the ground and pointed out Chub's horse tracks. Dane nodded.

He was glad Joe was riding with him. He was a tracker, after all. And if anyone could find Concho on that vast plain that stretched into Kansas and beyond, it would be the Cherokee.

Concho, he thought, was as good as dead when they caught up to him.

CHAPTER 29

Randy lay on his stomach next to a jagged tree stump. It was still dark and rocks dug into his knees and upper legs. Ants crawled over his hands, and the rifle was covered with them. Red ants. Somewhere nearby was an ant hill and he couldn't see it. He didn't dare move either.

This was where Concho had brought him and told him to stay hidden and wait for the head of the herd to pass by as soon as it turned daylight.

"You'll hear that bell a-clankin' and when you see that lead cow, you take aim and put a bullet right behind its left leg where it jines the ribs. You'll get it in the heart. It may run and jump for a hunnert yards or so, but it will be a killin' shot. You got that? Just like a deer, Randy, only slower."

"Yeah." He shivered, even though he wore a sheepskin-lined denim jacket. He could smell the cattle and he heard them lowing in the distance, far off to his right.

Concho had planned all this, he knew.

Randy also knew that Lyle was going to pick off another drover after he shot the lead cow. If he shot the lead cow.

He didn't want to do it, but he knew that Concho would have killed him if he had refused.

"This is your growin'-up party, Randy boy," Concho had told him earlier that morning. "You do this and the whole gang will think you're a man. And you will be a man."

"I don't know," he had said. "Killin' a cow ain't my idea of what a man should do."

"Would you rather kill a man in the morning?"

"No, no," Randy had said. "I ain't ready to go that far yet."

"Well, you stick with me and you will be. And right soon."

Randy's teeth chattered in the chill. He clamped them down tight and looked at the eastern sky. It was still dark as a sea of pitchblende. The birds were quiet too, and he hadn't heard a coyote in ten or fifteen minutes, at least.

He felt all alone.

He almost laughed at that thought.

He was alone.

And lonely for something he couldn't put into words. He didn't really have a home of his own. When he was working on the Circle K, that had felt a little like home. Except that he had been ashamed of himself for being so secretive and deceptive, not only to Dane Kramer, but to all the men in the outfit. He was nothing but a liar and a spy. Now he wasn't even a spy. He was caught up in something that scared the hell out of him.

He listened to the cattle. They did not seem to be stirring and he didn't hear any hoofbeats or the clank of that copper bell.

He thought he heard one of the nighthawks humming some old song, but whatever it was soon faded and though he strained to hear a man's voice, a horse's whinny, or a mooing cow, he heard not a sound.

And the silence deepened around him. He brushed away gravel under his legs, but it was no use. Little stones and grains of sand still dug into the flesh of his calves and he felt something crawling on his neck. He slapped at it, then cringed at the sound.

He stared into the darkness. He tried to see the darker shadows of the bedded-down herd, but he saw only blackness on the ground, the horizon. He looked up at the stars and they seemed so dim and far away that their light was not strong enough to illuminate either the terrain or the cattle.

Then he saw something out of the corner of his eye. Faint sparks way off in the distance. Had he imagined that he saw the flashing lights of fireflies? Or was there something else? He struggled to see where the sparks had been, but, again, there was only the deep dark of night.

There it was again. Small orange sparks. A shower of them, maddenly brief.

Moments later, Randy saw something that made his heartbeat quicken. A small flame where the sparks had been. He let out a breath that he had held for several seconds.

The flame grew larger, lashing into the darkness, orange and red, and a faint tinge of blue. He could not hear the crackle of the fire, but he could see it. And as he watched the flames grew larger and stronger, there were more sparks rising above the fire, burning embers that winked out almost as soon as he saw them.

A sign of life, he thought.

The fire fascinated him, even though it was far away and he could not feel its warmth. It told him that the camp was stirring, that the cook was building a fire to cook breakfast for the hands, make coffee, and warm the hands and bodies of those who came to it from their damp bedrolls. Randy felt his heart quicken and there was a pang of regret that he could not walk over there and partake of the companionship of men he had known when he worked on the Circle K.

He took his gaze away from the fire and looked at the eastern horizon. There was no sign yet of the dawn to come.

Ten minutes went by, then ten more, and the flames from the campfire wavered and broke up as shadows passed between the fire and Randy. Shadows of men and now and then, he heard a snatch of conversation, words that traveled on the high air but could not be understood.

Still, Randy waited and grew colder as the fire seemed to grow more distant. He felt a dampness on his face and realized it was dew. There seemed to be a fine, invisible mist in the air as he strained to hear what the cowhands were saying. He thought he heard someone laugh, and once, he heard what sounded like the clatter of a plate and eating utensils. He felt lonelier than ever as the night clung to the land and the cattle stayed bedded down.

Then the distant whicker of a horse jangled Randy's senses and he saw a faint flicker of pale light appear on the eastern horizon. The light grew longer and wider, and he looked up to see stars slowly disappear in a blue vapor, as if they were being wiped out by an unseen hand.

Distant clouds on the eastern horizon turned to ash, then seemed to burst into flame as the sun spewed more light on the sky. A few minutes later, those same clouds turned a fiery red and orange and all of the stars were gone and the sky had turned a pale blue that grew deeper and bluer by the minute.

He saw ants crawling on the backs of his hands and he shook them off, jiggling his fingers. He knocked ants off his rifle and blew two off his stock. He saw the anthill a few feet away and snuggled closer to the rotting tree stump. Bugs crawled out of the pulp and climbed up and down the gray husk that had been stripped of its bark a long time ago.

Then Randy heard hoofbeats and he saw the silhouettes of riders pass by the fire. There was the distinct sound of clanking pewter plates and the rattle of empty coffee cups. The land lit up and he felt naked and exposed as the shadows shrank and he could see green grass sprinkled with the tiny opals of glistening dew.

He lifted his rifle and seated it against his shoulder just to see if he could do it. He knew that his life depended on him shooting that lead cow.

What he didn't know was what would happen after that.

Would Concho ride up with his horse and help him get into the saddle so that they both could ride away before anyone shot at him? He didn't know. Concho had said nothing about how he could escape.

Perhaps, Randy thought, Concho had meant for him to die after he shot the belled cow.

Randy shuddered with the thought that he might die. Die the way Tolliver had died, with a bullet in his heart.

The fire went out and Randy thought he heard the faint hiss of water as it doused the flames. He heard men shooting to get the cattle moving.

Then he heard the clank of the cowbell.

He raised himself up on his elbows for a better look and saw the herd, part of it. He saw the humps of the cows' backs and they were moving forward, away from where he saw the roof of the chuck wagon. He heard the cattle bellowing and mooing, the neigh of horses, and the shouts of the men urging them on.

Then he saw the first white faces and the sea of horns, the bobbing heads of cattle. The clank of the cowbell grew louder.

He waited, the rifle nestled snug against his shoulder. He had a Sharps carbine and it felt like a lead sash weight in his hands.

The cattle moved closer and he could see them better. Ahead of the herd, there was a man riding point. The man looked over his shoulder every now and then to see if the herd was following his path.

Randy did not recognize the point rider, but he saw him light a cigarette as he rode and figured out that it must have been Skip Hewes. He thought he saw some strands of straw-colored hair poking out from under the man's hat. He was the right size and bulk and the way he sat his horse reminded him of Skip when he had seen him riding on the Circle K a thousand years ago.

Then the lead cow came ambling into view. It swayed from side to side, and every time she moved her forelegs, that bell clanged. He lined up his sights, holding the front blade sight on the cow and lining up the rear buckhorn. He knew he would have to lead her a tad. He had shot deer before and they were either standing still or stepping cautiously through the woods, a step or two at a time. The cow wasn't moving fast, but it was moving. He waited until it had come parallel to his position and then lined up his sights just behind her left front leg, about midway up her rib cage. He swung the barrel just a tad and held his breath.

He squeezed the trigger and felt the rifle butt buck into his shoulder. Smoke flew from the muzzle and he heard a *thunk*. As he stared through the haze of smoke, he saw the cow stagger and stumble. She jumped a half foot and let out a mournful bellow. He could not see where he had shot her but knew she had been hit. She ran for a few yards, then chased her tail in a circle until she dropped.

Skip turned around and saw the lead cow go down. He turned his horse on a dime and raced to where the cow had fallen. She lay on her side. She kicked her legs a few times and then lay still, her bell silent.

Randy shrank to the ground, flattening himself and his rifle.

There was yelling from the other hands, and a pair of riders rode out to where the cow lay dead.

Then all three began looking around. Skip looked straight at the stump. Randy looked up without moving his head to see if there was any smoke hanging over him. It had all dissipated and he held his breath, hoping no one would see him.

"Where'd that shot come from?" Paddy yelled from farther away on the herd's left flank.

Skip pointed in Randy's direction.

"Come from over yonder, I think," he shouted back at Paddy.

"Well, get on it, Skip. And you boys too," Paddy shouted.

Three riders turned their horses and started riding slow toward the tree stump.

Randy recognized Skip, but not the other two.

He rolled over and looked back to see if anyone was coming from Concho's bunch to help him get away.

He was on foot. Concho had his horse.

He was trapped.

Randy didn't know what to do. He rolled back on his stomach and saw the riders fanned out, heading straight for him.

He left his rifle on the ground and sprang to his feet.

He began to run back toward where he thought Concho and his men must be. There was only an empty plain.

He heard one of the drovers call out to him.

"Stop," the man yelled.

Randy kept running. He ran as fast as he could command his legs to move.

He ran until he heard a rifle shot.

It sounded like the crack of a leather whip. It sounded as though it would never go away. It seemed to linger on the morning air for an eternity.

It was the last sound Randy ever heard.

CHAPTER 30

Lyle Fisk crept along the bank of the narrow creek while it was still dark. He had changed out of his boots and now wore Sioux moccasins he had bought at a trading post in South Dakota some years before. His horse was ground-tied a half mile away, out of sight of the Circle K men. It grazed in a shallow ravine he had scouted out the day before when he had left Concho's gang to spend the night out on the prairie.

"You know what you're doin', Lyle," Concho had told him, "but if I were you I'd wait until that kid shoots off his Sharps and then you take another of them cowboys down right soon after that."

"I've got it all figgered, Conch," Lyle had said. "Don't you worry 'bout me. I'll see you and the boys by noon tomorrow."

Just before dawn, Lyle sharpened a forked stick he had found near the ravine. He had sharpened the longest part of the branch.

He was close to the herd and knew where the nighthawks crossed paths during the night. He rammed the pointed end of the stick into the ground, then pushed on the apex of the fork to drive it firmly in the ground. He had done this before when he hunted buffalo up in Wyoming and Montana for their hides.

He leaned his heavy Henry "Yellow Boy" so that the barrel rested in the fork. He squatted and settled into position. He knew he would only get one shot. But it would be daylight by then and he'd have the sun at his back.

He was very close to the herd. He could smell them and he could hear them breathing. The shadows of the two nighthawks passed within twenty or twenty-five yards of his position. He knew they could not see him, but he knew just where they would pass as they made their rounds.

He only wanted to drop one of them.

And he wanted to get away clean.

But Lyle was sure that he had it all figured out. If the kid did his job, then every one of the cowhands would be looking in Randy's direction. Timing was the key to his success. He didn't expect both night riders to cross in front of him after Randy shot at the lead cow. One would ride up to the head of the herd and the other would come along on his flank to catch up. By then, of course, the herd would be up and moving.

He felt the dampness of the dew on his face and hands. He pulled a bandanna out of his pocket and dried his hands off, then wiped his face.

It was close to dawn, he knew. He was ready.

The sun rose below the horizon and emblazoned the eastern sky. The herd rose to its collective feet as the hands prodded them awake. He heard the clank of the cowbell and the shouts of the men urging the cattle to follow the leader.

Lyle squeezed the trigger of the Henry gently, then cocked it. The pressure off, the hammer made only a slight sound as it came to full cock.

Light crept across the prairie. Lyle shouldered his rifle and sighted on a steer that was on the edge of the herd.

"Perfect," he said to himself.

He had a clear field of vision. There were no obstructions in his line of sight.

He looked both ways for the night riders. They were out of sight, but he saw that there was a commotion at the tail end of the herd as one of the hands pushed to get the cattle moving.

A moment or two later, he saw one rider round the tail end of the herd and come his way at a slow walk. His horse was bobbing its head and shaking it as if flies were already dipping into the fluid in its eyes.

He turned the other way and saw the other night rider emerge from the front of the herd and head for his station on the flank.

The cowbell clanked and Lyle gritted his teeth.

The sun was up and the sky was red.

"When is that kid going to shoot?" he whispered to himself.

Then he heard the shot and there was a second or two of absolute silence as the crack of the rifle seemed to vanish into a vacuum.

Cowhands shouted and the rider on his left rose in the saddle and stood in his stirrups, staring at the front of the herd and the other rider on Lyle's right. That rider turned his horse and went back to the head of the herd. Lyle heard one of the men, probably the trail boss, order someone to find out who had shot.

The cowbell was silent.

Lyle curled his finger around the trigger inside the guard and watched the rider on his left put his horse into a slow trot.

The rider came closer. Lyle sighted on him and waited. When the horse and rider were directly opposite him, he held his breath. He lined up his sights and led the rider a half foot.

Then he squeezed the trigger with a gentle pull of his finger. The rifle bucked against his shoulder as it belched lead and ignited powder into a multitude of firefly-sized sparks.

The bullet struck the rider in his side, heart high, knocking him sideways in the saddle. His right arm dropped to his side and the reins slipped from his grasp. He gurgled in his throat as blood gushed from his mouth.

Seconds later, the nighthawk slumped, then toppled from his saddle. The horse, suddenly deprived of the weight on its back, bucked, then skittered forward for a few yards, dragging its reins.

Lyle knocked down the forked stick and pulled his rifle free.

He duck-walked away from that spot toward the path he would take back to where his horse was tethered.

Men shouted and horses raced to the front of the herd. None of them were looking in his direction.

In moments, Lyle was well away from the

herd and running toward the ravine. A few minutes later he was atop his horse and rammed his Henry into its scabbard.

He did not look back but rode a wide loop to the other side of the herd.

He didn't care about the kid. Neither, he knew, did Concho.

"I don't care what happens to him," Concho had said the night before. "He's served his purpose."

Lyle hoped the kid had gotten away. He was harmless and not a bad kid as far as he knew.

But the truth was, he didn't give a damn about Randy either.

Out here on the prairie, a man's life wasn't worth much. That's the way the West had always been and that's the way it was now.

One less kid in the world didn't make much difference.

Not in Lyle's book.

Not in Concho's either.

CHAPTER 31

Paddy looked down at the body of Randy Bowman.

" 'Tis a cryin' shame," he said. "A good boy gone bad. Fallin' in with thieves like he did. And now it's come to this. The poor lad is dead long before he reached his prime."

"Paddy, that boy shot Bossy, our lead cow," Whit said.

"And who put him up to it, I ask?" Paddy said. "Concho and Throckmorton, the lowest scoundrels on the face of the earth."

"It's real sad," Chub said. "To die over killin' a damned cow."

"I guess that's life," Whit said as he shouldered his rifle.

Paddy turned to walk away.

"I got to get that bell off Bossy and get me another lead cow," he said. "I'll get Alfredo to butcher that dead cow. No use lettin' the meat go to waste. But we ain't gonna get the herd movin' like we should."

"Are we goin' to bury the boy, or just leave him out here for the buzzards and coyotes?" Whit asked.

"Bury him," Paddy said. "But be quick about it."

He had started to walk back to the herd when they all heard the boom and snap of a rifle shot.

"Now what?" Paddy exclaimed.

They heard the drovers shouting and Paddy took off at a dead run while Skip and Whit stood there like statues.

There was a ripple through the herd as cattle on the right flank pushed against those in the middle and on the left flank.

Paddy stopped and turned around. "Whit, you and Chub better get back to the herd. They look like they're trying to stampede."

The two men nodded and mounted up. They rode to the herd, which was still moving. They started to turn those cattle that were trying to bolt.

Paddy knelt down beside the dead cow and unbuckled the collar with the bell on it. He held the clapper so that it wouldn't clang, then yelled to one of the hands to bring up his horse.

There was pandemonium and confusion all up and down the line as riders lashed their horses to keep the herd from breaking up and starting out on a stampede.

Dewey Rossiter, one of the younger hands, brought Paddy a saddled horse.

"Here, Dew," Paddy said as he handed him the collar with the cowbell. "Put this in the supply wagon for the time being. What's goin' on?"

"Other side of the herd. I think somebody shot at a wolf or a coyote."

"Bullshit," Paddy said. "We don't shoot wild dogs when the herd is movin'."

"Hell, I don't know, boss. Everybody's runnin' around like their heads was off."

"Git," Paddy said, and shooed Dewey away. He climbed into the saddle and galloped around the front of the herd.

Dewey rode back toward the supply wagon like a pony express rider at full speed.

The first man Paddy saw on the east flank was Lester Pierson.

"Lester," he said, "can you tell me what's goin' on?"

"I got my hands full keepin' this herd from runnin' off in all directions, Paddy, but I think somebody shot Steve."

"Steve was ridin' night herd," Paddy said.

"Hell, I don't know," Lester said as he let his cutting horse have its head to turn back a wild-eyed steer that was trying to run off from the herd.

When Paddy rode up to the cluster of men gathered around the fallen night rider, he saw right away that it was not Steve Atkins lying there on the ground, but Cal Ferris.

Paddy swore under his breath and swung out of his saddle. Steve looked over at him.

"Did you see what happened, Steve?" Paddy asked.

"I was up at the head of the herd. Heard the shot and came ridin' over."

"You see anybody?"

Steve shook his head.

"Nary," he said. "I just heard the shot and saw Cal fall out of the saddle. Got here as fast as I could, but knowed it was too late when I saw him a-lyin' here."

"Shit," Paddy said.

"Cal didn't have no chance," another drover said. "Bushwhacked, just like Tolliver."

"Shut up, Summers," Paddy said to Pete Summers, who was going to ride drag that day in Tolliver's stead. "Let's not jump to no goldarned conclusions."

"Well, it warn't one of us what shot Cal," Summers said. His thin face contorted into an indignant snarl.

"I told you to shut up," Paddy said. "Go get a damned shovel. Steve, take off his gun belt and go through his pockets. One of you other men strip his horse and take it into the remuda."

"Where do we put Cal's stuff?" Steve asked.

"Supply wagon for now. One of you help Summers dig a hole. The damned blowflies are already at him, for Christ's sake."

The flies were at Randy's body too. The men could hear them buzzing as they dug a grave. They stripped off his pistol and gun belt, picked up his rifle. When they went through his pockets, all that he had was a twenty-five-cent coin.

Alicante spread a tarp out in the open and got one of the hands to drag the dead cow over to it and help him lift the cow onto the canvas. He took a long sharp knife and cut from the throat to the anus, then began to peel back the hide. The cattle moved off as he butchered the cow and packed the smaller cuts of meat into wooden boxes. He wrapped the legs and haunches in damp cheesecloth, then wrapped the fabric with butcher paper. He loaded these on the chuck wagon. By the time he finished, the herd was out of sight. All that remained of the cow was the head, hide, and tail, along with the windpipe, lungs, four-barreled stomach, a pile of intestines gleaming like

301

oiled eels in the sun. Four cloven hooves lay in a separate pile, guillotined from the legs by Alicante's meat cleaver, and as he drove by, the blowflies were crawling over the cow's face, sipping from the eyes and crawling into its nostrils and streaming along the raw remnants of its hide.

An hour later, the herd had moved a mile or more and Paddy watched the cows in the lead jostle for dominance. One cow seemed to want to lead, so he sent a man back to get the cowbell and collar.

It took three of them to bulldog the cow and wrestle it into submission so that Paddy could attach the bell collar.

"Now, let's see if Bossy Two can lead these cattle north," Paddy said as they released the cow. It bellowed and staggered to its feet, then took to the trail.

The men gave out hoorahs and returned to their positions on the flanks.

Skip rode with Paddy on point. They both looked in all directions as they rode, looking for any movement, any sign that they were being watched by Concho and his dry-gulchers.

"Do you think Concho and them other rapscallions is watchin' us, Paddy?" Chub asked.

"I been thinkin' on it," Paddy said.

" 'Pears to me that Concho is tryin' to scare hell out of us by pickin' us off one by one."

"Well, he's scarin' hell out of me," Chub said.

"You can't let that get to you, Chub. Long as we keep our heads and don't get rattled, we got a chance."

"Tolliver tried to spot them boys with the spyglass you lent him. Didn't do no damned good."

"I figger this Concho's pretty smart. Like most back-shooters. He sneaks up on a man in the dead of the night. So that makes him a coward in my book."

"A coward who's a killer," Chub said.

"Well, keep your eyes peeled, watch your back, and be ready to shoot anybody who don't look right."

"You can't never see no sneak," Chub said.

"But a coward like Concho is goin' to make a mistake sooner or later. He'll think he's brave one of these days or maybe that he's invisible. Then we'll get him."

"You think so?"

"Yeah, that's what I think, Chub."

Chub looked back over his shoulder at the long line of whitefaces, their heads bobbing, their horns glinting in the sunlight. The sky to the northwest was filling with large white clouds just drifting over the horizon. In the wake of the cattle he saw buzzards circling in the sky, wheeling on unseen currents of air, their wings widespread.

There were buzzards in the air, he thought, and buzzards on the ground. It was the ones on the ground he was worried about. They didn't wait for something to die. They were killers, and their leader was a savage bastard named Concho.

CHAPTER 32

Lyle didn't eject the empty cartridge from his Henry until he had rejoined Concho and the others. He cranked the lever, and the brass hull spun out of the chamber and struck the ground with a clang. Another cartridge slid into the firing chamber when he returned the lever to its former position.

"One shot?" Concho asked.

"You didn't hear it?" Lyle said.

Concho shook his head.

"One shot. One dead cowboy."

Concho laughed.

"I coulda dropped two," Lyle said. "Might have been a tight squeak, though."

"A cowpoke a day is my motto," Concho said.

Lyle laughed. "Anyways, I think the kid got the lead cow. I didn't hear no cowbell after he shot."

"What about the kid? I ain't seen him."

"I heard another shot. Figgered they shot

him. Like you figgered, right?"

"Yeah, I didn't think the kid had much of a chance to get away. He never come back for his horse, so we got one extry."

"No, I'm pretty sure them drovers got Randy. Or I would've seen him."

"Good riddance, I say," Concho said.

"Who's trackin' the herd, Concho?" Lyle asked.

"I sent Logan to see what all went on after you and the kid finished up your business."

"What's next?" Lyle asked.

"We'll hit 'em once more, maybe when they're crossin' the Verdigris. Then I figger Paddy will follow the Caney up into Kansas before he cuts over to the Missouri."

"So?" Lyle said.

"We'll rustle the whole herd up on the Caney River."

"Kill 'em all?"

"Kill 'em all, if need be."

"You think some of the cowhands will turn tail and run?"

"Don't make no difference to me. Better to kill all of them, though."

"How come?" Lyle asked.

"No witnesses," Concho said.

"Yeah, I get what you mean, Concho."

Late that same afternoon, Logan caught up with them. His horse was lathered and breathing hard when he rode up to Concho and Lyle.

The first thing that he did was hand the binoculars back to Concho. "Thanks, Concho," he said. "They helped a lot."

Concho stored the field glass in his saddlebag. "What did you see, Logan?"

"Two fresh graves and a butchered cow," Logan said.

Concho smiled. "So the kid did kill that lead cow."

"Paddy's already belled another and the herd is moving north."

"A few more days and we'll be taking that herd south," Concho said.

"It'll be a pleasure," Lem said. "Payday."

"Yep," Concho said. "I got a promissory note in my pocket signed by Throckmorton, to pay us ten dollars a head for all the cattle we bring back. Throckmorton balked at my demands, right off, but I told him that we were takin' all the risks. He was just puttin' up a small amount of cash while we were puttin' our lives on the line. So he gave me the guarantee I asked him for. I've got Throckmorton by the balls. He don't pay, he don't get no cattle. It's that simple."

"That's serious money," Logan said. "If Throckmorton pays us right away."

"He will," Concho said, "and when he

goes to sell them, we'll do the drive and make even more money."

"I'd rather drive 'em than steal 'em," Lem said.

"Well, we'll do both. Soon as Paddy gets that herd into Kansas, we'll take the cattle off his hands."

"What about Kramer?" Logan asked. "Ain't he comin' up behind Paddy with the rest of the herd?"

"Far as we know, he is," Concho said. "We'll probably run into him on the way back. He won't know what to think when he sees two herds comin' to meet him."

"By the time Kramer figgers it all out," Lem said, "we'll have his herd mixed in with ours and he'll be wolf meat."

"That's the way I look at it," Concho said.

The four men caught up with the rest of the band, and the others all looked to Concho for more revelations of his plans. They were envious of Lyle and Logan and wished they'd had more to do with the killings.

"You'll all get your chance," Concho said. "We'll let Paddy get the herd up across the Kansas line and then take him down, steal all the cattle."

"We still goin' to thin his crew down before that?" Mitch asked.

"When he gets the herd up to the Verdigris, we'll shoot at least one more man."

"Then I claim it's my turn," Mitch said.

"How do you figger that?" Skip asked.

"I just claim it, Skip."

The two men glared at each other.

Skip, enraged, swung a fist at Mitch. Part of his knuckle grazed Mitch's chin.

Mitch got enough of a sting from the blow that he leaped toward Skip, his arms outstretched. He grabbed Skip by the arm and jerked him so that Skip lost his seating in the saddle. He toppled toward Mitch, who dragged him to the ground as he fell from his perch.

The two started swinging fists at each other as the other riders halted and circled the two pugilists.

"Bastard," yelled Skip.

Mitch cracked him across the chin with his fist and Skip sagged backward into his horse. His horse sidled away and Mitch charged at Skip in an attempt to tackle him and throw him to the ground.

Skip sidestepped Mitch's charge and brought a hammering blow down on Mitch's neck. Mitch fell to the ground as if poleaxed. Then he rolled away and regained his footing.

Skip, panting hard, swung a roundhouse left at Mitch. His fist struck Mitch in his right ear.

Mitch roared in pain and grappled with Skip.

"Cut it out, you pecker heads," Concho yelled at the two men.

They ignored him and kept swinging at each other.

And missing.

The riders flexed in and out of their spectator circle as the two men scrambled to tear each other's heads off or gouge their eyes out. Some of the men were laughing.

"Damn it," Lem yelled, "stop it, you two, or I'll take the quirt to you both."

Mitch was breathing hard by then, and there were scratch marks on his face. Each mark trickled droplets of blood down his cheeks. Skip's left eye had started to turn purple underneath the lower lid.

The two men wrapped arms around each other and butted heads. They fell to the ground and rolled over and over, punching and gouging each other with fists and fingers, drawing blood, bruising flesh. They yelled and hurled epithets at each other while the men on horseback looked down and cheered them both on, first one, then the other.

"Grab his nuts, Skip," one man yelled.

"Kick him in the eggs," hollered another.

The two got up again and staggered as they circled each other like two punch-drunk pugilists.

"All right," Concho boomed, "you both got blood in your eyes. Enough. Save your fight for another time."

"Yeah," Lem said. "Save it for the cow-hands."

Skip and Mitch, both out of breath, and bleeding from dozens of scratches, stood there like two worn-out boxers, their arms hanging down at their sides, a pair of bedraggled roosters with most of the fight gone out of them.

"Shake hands," Concho ordered. "Mitch gets the next kill, Skip. You can have the one after that."

"Fine with me," Skip panted. He let his head drop and grabbed his legs above both knees to steady himself.

Mitch patted him on the back and when Skip stood up, he offered his hand. The two men shook hands.

"Mount up," Concho said. "We'll crack another jug of whiskey at sundown."

"Hooray," shouted some of the others on horseback.

Skip and Mitch crawled, wounded, into their saddles and slumped over as they recovered their breaths.

311

Later, Concho sent Will Davis off to the east to track the herd.

"Come back after Paddy beds 'em down for the night," he told Will.

"I don't get a shot?"

"You'd better not. I want ol' Paddy to have enough hands to get that herd up into Kansas."

"I never get to have no fun," Will said as he took the glass from Concho.

"Play with yourself, Will. That'll be the most fun you have this day."

Will laughed and rode off toward the east.

Concho caught up with the others, but he had his eye on the western sky and the huge thunderheads to the northwest. They billowed out like the huge sails of sailing ships and drifted across the blue ocean of the sky in their direction.

"When those clouds turn black on their underbellies," Concho told the others, "we're in for a real gully washer. We better start lookin' for high ground."

The men all looked at the sky and nodded.

They rode north in sunshine, but they all knew that by dusk they'd be in shadow and it would be time to break out the slickers and the jackets. In the distance, they saw both broken land and patches of farmland,

312

an occasional farmhouse, and a barn or two. They saw milk cows and horses, mules, and goats. All far away, all beyond their caring or their understanding.

They knew who they were and why they were riding their horses.

They were not sodbusters, by golly. Not by a long shot.

They were free men, not bound by the land or the law.

CHAPTER 33

It was well before noon when Joe Eagle
spotted the lone grave on the prairie. He
and Dane rode over to it.

"That's got to be Tolliver under there,"
Dane said.

"See coyote tracks," Joe said, pointing to
the hieroglyphs around the dirt mound.

"I see 'em, Joe."

They had walked, trotted, and galloped
their horses to gain time and distance. Dane
knew that a man could walk four miles in
an hour and he wanted to cover at least
thirty miles by sundown. The horses had
never been taxed, and were in fine fettle by
the time they came up on Tolliver's grave
site.

"Let's go on, Joe. We know what happened
here. You don't have to do any tracking to
find out more."

"Find herd?" Joe asked.

"By tomorrow, I hope."

"We go, then," Joe said, and the two rode on into the afternoon, following the wide swath of tracks left by two thousand head of cattle and several outriders. There were piles of dung littering the plain in the wake of the herd's passage, and the strong smell of urine drifted up from the ground and stung their nostrils.

Beyond the bedding ground, at the deep fork of the Canadian River, Joe spotted the stone cairn and the two men crossed there. Joe began to read sign and saw where Paddy had let the cattle drink on the other side and then got them moving again.

Dane kept the same pace as he had that morning and they ate up ground. The land was changing. There were farmlands, but there were also open stretches of prairie that were broken up by gullies and ravines. It looked as if the back of the land had been flayed by a giant wielding a cat-o'-nine tails whip and gouged out great wounds on the plain.

It was near dusk when they came to a place where Paddy had spent the next night. Joe saw where the herd had been bedded down, where the nighthawks had ridden on their rounds.

"There," Joe said as he pointed off to the

right of the bedding ground. "Another grave."

The two rode over and Joe began to decipher the myriad layers of tracks surrounding the grave. He rode over to a place some yards away and beckoned for Dane to join him. He pointed to the ground when Dane rode up alongside him.

"Man wait here. Shoot rider like buffalo."

Dane saw the forked stick that had been shoved down and broken where it was stuck into the ground.

Joe rode in a straight line past the stick, peering at the ground. Dane followed him.

"Walk here," Joe said, and then turned his horse to follow the boot prints.

"He's on foot," Dane said.

"Him on foot. Go to horse. We find place."

Joe found the ravine where the bushwhacker had left his horse while he carried out his murderous deed. Joe examined all the tracks and saw where the rider had come in and where he had gone out. They rode back to the bedding ground, past the grave of an unknown cowhand.

Joe sniffed the air and then his gaze settled on the head of the slain cow. They rode over to where the entrails, head, and other organs lay strung out and ravaged by buzzards and coyotes. They could hear the *zizzing* of the blowflies several yards from where the cow had been butchered.

"They kill cow," Joe said. "Cook butcher."

Dane nodded.

Then Joe swept the western horizon with his eyes and spotted the rotting hickory stump. Beyond, he saw a fresh mound of dirt.

"Come," he said to Dane. "Joe read tracks."

Joe rode to the stump and examined it.

"Him lie down here," he said. He looked beyond, toward the fresh grave. "Him run. We see."

Joe dismounted and walked over the ground. He pointed to a patch of grass that was stained with dried blood. "Him shot here. Him buried there."

"What was he shooting at?" Dane asked, not expecting an answer. It was more of a rhetorical question to himself.

Joe turned around and lifted his arm. He sighted down it and saw the strung-out detritus of the butchered cow. "Him shoot cow. Maybe him shoot lead cow."

"There's sure a direct line from this stump to where Alicante butchered that cow."

"Grave small. Not deep. Not man buried here. Young boy."

"You think so?" Dane said.

"Small man. Boy."

"But who —"

Dane stopped talking in midsentence. Suddenly he knew. He knew who was buried there in that small grave. It could only be one person.

"Randy Bowman," he said softly.

Joe nodded.

He walked farther on, following tracks that Dane could not see. He was too stunned to make sense of anything at that moment.

"Him walk here. Him run. Cowhand shot him. Him die here."

"He wasn't supposed to get away, was he?" Dane said to Joe.

"No place to hide," Joe said.

"Concho sent that boy into certain death."

"Maybe," Joe said. "No can hide. No can run far."

"Concho wanted him to die. But first he wanted him to shoot that cow. That's the only explanation I can come up with, Joe."

"You explain good. Make sense. Boy shoot cow. Somebody shoot boy."

"I'd like to choke the life out of that bastard Concho," Dane said.

"Maybe you get chance, Dane."

There was a faint smile on Joe's lips, but Dane did not feel like smiling himself.

Randy was a thief and a coward, a sneak who had spied on him. But he didn't hate him. Not now. He was just a young boy who had gotten in a rough game and now he was dead. What galled him was that Concho had sent him to this place knowing Randy would be killed. As Joe had said, there was no place to run, no place for him to hide.

"Let's get out of here, Joe," Dane said.

"Sun set soon. Make camp," Joe said.

"Yeah. We'll catch up to Paddy tomorrow. I just hope we don't find any more graves."

They camped by the little creek that ran on the eastern side of the bedding grounds, but a mile or two farther on.

They spread out their bedrolls under some cottonwoods and willows, filled their canteens. They hobbled their horses on new grass and did not build a fire. They ate sandwiches and watched the night spread its dark blanket over the sky and sprinkle it with sparkling diamonds. It was a peaceful evening, but in the distance they heard the ominous rumble of thunder and saw streaks of lightning scrawl electric latticework in the dark thunderheads.

"Much rain come," Joe said as he crawled inside his bedroll.

Dane plucked tobacco from his pouch and chewed it as he watched lightning strike the ground in the distance, followed each time by the bellowing of loud thunder.

Finally he spat out the last of his chew and slipped into his bedroll. The horses whickered and the thunder rumbled.

He fell asleep just before the winds swept across the plains and whipped up the creek, ripped leaves from the trees, and brought the first soft patter of rain.

CHAPTER 34

The rain blasted across the plain in silver sheets, lashing the cattle and the nighthawks with stinging needles propelled by the winds that circled and gusted with a chilling fury.

Steve and Bill helped Alfredo lash down the chuck wagon, tying strong ropes to the back wheels and stringing them to the supply wagon.

"This is a frog strangler," Steve yelled above the thunder and surging wind.

The chuck wagon rocked as its canvas top was buffeted by the savage gusts.

Alicante, soaked to the skin, shivered and tied knots in the long rope. The supply wagon too swayed under the onslaught of wind and rain as its covering tarp rippled and rattled as if it harbored a box full of writhing snakes. The men bent to the wind as they tautened the ropes. Horses neighed as they clustered together, their rumps turned to the northwest as buffers. The cattle groaned and mooed, pressed against one another for warmth and protection.

Paddy came by and tested the ropes.

"It's a howler," he shouted, and the wind snatched away his words while he clamped his hands down on his hat to keep it from sailing into the darkness.

"How come you're ropin' the two wagons together, Bill?" Paddy asked.

"Case either wagon gets blowed off its brake, I figger the other'n will act like an anchor."

"Any of you seen Chub Toomey?" Paddy's voice was loud, but it was torn to shreds by the wind and the rain.

"Seen him a while ago with Dewey," Steve said. "Some cattle broke away from the middle of the herd and he's tryin' to round 'em up or drive 'em back where they belong."

"Yeah, him and Dewey were flappin' their hats and hollerin' at a bunch of steers makin' tracks for high ground."

"There ain't no high ground," Paddy yelled as he turned his back to the wind.

Wu finished hobbling the two horses that were still hitched to the chuck wagon, then ran his hands along the harness clear to the brake. The pots and pans inside the wagon rattled and clanged like some mad symphony that was off-key and off-tempo. The cook fire was out and the fire ring was filling with water. Burned and charred chunks of firewood began to float and churn and there was a thick soup of ashes that danced under the peppering downpour of rain.

"I go inside," Wu said as he struggled against the wind alongside the wagon. "Too much rain. Too much wind."

Paddy shooed him toward the back of the wagon.

"Go on, Wu Ling," he yelled.

Wu nodded and made his way to the rear of the wagon.

"Horses okay, Alfredo?" Paddy asked the wrangler.

"Wet and cold," Alicante said. "All hobbled and shivering like the rest of us."

"Bill, you and Steve come with me," Paddy said. "If we've got strays, Chub and Dewey might need help."

"Sure thing, Paddy," Steve said. "Do we ride or walk?"

"Walk for now. But bring your horses."

The two men walked to the other side of the supply wagon and untied their reins from the rear wheel. They led their horses around the wagon and followed Paddy, who looked like a downhill skier as he braced the wind and plodded forward toward the middle of the herd.

His horse was tied to a short tree stump with jagged edges around the cut top. He unwound the reins and the three men continued on their way. Rain stung their eyes. They bent their heads and held their hats down.

"My makin's are all wet," Bill said, but neither Paddy nor Steve heard him. The wind blotted out all normal conversation, and the din from the chuck wagon mingled with the thunder to muffle any but the strongest voice. Lightning stabbed the ground a few miles away and stitched the elephantine clouds with jagged forks of mercurial light that flashed and vanished as peals of thunder rolled across the skies.

Paddy came to a place where the herd was hemorrhaging cattle. He heard Chub and Dewey shouting at each other but could not see them.

He turned to Bill and Steve. "Mount up," he said. "We've got big trouble."

Paddy hauled himself into his saddle and fought through the rain to find Chub and Dewey. He followed the stream of cattle that had left the herd. They weren't running, but they were walking fast, following some new leader that evidently had struck out on its own.

At the next flash of lightning, Paddy looked down at the ground. What he saw in that brief flash was very disturbing. Water ran in rivulets in several directions. Fast water. Water that swept along clods of mud that disintegrated and formed small banks. Another flash of lightning showed him that the cattle were splashing through ankle-high water. They seemed to be unsteady on their feet. Their heads hung low and raindrops bounced off their horns and shoulders, splattered from their rumps. The wind blew hard and gusted even harder.

Behind him, Bill and Steve followed at a distance, their horses surging against the wind. Rain splashed off their chests. Their hooves were plopping into the tiny rivers of runoff, and water spattered onto their bellies.

Paddy pressed on with a strong feeling of dread at the amount of water he saw running across the ground.

Flash flooding was always a danger and a threat during a heavy rainstorm, especially when the plain was broken by gullies and ravines. And he knew they were very near the river he planned to cross into Kansas, the Caney.

Streaks of lightning etched a zigzag pattern in the distant thunderheads. That's when he caught a glimpse of Chub trying to turn a large steer back against the truant cattle behind it.

He called out at the top of his lungs, "Ho, Chub, we're right behind you."

Chub turned around in the saddle, but his face was dark under the hood of his slicker. He raised a hand in acknowledgment but did not try to say anything amid the peals of thunder and the roaring wind.

Paddy spurred his horse and charged toward Toomey. He did not see Dewey just then. He urged his horse in tandem with Chub's to drive the cattle back into the herd while avoiding their horns.

The lead steer swung its head and tried to gore Chub's horse. The horse sidestepped and danced out of range.

"Stubborn bastard," Chub yelled into the teeth of the wind.

"Where's Dewey?" Paddy asked.

"Up ahead. There's another bunch that we couldn't turn. They were runnin' like hell when they heard the thunder."

"I just hope the whole herd don't stampede," Paddy said, and reached down to grab one of the steer's horns. He grasped it at the boss, but the steer jerked its head and the horn slipped through Paddy's hand as if it had been soaked in oil.

Paddy cursed and his horse tried to turn the steer back, but the agile whiteface charged off in another direction. The cattle behind it followed it, pushing and crowding against each other, blinded by the blowing rain. Chub and Paddy were surrounded by milling cattle and had to spur their horses to break free of the crushing bodies that surged after the runaway steer.

"Don't know if we can turn 'em back," Chub yelled, once he and Paddy were free of the jostling cattle.

"Might have to shoot that steer to stop him," Paddy said.

"Wouldn't be no big loss," Chub said.

Bill and Steve rode up. They were drenched and dripping, but their expressions were crestfallen.

"There's a bunch more behind all these," Steve said to Paddy.

"They just keep on a-comin'," Bill said, shaking his head. Both men had their hoods up on their slickers now. Paddy did not and he looked like a drowned rat.

"Bill, go see if you can find Dewey and help him. If we can get part of the herd turned back, maybe the rest will follow."

"Where is he?" Bill asked.

"Up ahead of me," Chub said. "God knows where."

"Lot of water," Bill said. "We could get a flash —"

Paddy cut him off. "Don't say it, Bill. Just get your ass up there and help Dewey. Steve, you go with him."

The two men rode off through curtains of rain into pitch-darkness. It seemed as if the earth or the storm had swallowed them up.

Chub looked dejected.

"I don't know what we can do in this downpour," he said to Paddy.

"Mainly, about all we can do is let the cattle know we're here and try to keep them from running all over creation. Let's go after that damned steer and see if we can rope him."

"I ain't never roped in no storm like this," Chub said.

"There's always a first time," Paddy said. He pulled his hood up over his hat and loosed the tie-downs on his rope. He untied them enough so that he could just jerk one strand free and grab the rope when the time came.

Chub and Paddy trotted well ahead of the fugitive herd until they spotted the temperamental steer. It was heading blindly on a course that made no sense to Paddy. Whenever the lightning flashed, he saw no high ground, no hills. Still, he figured the steer was guided by some instinct that told it to move in a westerly direction, straight into the maw of the thunderstorm.

"Head him off, Chub," Paddy shouted.

He loosened the thong that held his coiled manila rope and grasped the strands. He shook out a loop and guided his horse alongside. The steer bucked and kicked out its hind legs when Paddy's horse came up alongside.

"I got you now," Paddy said as he widened the loop and dropped it over both horns. He rode on past. He jerked the rope taut, looped it around his saddle horn.

Then he reined his horse into a wheeling angle to the side. The rope tightened and there was resistance from the steer, but the horse was stronger. It dug in its heels as Paddy thrummed its flanks with his blunt spurs and yelled into its ear. He felt the weight of the steer as it tugged on the rope, but there was no escape for the animal.

"You got him," yelled Chub.

Then Paddy's horse responded to the spurs and his master's slaps on his rump and barreled forward. The horse jerked the steer to the ground and Paddy turned him again to drag the cow away from the others. It slid through water and mud, bawling and kicking, trying to get to its feet. It dug one horn into the ground and the horse pulled it free. The white face of the steer was spattered with mud so that it appeared to be freckled.

Paddy started taking up rope, loosening it from his saddle horn until the steer was nearly under his horse. He kept the rope tight.

"See if you can put a dally on that steer's hind legs, Chub," he ordered. He panted, nearly out of breath.

Chub grabbed a short piece of rope and jumped from his horse. He rammed into the steer's butt, sat on it, and grabbed both hind legs by the ankles. He jerked the rope from his teeth and bound the hind legs together, formed a slipknot, and jerked the rope until it was tight. The steer struggled, but it could only groan and lie there as the rain spattered on his wild eyes until he closed them and stopped struggling.

"Now let's turn them cows back into the herd," Paddy said.

He and Chub charged the oncoming cattle and turned them. Cows in the rear began to turn and trot back to the main herd.

Paddy turned loose of the rope and let it fall with a splash onto the wet ground.

He and Chub got the cattle into a run. He thought that the thunder behind them helped. When they saw the herd, it was up and moving north, very slowly. The cattle they had rounded up melted into the flow of cattle, and both men turned their horses.

"Now what?" Chub asked.

"Let's go back and help Dewey."

"This rain is like a cow pissin' on a flat rock," Chub griped. "I ain't never seen so much water fall all at once."

"This is just a regular spring rain," Paddy cracked, but when he saw Chub's drenched face, he nodded in agreement.

The two men rode back toward where they thought Dewey and the other two hands might be. As they passed the hog-tied steer, both looked at it as they passed.

"What about Frisky there?" Chub asked.

"We'll pick him up when we've got the other loose cattle back in the main herd," Paddy said.

They heard shouts from up ahead and soon they saw Dewey, Bill, and Steve surrounding six or eight head of cattle. They had them turned and were driving them back toward the main herd.

"You got all of 'em, Dew?" Paddy asked.

"I think so. Hard to see in this wet stuff."

"Good job," Paddy said.

He and Chub took opposite flanks and the cattle responded to the herding by heading out single file as docile as farm-bred Guernseys.

Later, he and Bill returned for the steer that was drowning in mud and water. Bill jumped down and removed the dally. He handed the rope up to Paddy. Paddy jerked the steer to its feet and they led it back to the rear of the herd, where Pete Summers was riding drag.

The wagons and the remuda remained where they had been as the herd moved on like sleepwalkers, their heads drooping, their hides soaked, their feet plopping into puddles of mud and water.

The storm clouds moved over them and drifted eastward. Lightning lashed at the prairie, and the thunder rolled toward the east, its booming roars fading in the distance.

Chub and Paddy took the point, staying close to the lead cow with her clanking bell sounding like a buoy off some lonesome seashore.

The rain continued to pelt down, but the wind eased up around midnight.

"Should we bed 'em down, Paddy?" Chub asked as he began to see a few stars break through in the western sky.

"Give 'em a while yet," Paddy said. "I have a hunch we'll see Dane come mornin'."

"Think he'd be ridin' at night in weather like this?"

"I don't know. Dane is his own man. If he's ridin' alone, he might. If he's got Joe Eagle with him, maybe not."

"Why not?"

" 'Cause Joe would find some shelter and wait it out, I think."

"Why?" Chub asked.

" 'Cause Injuns don't like rain and they don't like dark."

"Hmm," Chub snorted.

Paddy didn't know if he was right, but he knew he would begin to feel better if Dane did come and join them. Two of his men had been killed already and he didn't want to lose any more hands. Yet he knew he had to get the herd to Omaha and couldn't stop to fight off a bunch of rustling gunfighters.

Dane, likely, would know what to do.

And, after all, it was Dane's cattle that they were driving. He had more to lose than any of them.

Paddy knew too that Dane did not like to lose.

Chapter 35

Daybreak.

A wan sun rising in the east on a pale cool dawn. Disgruntlement in the outlaw camp. Soggy bedrolls, wet socks, soaked clothing, water on the ground, horses shivering, men complaining, Concho's mood as dark as the night had been.

"We'll never get dried out," Lyle said, pouring water out of his boot.

"Firewood's all wet," Mitch said.

"Blow on it," cracked Logan.

"Fan it with your wet hat, Mitch," Will said as he squeezed water out of his own battered Stetson.

"Where's Skip?" Concho asked. He had his shirt off and was putting on a dry one he had found at the bottom of one of his saddlebags.

"Should be ridin' in with his report pretty soon," Lyle said. "He lit out about an hour or so ago. I could hear his feet squishing inside his boots."

Nobody laughed.

They had all spent a miserable night, with no shelter from the wind or the rain. Concho had ordered Skip to check on the trail herd before sunup. The rest of them had huddled together with their slickers pulled up over their faces, their heads on rolled-up saddle blankets. Horses that were hobbled jumped at every lightning bolt or rumble of thunder. Miserable.

The sky was still overcast. Layers of gray, batten-shaped clouds lay from horizon to horizon, silent and brooding, somber as dirty cotton.

"Can anybody start a damned fire?" Logan asked.

The men shook their heads. There was no paper, no dry firewood, no kindling.

Logan rubbed his hands together and shook each foot in turn to warm his toes. That didn't work, so he stomped around in a circle, stamping each boot down hard.

"Rider comin' from the east," Mitch announced.

They all looked and saw a solitary rider, his horse at a fast walk, break the bleak line of the horizon. He was bent over in a slump, but they recognized him.

"That's Skip, I reckon," Will said. His lips

were bluish and his complexion was as bland and empty as a bowl of oatmeal. His arms were wrapped around his waist for warmth, but his fingers were gaunt and bloodless, the skin wrinkled as if he had soaked them in cold vinegar.

"He's sure takin' his sweet time," chimed in Lyle. He held up his bedroll and shook it. Water drops flew in the air like tiny beads of sweat.

"He looks like a drowned rat," Mitch said.

Concho scowled but said nothing.

Skip rode up a few minutes later. His eyes were red around the rim of his iris, and there were dark smudges under both eyes. He dismounted and his legs gave way. Concho caught him before he fell.

"Lord, what a night," Skip said. "I never saw so much rain and the wind like to have blown me off my horse."

"There ain't no hot coffee, Skip," Concho said, "so tell me what you saw, where the herd's at, and what all happened last night."

Skip managed to stand on his own and he broke away from Concho. Lyle took his reins and began to rub the horse's neck and withers. Water pooled up with each scrape of his hand and dripped to the ground.

"That herd started movin' right after the storm hit," Skip said. "Some of 'em run off and the hands had a hell of a time roundin' 'em up. Herd kept movin' and they're headed for the Caney. I reckon they'll cross into Kansas by tonight or tomorrow."

"They moved the herd all night?" Concho asked.

"They didn't move fast, but they didn't stop movin', Concho. I swear. You couldn't see five foot in front of your face, but I follered the cattle by listening to the hands all a-yellin' and chasin' back strays. Just before I come back, they got their wagons movin' and I saw that Mex take the hobbles off the remuda and get them a'movin'."

"So they're headed for the Caney," Concho said.

Skip nodded. "They ought to hit it by noon or soon after," he said.

Concho turned to Mitch. "This looks like your chance, Mitch. You ought to catch up with that herd in an hour or so. Take one man down."

"Any man?" Mitch asked.

"No. Don't shoot Paddy and leave the cook and the wagon driver alone. Same with that Mex wrangler. You knock down one of the outriders. Make it easy on yourself. Plan it all out so's you can get away and leave a dead man lyin' in the rain puddles."

"I can do 'er," Mitch said. "I'll saddle up."

"The rest of you saddle up too," Concho ordered. "I want to get up into Kansas and find a place along the Caney. Maybe we can grab that herd just when that Mick Paddy is startin' to cross it. We can turn the herd before they hit the ford."

"Maybe we can find some dry firewood up in Kansas," Lyle said.

"Don't count on it," Concho said.

Mitch saddled his horse before any of the others and started out after he checked his rifle and wiped it down with a dry bandanna.

"So long," he said.

"See you up on the Caney, Mitch," Concho said. "Look for us west of the river."

Mitch nodded and rode off.

The others finished saddling their horses. They set their saddles on wet blankets and wrung out their clothes and bedrolls. A half hour later, they were riding north toward the Kansas border under a sky as gray as a dove's wing. They rode single file with Concho in the lead. He was veering ever eastward a few degrees at a time.

There was no need to hurry, Concho knew. If Mitch did his job, that would slow the herd while the Circle K hands buried another cowhand. He figured that Paddy would not try to go around the Caney, but

338

would take the herd up along the river so that the cattle could drink before he looked for a ford. That was the time and place to hit him. On the way back to Shawnee Mission, they could rustle the other herd and he'd have three thousand head to hand over to Throckmorton. Then he would collect thirty thousand and divide the money among the men. He had already planned to keep the lion's share of the money for himself. But his men would have a decent payday, and if any of them didn't like it, they could eat lead and forfeit their shares.

He felt good that they were getting close. That storm had taken a lot of the fire out of the men and they needed to dry out and do some work.

"You know," he said to Lyle, who rode alongside him, "I feel like Robin Hood."

"Robin Hood?" Lyle said, surprised at the statement.

"Yeah," Concho said. "You know the English outlaw, that old story."

"I remember it. He used a bow and arrow, I think."

"Don't make no difference. I'm just like him."

"How so?" Lyle asked.

"I rob from the rich to feed the poor."

Both men laughed.

The others, riding behind them, wondered what was so funny. They were all cold and wet and saw nothing to laugh at. They made faces at one another and shrugged their shoulders.

The horses splashed on past small lakes of standing water and bare spots where flash floods had arisen and swept the rocks and brush into the gullies and ravines.

The land there was desolate and empty, with no signs of life.

Doves flew past, their wings whistling, and they flushed a rabbit or two. In the distance, they heard the whistle of a prairie dog sentinel and then it was quiet except for the *thunk* of the horses' hooves and the rustle of their clothes drying out under the lash of the fresh breeze that sprang up out of nowhere.

Skip rode in the rear, exhausted.

When he looked at the line of men on horseback, he thought to himself that they resembled somber men in a funeral procession.

And he felt like one of the mourners.

CHAPTER 36

Joe Eagle read part of the story in the muddy tracks when he and Dane came upon the place where Paddy had bedded down the herd the night before.

The muddy ground was littered with cow and horse tracks. As Dane watched, Joe rode all over, sometimes disappearing, only to reappear. Dane looked at the maze of tracks and knew that he could never figure out what had gone on there. But at least, he thought, there was no fresh grave anywhere that he looked.

Joe finally rode back and reined up his horse next to Dane's.

"You saw things I didn't, Joe. Is there a story to tell here?"

"Hmm. Me read story. Herd not stay here long. Cattle run off. Men drive cattle back. Wagons stay long time, then move."

"No graves, right?"

"No graves. Storm scare cattle. Some

cattle run. Hands get back. Then herd walk north. Slow."

"Let's ride on, then, Joe. If you see signs of any trouble, let me know."

Joe nodded.

The two rode on under a gray sky. They followed the tracks of the herd, but stayed on the left flank. The ground where the cattle had passed was churned up, muddy, and there were many cow pies and horse apples strewn along the herd's path.

Their clothes were drying out in the light breeze and the clouds were thinning. The sun rose above them, so they had shade. Dane knew that they had gone through a violent storm. He and Joe had been aroused by the heavy thunder and both saw the lightning. Dane knew that it was a prime situation for a stampede and worried most of the night.

He felt relieved that only a few head of cattle had run off from the herd and that Paddy and his men had gotten them all back. They saw no stray cows and no dead ones. So he had worried needlessly.

"Tracks fresh," Joe said after they had ridden more than an hour.

"How fresh?" Dane asked.

"Three hour."

"We should catch up to them by noon, then."

"Cattle move slow. Noon maybe."

The sun climbed and the clouds began to break up and leak shafts of sunlight. They saw a few jackrabbits, and off in the distance, a red fox scampered over the puddles and mud mounds. Bobwhite quail flushed and took flight, and a red-tailed hawk floated over the rain-soaked land, riding the wind currents high above them.

Snakes slithered across their path and they heard a warning rattle, but never saw the serpent. The horses sidled away from the sound, their heads held high, their eyes bulging, ears twitching.

Joe scanned the countryside and still looked down at the ground to read sign. They rode at a walk for a half hour, then trotted for a half hour and ran for about fifteen minutes at a fair gallop.

Dane saw a bleak and empty landscape, places that had been flattened smooth by small flash floods, and belts of mud that had been piled up during the storm. He could smell the sharp tang of urine and the musky aroma of the fresh cow pies and horse droppings. He felt at home in a strange land.

Around noon, the tracks grew even fresher. Even Dane could see the sharp edges of the tracks left in the mud by the cloven hooves of the cattle and the inverted U's that the horses left preserved in drying mud.

"Soon," Joe said.

They rode in silence as the sun reached its zenith and began to beat down on them. Joe stood up in the stirrups to look farther ahead of them every so often.

The scent of cattle grew stronger by the minute.

Then, in the distance, they heard the unmistakable sound of wagon wheels. Soon they both caught sight of the lumbering chuck wagon. It swayed on its frame and the wheels spat out clods of mud and splashed water as it ran through small puddles of water.

The wagon increased in size as they gained on it. Well ahead of the chuck wagon and the supply wagon, they saw the horses in the remuda. And fifteen minutes later, they saw the tail end of the herd with a rider on drag.

"Me smell river," Joe said. He pointed ahead of them as they continued to walk their horses now that the herd was in sight.

Dane sniffed the air. "I don't smell any-thing but mud and cow shit," he said. The breeze had shifted and was striking them in their faces.

"Cattle move fast," Joe said. "Cows smell river."

It was true. The cattle broke into a trot and surged forward ahead of the wagons and the remuda.

"Let's catch up to 'em," Dane said.

Joe spurred his horse to a trot and Dane followed. They began to close the distance.

Then they both reined up fast as they heard the distinct crack of a rifle.

Joe turned his head in the direction of the shot.

So did Dane.

They saw nothing but empty plain.

Seconds later, they heard a man shouting, but could not make out any of his words.

"Come on, Joe. Nobody on the drive should be shooting."

"Shot come from west," Joe said. He stretched out his arm and pointed to the left.

"You see anybody, Joe?" Dane asked.

"No see," Joe said.

But he kept looking. They spurred their horses again and rode on. Men shouted and they saw riders dashing along the left flank of the herd.

Joe stood up in his stirrups as his horse galloped ahead.

Dane kept looking off to his left every other second.

Then Joe broke away just as Dane saw the tiny figure of a man carrying a rifle. He was running and then disappeared behind a low hill. Moments later, they saw a rider atop a horse. The horse was running fast, away from the herd.

"Can you catch him, Joe?" Dane asked.

"Me catch," Joe said, and turned his horse. He galloped toward the retreating man while Dane rode on. As Dane came up on the herd's left flank, he saw men light down from their horses. They stood around something on the ground that he could not see.

His heart seemed to sink into his stomach. There was a flutter of winged insects in his belly. He knew what the men were looking at there on the ground.

Another dead cowhand.

Bushwhacked, he thought, and looked in Joe's direction. The rider he was chasing had disappeared, but Joe was hunched over the saddle horn, flying like the wind.

The men looked up as Dane approached.

"Who is it?" Dane asked.

Paddy stepped out and his face was grim. "Lester," he said. "Lester Pierson."

Dane swung out of the saddle as Reno

came to a skidding stop. He looked down at the man on the ground.

"Dead?" he asked.

"Stone dead," Paddy said sadly. "That Joe ridin' off?"

"Yeah. We saw the bushwhacker, Paddy."

"I hope Joe puts a bullet in him," Paddy said.

"I hope he cuts off his balls," Whit Hawkins said. "Lester was a pard of mine."

Dane said nothing. He looked down at the body of Lester, and his stomach twisted into a knot. There was a hole in Lester's left side and a large pool of blood beneath his armpit. The blood rippled in the breeze and began to soak into the damp ground.

"That's the third man Concho has kilt, Dane," Paddy said.

"I know," Dane said. "Joe and I saw the other graves."

He turned away as bile rose in his throat. He gulped in air, but his knees turned to jelly. He hoped Joe caught up with the killer. He wished he could be there to help him.

He turned around. The men all stared at him, perplexed and questioning looks on their faces. If they had asked him anything, he would not have been able to answer. Death was an ugly thing and especially when it happened to a friend.

347

There were no answers yet.

There were only questions and the fear of the unknown.

CHAPTER 37

Mitch tied his horse to a clump of bushes behind a small hillock once he saw the herd.

He walked to a good vantage point and lay flat. He measured the distance to one of the flanking riders. He jacked a shell into the chamber and sighted his rifle, allowing for windage and trajectory. Like Concho, he had sighted his Winchester in at twenty-five yards and knew the drop would be perfect at a hundred yards.

He figured the rider he had targeted was a little more than a hundred yards away most of the time.

He didn't look at anyone else. Just that one rider on the flank, who was riding back and forth on an invisible line to show the cows that he was there and they shouldn't try to bolt from the herd.

Mitch waited until the rider turned his horse and paused for a minute. He cocked his rifle, held his breath. He aimed for the head, expecting the bullet drop would hit a vital region. If he was right on, then the bullet would blow the man's head apart.

He squeezed the trigger. The rifle exploded fire and a lead projectile from the muzzle. The stock rammed against Mitch's shoulder. Smoke filled the air until the breeze shredded it into cobwebby wisps.

He saw the rider twitch when the bullet struck him in the chest, just below his left shoulder. The man toppled from his horse and hit the ground with a thud.

Mitch did not wait to see any more. He knew the rider was dying if he was not already dead. The bullet probably collapsed his left lung and ripped through his heart.

Mitch ran to his horse. He ejected the spent cartridge on the fly. Then he mounted up and put the horse into a gallop. He did not look back for an eighth of a mile.

When he did turn around, he saw two riders coming up on the rear of the herd. One of them pointed in his direction, then turned his horse to give chase.

Mitch slapped the ends of his reins on his horse's rump and jabbed him in the flanks with his spurs. The horse increased its speed, its head outstretched, its mane flying in the wind.

"Come on, boy," he yelled into the horse's

ear. "Give it all you got."

He slid his rifle back in its sheath and turned around again. The rider was still far back, but he was coming after him at full speed.

Mitch lay almost flat to cut down on wind resistance and felt the horse eating up ground.

He did not look back again. He was into gently rolling country now and his horse was running well. He knew he could not keep running at this speed, but he also knew that the rider who had come after him would soon see his own horse falter.

Long strings of yellow lather blew back and struck Mitch's legs. He slowed the horse, not wanting it to founder.

He looked back. The rider chasing him was stopped. He began to shrink as his own horse slowed to a walk.

"Close call," Mitch said to himself.

He was breathing hard and his horse was wheezing. He stopped and let the animal blow. When he looked back, he saw no one on his trail.

"Tough luck, feller," he said aloud, and his mouth bent in a smirk of satisfaction. He had done what he came to do. Now there was another notch to put on his rifle stock.

He walked his horse until its breathing returned to normal. He kept looking back until he turned north. He followed the tracks of Concho and the others. There was no hurry now. He would catch up and tell of his deed and get a few slaps on his back and maybe a slug of whiskey.

The clouds were thinning overhead and breaking up. Columns of sunlight broke through and lit patches of green grass and shone on small pools of water. It felt as if he were riding through an open-air chapel and that the light was shining through stained glass windows.

He dug out the makings and rolled a cigarette.

No one was following him.

He felt as if he owned the ground he was on and all the empty land around him.

CHAPTER 38

Pete and Whit were hard at it, wielding shovels for the grave where Lester would be buried.

Paddy had halted the herd, and the other outriders were keeping it in check while Dane and Paddy talked.

Dane was satisfied that Lester had not suffered.

"The bullet grazed his arm before it tore into his chest and blew his heart to pieces," Dane said after inspecting Lester's wound. He had not lost much blood because his heart had stopped pumping almost immediately after he'd been shot. "Bullet smashed through his right lung and came out through his right rib cage."

"You'd make a good coroner, Dane," Paddy said.

They stood a few feet away from the diggers and kept their voices low out of respect for the dead.

"I saw enough gunshot wounds when we fought the Yankees down in Texas at the end of the war. War was over, but we didn't know it. A couple of my friends got shot in just about the same place. I stood next to the surgeon who poked around in one of the men's chests. It's something you never forget."

"You must have been real young then," Paddy said.

"I was fifteen. Told everybody I was eighteen. I got my belly full of war in a real short time."

"I was at Vicksburg," Paddy said. "You ain't seen nothin' until you see what grapeshot can do to a man."

"I can imagine," Dane said. "But men die from most anything that comes at the end of explodin' powder, tacks, nails, dimes, pennies, ball bearings."

"You got that right."

As the men were shoveling dirt from the six-foot-long hole, Dane looked up and saw Joe Eagle riding back toward them. "Here comes Joe," he said.

Paddy looked in the same direction.

"Looks like he don't have no scalp hangin' from his belt," Paddy said.

"Joe wouldn't scalp anyone," Dane said.

"I was just jokin'."

They waited for Joe to ride up. Dane could tell from the expression on his face that he hadn't caught up to the bushwhacker.

"Him get away," Joe said. "Too far."

"Did you recognize him from town, Joe?" Dane asked.

"Too far. No see face. Fast horse."

"Light down, then," Dane said. "The hands have the herd under control."

Joe slid out of the saddle. His face shone with sweat and there were strands of foam on his horse's chest. He rubbed the gelding dry with the palm of his hands. He spoke soothing words to the horse as he patted him on the neck.

"Say, Joe," Paddy said. "What do you call your horse anyways?"

"*Swoghili*," Joe said.

"Swog what?" Paddy said.

"Cherokee word. Mean horse."

Dane laughed as Paddy gulped.

"You don't want to know what he calls you in Cherokee, Paddy," Dane said.

"No, I reckon I don't. I don't savvy Cherokee no way."

Joe walked away, leading his horse. He would walk him until the horse was fully recovered from the hard run.

"How deep, Paddy?" Pete asked.

"Two foot ought to do it," Paddy said. "I want to get this herd up to the Caney before sundown."

"We got about a half foot to go," Whit said, and the two men continued to dig down into the earth and pile dirt next to the grave.

"There's no hurry, Paddy," Dane said. "When we make the Caney, I want to hold the herd until Len Crowell catches up to us."

"How far behind is he, do you reckon?" Paddy asked.

"Maybe a day, day and a half."

"You lose any men on the ride?"

Dane shook his head. "No. I don't know what Concho's got on his mind exactly, but it looks to me like he's thinning you down, Paddy, before he jumps the whole bunch of you."

"That's the only thing I can figger. He'll pare us down to just a few men and then jump us somewhere. God knows where."

"Maybe he's waiting until you run the herd over the border into Kansas."

"Why?"

"My hunch is that Throckmorton wants these cattle rustled a long ways from Shawnee Mission. A way of keepin' his hands clean, you might say."

"I don't see that it makes much difference. Oklahoma or Kansas seems about the same to me right now."

"Out of sight, out of mind," Dane said.

Paddy tilted his hat back off his forehead and scratched a patch of hair above his left ear. "You think maybe Throckmorton's countin' on having folks think we was rustled by Kansas jayhawks instead of Oklahoma Sooners?"

"Maybe," Dane said. "You got to think like Throckmorton. He's as devious as a Texas sidewinder. And now I got to think like Concho."

"How do you think like Concho?" Paddy asked.

"It's hard, but from what I've heard about the bastard and the way he's attacking your hands, makes me think he's a damned coward, deep down."

"What makes you think he's a coward, Dane?"

"He's a back-shooter and a dry-gulcher. His tactics with you prove me right. His reputation proves it even more. A man who is not a coward doesn't sneak up on a defenseless man and shoot him dead. That's the coward's way. He never risks his own life. He only takes the lives of others."

"You may be right," Paddy said.

"If a man like Concho has a disagreement with someone, say at a saloon, or anywhere, he doesn't call the man out to his face. Instead, he waits until dark and then continues the argument with a six-gun, a bullet in the back of the head resolves the disagreement and Concho walks away the winner in his mind."

"Well, he's right dangerous, that's for sure. I'm feelin' real bad at losin' men when I can't even fight back."

"Well, Paddy, you are going to fight back. We all are. That's why I want to wait for the rest of the cattle to catch up to us. We'll have more guns and we'll probably outnumber Concho and his band of outlaws."

"But Concho don't fight fair, Dane."

"No, he doesn't," Dane said. "And neither will we."

"How you gonna beat Concho, even with more guns?"

"I'll let you know when the time comes, Paddy. I'm still studying on it. In a way, my plan depends on thinking like Concho and knowing where he will strike next."

"You ain't no mind reader, Dane."

"No, Paddy, I'm not. And neither is Concho. But I'm a man reader and I know he's going to pick the best place to jump us, someplace where we can't run and can't hide."

"Where might that be, Dane?"

Dane chuckled. "You ask too many questions, Paddy. I have a good idea where Concho will hit us, and you'll recognize it when we come to it."

"You know, Dane, sometimes you're so damned mysterious, nobody can figger you out."

"I get that from my daddy. He's so full of secrets he has to keep his cane handy to beat 'em back from leakin' out of him."

"I always thought your pappy was real open and honest, Dane."

"Oh, he is, Paddy. But he's good at keepin' secrets too."

"Hmm. Well, I guess you know him best."

"I'm his son, Paddy. A son gets to know his father. It might take a lifetime, but I'm gettin' smarter about him by the day."

The two men finished digging and looked over at Paddy and Dane. They leaned on their shovels beside the grave to show that they were through digging.

"Take off Lester's gun belt and go through his pockets, then set him in the grave," Paddy said.

"Shouldn't we wrap him a blanket or something?" Whit asked.

"See what can you find in the supply wagon," Paddy said. "And tell anybody you see we're layin' Lester to rest, case they want to show their respects."

Whit nodded and dropped his shovel next to the pile of dirt. Pete knelt down beside Lester's body and unbuckled his gun belt. Then he searched through his pockets and laid cigarette papers, matches, and a bag of makings beside the holstered pistol. He found some change in one of his front pockets and hefted it as he stared at the coins.

"He didn't have much," Pete said.

"No wallet, no greenbacks?" Paddy asked.

Pete shook his head. "Nary," he said.

"Put all his stuff in an empty flour sack and stow it in the supply wagon," Paddy said.

Joe Eagle returned a few minutes later. He stood with Paddy and Dane as Pete and Whit cut up two potato sacks and wrapped Lester's face and torso with one, his legs with the other.

"That'll have to do," Whit said. "You get his feet," he said to Pete.

The two men lifted the corpse and laid it in the shallow grave. The body looked grotesque with the sacking material wrapped around it. They straightened Lester's body and crossed his arms across his midsection. They picked up their shovels, but neither man wanted to be the first to throw dirt on his friend.

"You go ahead, Pete," White said.

"No, you do it first, Whit."

Whit filled his shovel with dirt and swung it over the grave. He tipped it so that the dirt fell on Lester's boots.

"That's a start," Paddy said dryly. "Get on with it. Lester don't feel nothin'."

There was the scrape, the rustle of sand hitting the body, and at the last, Whit covered Lester's burlap-swathed head and cringed as the dirt covered up the last glimpse of Lester's dead body.

"Rest in peace," Paddy said as he removed his hat.

The others took off their hats. Joe stood there like a statue, his face rigid as iron. He did not remove his hat, but he looked up at the sky and closed his eyes for a brief moment.

Pete and Whit shoveled the rest of the dirt over the grave until there was a mound of dirt.

"Better cover that dirt with some rocks," Paddy said. "Make it harder for the critters to get at it."

Pete and Whit scouted for rocks and

finished off the grave with what they had found.

"Okay, boys," Paddy said. "Get on your horses and get this herd movin'. Me and Dane will ride point. Joe, you can come along if you like."

"I ride flank," Joe said. "Ride for Lester."

Dane was deeply touched by what Joe Eagle had said. He could not think of a finer tribute for Lester than to have a man take his place so that few would notice the missing man.

He felt tears well up in his eyes and turned away to get on his horse.

"Let's make the Caney, Paddy," Dane said as they took the point. "Camp there tonight and cross into Kansas tomorrow after the other herd catches up with us."

"Good," Paddy said. "We could all use a little extry rest."

"Tonight, double up on the nighthawks, and nobody sleeps," Dane said.

"That what you call rest?" Paddy asked.

"I call it a precaution, Paddy."

"That's a two-bit word for certain sure," Paddy said.

Dane let out a small laugh.

The Caney River was not far, he knew, and yet he also knew that with each mile the herd traveled, the more danger they were in. If Concho had any hint that the other herd was going to join up with them, he could strike at any time. He might not even wait until they got over the border into Kansas.

The only thing worse than a skulking coward like Concho was a desperate one. Greed drove men like Throckmorton and Concho. Greed for other men's possessions. Neither man would stop short of his avaricious goals.

And Dane was bound to stop them and make them pay for what they had done.

As he rode, he formed mental pictures in his mind, and the jigsaws of his ideas all began to fall into place and fit neatly into a plan of battle.

A battle to the death, with no quarter given.

CHAPTER 39

Just south of the Kansas border, Dane saw the Caney River shining in the late afternoon sun. He rode well ahead of Paddy and the head of the herd. He stopped his horse with a gentle tug on the reins. Reno whickered low in his throat.

"Thirsty, boy?" Dane said as he patted the gelding's withers.

There was an answering whicker, more pronounced this time.

He surveyed the land bordering the river and then turned his horse to ride back and talk to Paddy.

"Good graze, Paddy, and water. Let's bed the herd down up yonder."

"Good country," Paddy said. "I'll pass the word."

Even though it was early in the day, they drove the cattle to the river and let them stretch out the caravan and drink. Alfredo brought the remuda up and let the horses slake their thirst. The skies had cleared and there was blue, dotted with puffy clouds floating in all directions. The chuck wagon pulled up in the wide meadow and Wu set the brake, hopped down, and began searching for stones to make a fire ring. The supply wagon, with Charley Moss at the reins, pulled up behind the chuck wagon. Charley set the brake and wrapped the reins around the handle. He glared at Wu Ling but said nothing. He started scraping the mud off the fetlocks of the horses pulling the wagon and checked their shoes for caked dirt.

Drovers drifted away from the herd and rode back to where the wagons were parked. They dismounted near Charley and watched as Wu scoured the bank of the river for driftwood.

"Ain't any of you boys goin' to help that Chink gather wood for the campfire?" Steve asked.

"I ain't helpin' that Chinese do nothin'," Charley said. "Let him gather firewood and kindlin' all by hisself."

The other men looked at Charley and nodded in agreement.

"How come?" Steve asked. "He ain't done nothin' to you, has he, Charley?"

"He's a damned jinx," Charley said.

"Huh?" Steve said.

"Yeah, I think Charley's right," Dewey said. "We lost three men and Wu there is just plain bad luck. We ought to have brung Gooch with us to cook."

The other men had begun to grumble among themselves when Dane walked up to see what was going on.

"When that Chink cooked for Len Crowell, they lost their whole damned herd," Charley said. "We got us a real Jonah with us."

"Not so loud," Steve said. "He might hear you."

"I don't give a damn what he hears, that slant-eyed son of a bitch," Charley said. "I tell you he's got us all jinxed."

"What's all this about?' Dane asked. "Are you talking about Wu Ling?"

"Charley thinks Wu is a jinx," Steve said.

Dane looked at Charley. "That's a serious claim, Charley," Dane said. "Maybe you'd better explain where that's comin' from."

"Hell, it's as plain as the nose on your face, Dane. You switched cookies on us, and we got the Chink. Since he come here, we've had three good men shot and kilt. Now, it don't take no tea leaves to tell me Wu is the cause of all this. Hell, if Barney had been our cookie, none of this would have happened."

"What makes you think Wu is a jinx?" Dane asked. More men began to gather around, drawn by the loud voices. Even Paddy rode up when he saw what he thought was some kind of argument or gripe session among the drovers.

"What happened to Crowell's herd on his first cattle drive, and now he's lost his home and his spread and dumped his cook on us. I tell you, we got us a Jonah here, Dane. Wu's brought us nothin' but bad luck."

"Charley," Dane said as he looked not only at Charley, but at all the other men, "you're plumb full of shit."

Charley reared his head back as if he had been slapped with a wet shaving strop. He sputtered and spluttered.

Paddy, who had overheard the last exchange, shouted down at his men, "Well, if you think that, boys, why don't you ask Len Crowell? There he is yonder, comin' up on us with a thousand head of cattle." Paddy pointed back down the trail they had traversed.

All heads turned to see Len Crowell riding point and a wave of white-faced cattle in his wake, their horns shooting off sparks of sunlight as if they were an army charging into battle, waving swords above their heads. The men were silent for a long moment, then loosed a rousing cheer.

"And anyway," Paddy continued, "it wasn't Len what foisted Wu Ling on us, but Dane who made the switch. Ain't that right, Dane?"

Dane spoke up as Len continued to get closer to them.

"That's right," he said. "I made the decision, and Wu didn't have nothin' to do with Crowell losin' all his cattle or his ranch. Wu had nothin' to do with either, and you boys ought to be ashamed of yourselves for accusin' a man like you're doin'."

"Well, let's just ask Len what he thinks," Charley said.

"You go right ahead, Charley," Dane said. "But if Wu quits on us, I'll blame you, and by the gods, you'll draw your pay and head on back home."

Dane walked away from the group and went out to meet Len. He held up his right hand in greeting.

"What's goin' on, Dane?" Len asked as he rode up. "You boys havin' some kind of meetin'."

"Sort of. Come on over and join the discussion. Good to see you. Just run your cattle in with the other herd. We'll finish the drive with all three thousand head."

Dane turned and walked back to the supply wagon. Len followed on horseback.

"Howdy, Len," Paddy said.

"Howdy to you, Paddy," Len said.

"One of the boys has a question for you," Paddy said. "Charley, go right ahead and ask Mr. Crowell, does he think Wu Ling is a jinx?"

"What?" Len exclaimed. He pushed his hat back on his head.

Charley stepped out.

"I think that Chink cook is bad luck," he said. "We've had three men kilt since he come on. I don't know if he sends signals to Concho and his outlaw killers with the cook fire or what. I think he jinxed your herd too."

"Well, I'll be damned," Len said. "That's the craziest thing I ever herd. Wu Ling is one of the best cooks in the territory, and I'd take him on any drive I made if I had cattle to sell."

"See, Charley?" Dane said. "You better shed that cockeyed idea of yours. Concho is the damned jinx. And he's in cahoots with that crooked banker, Earl Throckmorton. Wu Ling doesn't have anything to do with the killings. You're blamin' the wrong man."

"Well, I don't know," Charley said. He looked down at his boots and started worrying the grass and the dirt with a scuff one his heel.

"Oh, Charley," Steve said, "swaller whatever you got in your damned craw and lay off the Chinese cook. What happened to us ain't none of his doin'."

The others grunted in assent and Charley looked sheepish. "I guess it don't make no difference what I think," he said, but his voice was barely audible.

The cattle herd started running to the river as Len waved them on. Soon the whitefaces were streaming past on both side of the wagons and merging into Paddy's herd.

Paddy drew Len aside and Dane walked over with them.

"I saw the graves," Len said. "Tough luck."

The three of them watched as the other men, including Charley, walked to the river and started walking along the bank and snatching up pieces of driftwood. Wu began to stack the wood in separate piles, the driest ones in one pile, the soggy ones in another.

"Looks like we done got through that briar patch," Paddy said.

Dane looked up at Len. "We're beddin' down the herd early, Len," he said. "From now on, we got just one herd. Tonight, all hands will ride nighthawk rounds and do guard duty."

"You think Concho's going to try and rustle all the cattle?" Len asked.

"Yes, but not now. Soon enough, he'll see that we have all the herd together and more men to fight him."

"So he won't attack us?" Len said.

"I think he'll wait until we're over the border. Maybe tomorrow, or the next day. He wants these cattle. Throckmorton wants them, and he wants the Circle K. So Concho won't give up. But I've got a surprise for him."

"You do? What?" Len asked.

Dane smiled. "When the time comes. I'm still working things out in my head."

Chub waved to Dane and Paddy as he rode past on the way to the river. The firewood piles grew higher.

"I'll let my horse drink and see you later," Len said. He followed Chub to the river.

"It feels good to have the whole herd all together," Paddy said. "It' almost feels like we're back on the Circle K."

"Water your horse, Paddy. I'm going to set down near the chuck wagon and wait for Wu to make some hot coffee."

"See you in a while, then, Dane."

Paddy rode off and Dane walked over to Wu. "Need any help, Wu?" he asked.

Wu bent over the fire ring and, with his

knife, started shaving sticks into dry kindling. He looked up at Dane, his moon face devoid of expression.

"Me no jink," he said.

"Jinx, Wu, jinx."

"No jinx." He grinned.

"No, you're not. The men are just itchy, that's all. They got to blame someone for all the bad that's happened, and you were just right handy."

"I know. It is the same in China. Man get mad at other man. Other man not there. So man get mad at wife. Wife not there, man get mad at kids."

Dane laughed. "I guess it's the same everywhere. We have to blame someone for our troubles. Sometimes we pick the easiest target."

"Wu get mad, he kick can, or hit pan. Anger fly out door."

"You're a wise bird, Wu," Dane said.

"You kill Concho?"

"I'll kill him if he comes after me or any of the men."

"Good. No kick can. Kick Concho."

The two men shared the next laugh.

"Make coffee soon," Wu said. "Cook big meal tonight."

The other cook wagon rumbled up. Barney Gooch waved and halted behind the supply wagon. He set the brake, wound the reins around the handle, and jumped down. Behind him rode the two Mexicans and the remuda, and behind them the supply wagon rolled to a stop behind Gooch's wagon.

"Looks like a danged rendezvous," Barney said. "Howdy, Wu. Need any help? We got dry wood in the supply wagon. Been gatherin' it all day."

"Sure," Wu said. "Make big fire. Cook many meals."

Barney laughed. "God, it's good to be with all my friends," he said.

"Make yourself at home, Barney," Dane said, and sat down with a wagon wheel at his back.

He looked out at the western sky. The clouds were turning pink and gold on their undersides, and the sun threw long shadows across the prairie. The grass was almost belly-high and the cattle grazed like slow-moving statues. It seemed a land of peace and contentment at that moment.

Dane plucked a chaw from his pouch and closed his eyes as he chewed.

It was enough to make a starving man feel full, although he had not yet eaten. He listened to the clank of pans and the soft fall of feet on the grass as Barney and Wu prepared to cook the evening grub.

If Concho was watching them, Dane thought, he'd know he needed an army to rustle three thousand head of cattle.

And even then, Dane knew, he would lose.

Wu wasn't a jinx.

He was a good-luck charm.

CHAPTER 40

Logan Heckler rode into Concho's camp in Kansas singing an old hymn.

"Shall we gather at the river?" he sang.

"What are you so jolly about, Heckler?" Concho asked. He and his men sat around a small campfire drinking stale coffee. One or two smoked quirlies, and one man, Dewey, was digging dirt out from under his fingernails with the tip of his knife.

"They done crossed into Kansas," Logan said as he swung himself out of the saddle and let the reins fall from his hand. "And that herd has done swolled. I'd say they got about three thousand head, easy."

"That was what Throckmorton said Kramer sold to the Omaha buyer. That second herd must have caught up with Paddy's bunch."

"I reckon." Heckler picked up an empty tin cup and poured it half-full from the battered coffeepot sitting on the coals at the edge of the small fire. "They ain't tryin' to cross yet, but are just moseyin' along, letting the cows and horses graze. There's lots of grass and lots of big old trees growin' along both banks. I don't see no place where they can cross real soon."

"Hell, that's welcome news, Logan," Concho said. "That river's nigh two hundred mile long and they got to find a ford."

"Well, we got time," Logan said. "They ain't more'n a mile or so from where we're a-settin', and there ain't no easy crossin' where they're at."

"Finish your coffee, boys," Concho said. "It's time we rustled us some cattle and killed us some cowpokes."

"Hell, we ought to take them horses too," Mitch said.

"Yeah, they ain't gonna need 'em no more," chimed in Skip. "We can sell 'em to the army or over in Texas. Kind of a bonus."

Heckler sat down and sipped his coffee. It wasn't very hot and it tasted like mud. "This sure ain't Arbuckles'," he said.

"Them ground beans are on their third pass," Mitch said. "I told Concho it needs a little whiskey to perk it up."

"It needs more than whiskey," Lyle said. "It needs a shot of tequila and some stout brandy."

The men all laughed. All except Concho, who was deep in thought. After a moment or two, he turned to Heckler.

"Is the herd pretty spread out, Logan?" he asked.

"Yeah, I'd say it's strung out for a mile or two and ain't nobody chasin' 'em. Out riders are just keepin' an eye out on the flank, like they was out for a Sunday ride."

"That's good for us," Concho said.

"How do you figger on gettin' them beeves and drivin' off the drovers?" Mitch asked Concho.

"We ride up in a bunch and count outriders that are closest to us. Then we fan out and start shootin'. If we have to drop a horse or two, that's just fine. Get 'em on foot and we can mow 'em down like wheat."

"Rifles?" Skip asked.

"First shots from our rifles," Concho said. "Then we go in close with six-guns and shoot anything that moves."

"There's some Mexes wranglin' the horses and now they got two chuck wagons and two supply wagons," Heckler said. "Wagons ain't movin'."

"Perfect," Concho said.

"It's goin' to be like a turkey shoot," Lyle said, licking his lips. He finished his coffee and shook out his cup. He placed it in one

377

of his saddlebags, then hefted it and slung it on the back of his horse.

"We got enough bullets in our six-guns to drop quite a few of them boys," Mitch said.

"They won't be expectin' us, that's for sure," Lyle said.

"Logan, did them hands look like they was watchin' out for trouble?" Skip asked.

"Hell no. They looked like they was just enjoyin' the sunshine and acted like they was back on that ranch."

Concho got to his feet.

"Let's ride," he said. He shook out his cup and stowed it in his saddlebag, which was still draped over his horse's backside.

Heckler walked over. He lifted the field glass from around his neck and handed it to Concho. "Anybody see you, Logan?"

"No, I don't reckon. I tied my horse up and sneaked along an old furrow, all hunched over like a beggar. I could see everything real good with that glass. I sneaked back and rode off. I was way out of sight when I got back on my horse."

"All right." Concho climbed into the saddle and began issuing last-minute orders. "Check your rifles. Jack a shell in the chamber and leave your gun on half cock. Make sure your six-guns have all the beans in their chambers. Get your pissin' done now."

There were the clicks of rifle mechanisms as the men chambered fresh rounds into the firing chambers of their rifles and the whir of six-gun cylinders as they checked the loads in the pistols. Leather creaked as the men mounted their horses. Then the whisper of leather reins and the jingle of roweled spurs.

Concho watched as the men lined up behind him. They all sat and waited until he gave the signal. Satisfied, Concho raised one arm and swung it forward. Then he touched spurs to his horse's flanks and they rode in a procession toward the Caney River.

Men adjusted their hats, and shadows floated onto their grim faces. The sun smiled down on them, and the sweet scent of grass inched into their nostrils.

It was, Concho thought, a perfect day.

It was a day when nothing could go wrong for him and his men.

It was a good day to kill cowboys and rustle a large herd of cattle.

CHAPTER 41

Someone had seen Logan Heckler when he surveyed the herd that day.

Joe Eagle climbed down from the large oak tree where he had been perched all morning. He didn't need a field glass to see the rider sneak up to a spot and dismount, then walk toward the herd with a pair of binoculars dangling from his neck.

Joe saw the man lie down and put the glass to his eyes. He saw him crawl back for a ways, then walk to his horse and ride off to the east.

Dane waited for Joe to walk up to him.

"Man come. Man watch herd long time. Man ride away."

"So Concho knows we're here," Dane said.

"Him know."

"All right, Joe, get on your horse. I'm going to tell Paddy and Len what I want them to do. You'll be with me."

Dane whistled. He put two fingers in his mouth and blew on them. The whistle was loud and piercing.

"That's the signal, Len," Paddy said. "We talk to Dane and find out what his plan be."

"I'm as nervous as a long-tailed cat in a roomful of rockin' chairs," Len said.

The two men rode down the line of cattle to where Joe and Dane were waiting. They dismounted and stepped in close.

"Paddy, Len," Dane said. "Here's what I want you to do. Line up all your men behind the herd at fifty-yard intervals. River at your backs. When I see Concho and his men ride into sight, I'll give one whistle. Your men will have their rifles loaded and cocked. I want all the rifles to go off at one time. One loud roar."

"Dane, that'll spook the cattle," Len said. "They'll stampede for sure."

"I want 'em to stampede, Len. When the cattle start runnin', the drovers will make sure they head east, away from the river. All of the men will follow and keep shooting their rifles."

"You goin' to run right over Concho and his men?" Paddy asked.

"Yes, but tell your men to shoot any of those rustlers within range. I figure they'll be too busy gettin' out of the way of all these cattle to do much accurate shooting at us."

"Pretty bold, if you ask me," Paddy said.

"I don't want to lose any hands or any cattle. If Concho means to rustle what we've got here, I want to run him down and trample him to death. Joe and I will be looking for targets and chasing cows their way."

"All right," Len said. "Your plan just might work."

"It will work if we all do what I ask. At my signal start shooting. Run the cattle as fast as they'll run and don't let anyone pass through the stampeding herd. If Concho starts shooting, he might be trying to drive them all back on us."

"Jaysus," Paddy said, "it's goin' to be pure hell out there."

"I hope so," Dane said. "Now get your men ready and wait for my whistle."

Paddy rode up the line to the north while Len rode along the river to the south.

"Let's get on our horses, Joe. Before all this starts, I want to make sure Wu and Barney get behind their wagons and aim their rifles to the east."

"Horses," Joe said.

"I'll tell the wranglers to take them over by the river, into the trees. No use putting any of them in danger."

They walked to their horses and climbed into their saddles. They rode to Wu's wagon.

"There's going to be some loud noise, Wu," Dane said. "And lots of lead flying. You get behind your wagon. Make sure your rifle is pointed away from the river. If anyone you don't recognize rides up, you shoot that man dead."

"Uh-huh," Wu said.

Dane told Barney the same thing and he told the Mexicans to hide the horses in the trees along the river.

"Will we get to go on the charge?" Montoya asked. "I want a crack at Concho."

"If you hurry, you can chase cattle right over them rustlin' bastards," Dane said. "Just make sure you fire your rifles when I give the signal. I want to hear just one loud roar. And I want to see three thousand head of cattle running at full speed right over Concho and his bunch."

The Mexicans all grinned and started leading the horses back into the trees along the Caney.

Joe and Dane took up positions at about the middle of the herd. They watched as Paddy called in the flankers. Len did the same on his end. Soon, when they looked, they saw men on horseback holding their rifles at attention up and down the line.

They looked like guerilla cavalry waiting for the order to charge.

Dane wondered how long they would have to wait. He looked up at the sun and saw that it was almost directly overhead. The cattle grazed peacefully on the lush tall grass.

"Can you see far enough, Joe, to spot any riders comin' over the horizon?"

"See long way," Joe said. "Me look."

The minutes dragged by and the plain beyond the cattle herd seemed devoid of all life. It was agony, the waiting, but Dane was ready. He wet two fingers of his right hand and held them close to his mouth.

A cloud passed over the sun's bright face and cast a large shadow on the prairie.

For a moment, Dane stiffened, wondering if he would be able to see anyone riding through that shadow.

Then Reno's ears stiffened as the horse stared into the distance. Dane looked at Joe. Joe stood up in his stirrups, the flat of his hand shading his eyes.

Dane gripped the lever and the stock of his Winchester. His hand began to sweat. His rifle was cocked, like Joe's, and it would take only seconds to bring it to his shoulder, slip a finger into the trigger guard, and squeeze the trigger.

After he whistled, he thought.

His fingers were poised to slip into his mouth.

Joe continued to stare past the cloud shadow. His horse whickered softly and its ears began to twist and twitch.

"Men come," Joe said. "Blow whistle."

Dane put the two fingers into his mouth and laid his tongue under them. He blew a single long ear-lancing whistle.

Time seemed to hang suspended for an eternity. There was a silence for a split second that seemed as deep as the eternal sea, a silence that was almost deafening.

Then all hell broke loose.

CHAPTER 42

More than a dozen rifles cracked the eerie stillness. Men shouted and cattle heads jerked up as if the cows had been lashed with three thousand bullwhips.

A moment later, the first cow bolted from the herd. It was followed by others. There was the sound of tramping hooves, and the grazing cattle flowed eastward, straight at the column of men led by Concho Larabee. The outlaws fanned out and began to shoulder their rifles.

More rifle fire crackled as the cowhands jacked shells into their chambers and fired again. The second time, they did not shoot straight up into the air, but started to aim at the approaching riders.

Bullets whistled past Concho and his men as they scattered. They began to yell too.

"Lord, would you look at that?"

"Holy cow, a damned stampede."

"Shoot 'em, boys," Concho yelled. "Turn

that herd back."

Dane glanced at Joe. "Let's get after them," he shouted above the din.

They both spurred their horses and charged into the scrambling herd, forcing their horses to part a path through the herd.

Dane saw Concho's men gallop their horses to avoid being overrun by the cattle, but he knew they would not make it. The herd was too wide and coming at them with such speed that their plight was a foregone conclusion.

The other cowhands charged into the herd and forged pathways through the herd. They fired their rifles at the rustlers, but it was difficult to take direct aim and their shots missed hitting any targets during that initial charge.

Some of Concho's men turned their horses and began to retreat. All of them had given up trying to shoot their rifles. They sheathed their long guns and drew pistols. They fired at the onrushing cattle and began to drop a few.

The herd bellowed and chased after the lead cow and swallowed her up in their fear-filled rush away from the exploding rifles at their rear.

Dane looked toward his right and swung his right arm to signal Paddy to turn the herd. Then he looked to his left and yelled at Len. He made the same gesture. Both men nodded and began to race ahead of the surging cattle and turn them inward.

Both flanks of the herd started to crowd inward in Dane's attempt to cut the rustlers off and corral them with cattle on both sides.

Concho turned his horse and realized he could not outrun the storm of cattle that was descending on him and his men. Bullets whizzed overhead and past his ear. He yelled at the men on both sides of him. "Don't run," he shouted. "Start shootin' to kill them cowboys."

He swung around in his saddle and took aim on a cow with his six-gun. He fired at it, saw the bullet strike it in the belly. Dust flew up where the bullet entered the body of the cow, but she kept running in a zigzag course as if nothing had happened. Blood streamed from the wound and still she ran, weaving on unsteady legs.

Concho fired again, aiming straight at its head, just below the boss. The bullet ricocheted off the thick ridge of bone and whined off into empty space.

He saw Will Davis out of the corner of his eye. Will was shooting at a phalanx of onrushing horned beasts. Then he saw a man aim his pistol at Davis from thirty yards away. The man looked like an Indian, with swarthy skin and black eyes.

Joe Eagle squeezed the trigger of his Colt and the pistol exploded, belching sparks and smoke.

Will clutched his chest, and his fingers turned red with blood. He slumped forward in the saddle; then a lone steer swung toward him and struck his horse's left foreleg. The leg snapped with a loud crackle of the bones, and the animal collapsed. As the horse went down, its momentum pitched Will from the saddle. He hit the ground, screaming, until the scream turned to a raspy husk and cattle trampled over him, smashing bones, flattening his head like a squashed pumpkin, ripping out muscle and sinew, cutting off his scream, and smashing his neck to a bloody pulp.

Dane picked out a rider and tracked him with his six-gun.

Logan Heckler saw Dane aiming his pistol at him and brought his up. Dane fired first and Logan felt something hard smack into his neck. He slapped at it and his hand came back into view all smeared with blood. He felt a light-headedness before the pain hit him as the bullet exited on the other side, just below his right ear. The land and the stampeding cattle blurred, and when he tried to yell, there was no sound from his mouth. He spit out a large clot of blood and then the sky turned coal black. He felt his heart pump fast and then he shuddered as it stopped. He fell from his saddle, and cattle streamed over him, slashing his body with cloven hooves until there was nothing left of him but shredded clothing embedded in a blood-soaked mass of flesh that was turning him into a skeleton.

Concho shot an onrushing cowhand who had angled his horse to cut him off. He could see the herd bending, turning in on him, but the cowhand was an immediate threat. He squeezed the trigger when Chub was twenty feet away and saw the bullet open a black hole square in the center of Chub's breastbone.

Chub's finger squeezed the trigger of his Remington six-gun, but the bullet went straight to the ground as Chub's breath left him and he could not draw any more air into his lungs. He felt a sharp pain as if he had been struck by a hammer and then his consciousness shrank to the size of a small glowing pea and then winked out like a crushed firefly. His pistol dropped from his hand and he followed it to the ground a moment later. He hit the ground with a thud and never felt the slash of hooves as cattle swarmed over him and dashed on in their headlong rush away from the constant thunder of firearms.

Carlos Montoya saw Concho and started to angle through the herd to get at him. But there was another would-be rustler blocking his way.

Skip saw the Mexican charging toward him, struggling to get through the herd without being knocked from his horse or having his horse bowled over by a mass of horned white-faced cattle. He swung his horse around and cocked his pistol.

Carlos saw red. He watched Skip, and gave his horse its head as he dug spurs into its flanks. The horse bucked away from the cattle and charged on a clear path toward Skip.

Skip fired at Carlos from thirty-five yards. Even as he squeezed the trigger, Montoya's horse swerved and jumped ahead of a pair of steers and headed straight for him.

Skip thumbed back the hammer of his pistol.

Too late.

Carlos fired his own six-gun from twenty-five yards straight at Skip. The shot was low and blew a hole in Skip's gut some four inches above his belt buckle.

Skip felt the bullet strike him like a sixteen-pound sledgehammer. He touched a hand to the wound, and blood gushed onto his palm and over his fingers. He fired his pistol again, but the Mexican was only a blur and wavering out of focus as if he were only a reflected image in a pool of water.

Carlos rode in closer and fired his pistol again, almost at point-blank range. He saw the bullet smash into Skip's forehead, just above his left eyebrow. A saucer-sized piece of bone exploded from the back of Skip's head and flew away from him in a cloud of misty crimson spray.

Skip's eyes glassed over and froze in a fixed empty stare as he slid from the saddle square into the path of a dozen whitefaces. They swerved to avoid the fallen man and his horse, but the cattle behind them kept on coming and turned Skip's body into a bloody smear of flesh and clothing that was soon pounded into the soil like so much fertilizer.

Concho saw Skip go down. He recognized Carlos and was boiling with anger. At the same time, he saw Dane's hands turning both ends of the herd to encircle him and the rest of his men. Carlos was riding toward an open place, trying to outrun the cattle that were streaming all around him.

"There Concho," Joe said, pointing to the leader of the outlaw band.

"I see him, Joe," Dane said.

"We go?" Joe asked.

Dane saw that there were yards and yards of cattle between him and Concho. He didn't see how they could ride through without injuring their horses or getting thrown from their horses. He didn't fancy getting trampled to death, but he wanted to get close enough to Concho to get a clear shot.

"If you see a way through, Joe, go to it. I'll follow you."

Joe nodded. Then he rode up behind a running steer and sideswiped him with his horse. The steer swerved onto a different path, but more cattle filled his empty spot and ran headlong toward the open plain.

As Dane hugged the path directly behind Joe, he watched as Eagle kept inching his horse toward Concho.

Then two men in Concho's band turned their horses and started emptying their six-guns into the cattle rushing toward them. One cow fell, another staggered with a bullet in its lung, and the cattle behind them veered away from the injured animals.

Mitch and Lyle dropped two head, then retreated a few yards and began to shoot at other cattle. They rode up to where the cattle had fallen and tried to stack other cows behind them. They fired until their pistols were empty, then quickly ejected the spent cartridges and reloaded.

Concho saw a rider heading toward him.

It was Bill Coombs and he rounded the far edge of the herd in an attempt to come up behind Concho.

Concho aimed his pistol at Coombs and fired. He thumbed back the hammer and fired again. Two quick shots.

Dane watched in horror as Bill clutched his chest and swayed in the saddle. He lifted his six-gun to fire at Concho, but the second bullet hit Coombs in the abdomen and he doubled over, mortally wounded. His pistol went off and the bullet plowed a furrow through the grass and soil a few yards ahead of him. He fell from the saddle, spewing strings of blood from his two wounds. He screamed once before he was overrun by a half dozen head of cattle that seemed disoriented.

Dane swore under his breath and Joe forged head, slapping whitefaces with the tips of his reins. The cows seemed impervious to the stinging blows from the leather.

Alicante joined Montoya amid the thrashing sea of cattle and they bore down on

Mitch and Lyle, who were edging toward Concho and shooting at cattle right and left.

The Mexicans held their fire while Mitch fired a shot at them. Both men ducked. Lyle swung his gun hand around and squeezed the trigger. His firing pin fell on a spent round.

"Damn," Lyle exclaimed. "Out of bullets. I got to reload."

"Me too," Mitch said.

Both men opened the gates on their pistols and with agonizing slowness, pushed the ejection lever through each chamber. Empty .45 hulls pinged on the ground as Alicante and Montoya, still holding their fire, continued to close the gap to get within firing range of the two outlaws.

Mitch started to cram fresh cartridges into each cylinder, one chamber at a time, until all six chambers were full. He closed the gate while Lyle was dropping fresh cartridges from his nervous fingers.

"Shit, they're on us," Mitch exclaimed.

Lyle had four chambers filled with fresh rounds and he closed the gate and looked up to see the two Mexicans raise their pistols and take aim.

"Damn it all," Lyle spat, and thumbed the hammer back to cock his .45.

Mitch squeezed off a shot just as Alicante

and Montoya split and fired their weapons. His shot fried the air between the two Mexicans, missing them clean.

Carlos saw his bullet strike Mitch first. It ripped into his left shoulder with a hard smack. The impact twisted Mitch in his saddle, and his gun hand went out of control.

Alicante's bullet ripped into his right lung, cracking ribs and pulping the lung, until it collapsed and robbed Mitch of a full breath. The bullet smashed through and out his back, leaving a hole the size of a tennis ball.

Mitch screamed in pain with his last short breath.

Blood stained the front of his shirt, and his eyes glazed over with the frost of death as if they had been frozen into solid ice.

Lyle fired his pistol, but it struck a white-faced steer and rocked it off its course.

Carlos swung his Colt to bear on Lyle. He halted his horse for a moment, despite the jostling of the cattle as they brushed past his horse. He held his breath and squeezed the trigger. Smoke billowed out of the six-inch barrel, and sparks flew on the heels of the lead projectile.

Lyle thought he could see it coming and started to duck.

Too late.

The bullet smashed into the top of his head as he bent over his saddle horn, and it turned his brains to mush. Blood spray filled the air with a scarlet haze and he moaned as if it were some kind of afterthought. He continued his slump and rolled out of the saddle, stone dead.

Dane prodded Reno in the flanks and the horse jumped a foot straight toward Concho. Several head of Herefords rammed into Joe Eagle's horse and shoved him out of the way.

Concho glared at Dane and lifted his gun to take aim.

Dane hunkered low in the saddle and sighted his pistol along the horse's neck.

It would be close, he thought. A tough shot for him and maybe for Concho as well.

He saw the outlaw in slow motion as if his mind had locked on to the man and turned him into a mannequin that did not move for a split second that stretched into an eternity.

He was close now and Reno seemed to sense that it was time to stop running and hold steady. Reno moved his head slightly to the right and Dane had a clear vision of Concho aiming his pistol at him.

Then the mannequin came to life and Dane squeezed the trigger as he hugged the saddle horn and caressed it with his left hand.

The explosion made Reno jump.

Dane held on tight and thumbed back the hammer of his Colt.

Just in case, he thought.

Then he heard Concho's gun boom. Dane felt as if he were riding into a private hell where neither man would come out alive.

CHAPTER 43

Dane jerked the reins taut. Reno halted in his tracks as cattle avoided him and streamed around on both sides.

He sat up straight in the saddle even as he heard the keening whine of Concho's bullet as it *zizzed* past, inches from his ear.

Concho just sat his horse for a long moment as if he were untouched.

Dane thumbed the hammer of his pistol backward to full cock, prepared to fire again. Then he saw a small black hole at the base of Concho's neck. Concho dropped his pistol and reached upward. His finger touched the wound. His mouth opened, but nothing came out.

No scream. No sob. No words.

Nothing.

Dane drew a bead on Concho to finish him off, but Concho's arm dropped lifeless to his side. His eyes flapped closed. Then he fell sideways out of his saddle and hit the ground with a resounding thud. His horse jumped as if electrocuted and ran into three cows that knocked him to one side as they passed. The horse kicked up its heels and scampered around in a circle, confused and disoriented. A slash of red appeared on its side. One of the horns had grazed its ribs and left a bloody streak of white flesh.

"Him dead," Joe said as he rode up alongside.

"Hold the cattle off me, Joe," Dane said. "I want to go through Concho's pockets."

"Be quick," Joe said as Dane let his hammer drop back to half cock and holstered his pistol.

He ran to Concho and turned him over. He put two fingers to his throat, just under the ear.

"He's dead, Joe. The bastard is dead."

Joe nodded.

Dane straddled the legs of Concho and bent over. He went through his pants and shirt pockets. He pulled out a wad of greenbacks from a front pocket, a worn brown wallet from his back pocket, a pouch of chewing tobacco out of the other back pocket. In his shirt pocket, he drew out a square piece of cardboard folded in half. He opened the cardboard and saw a note that was also folded over. On the note were handwritten words and a signature that he recognized.

The heading stated PROMISSORY NOTE in block letters.

The text read as follows:

I, Earl Throckmorton, President of the Prairie Bank of Shawnee Mission, Oklahoma, do hereby promise to pay the bearer the sum of $10.00 (ten dollars) per head for any cattle returned to my custody upon the successful foreclosure of the property known as the Circle K Ranch, formerly owned by Dane Kramer. It is understood that these cattle came from Kansas and had been abandoned by the former owner, one Dane Kramer.

The note was signed *Earl Throckmorton* in florid cursive script.

"I'll be damned, Joe. That tinhorn Throckmorton was payin' Concho ten dollars a head for my cattle."

"Concho no have cattle," Joe said.

"No, but he tried to rustle them."

They heard Paddy yell orders. The firing had stopped.

"Round 'em up," Paddy hollered. "Head 'em all back to the river."

The call was repeated by several cowhands including Len Crowell.

Men on cutting horses started turning the

herd back as Dane stood up. Cattle were scattered all over the prairie, but they were no longer running. They were, instead, panting and docile, worn out from the stampede.

"You know what this paper means, Joe?"

"White man's words."

"They mean that I can have Throckmorton put in prison for trying to rustle my cattle. I might even get him put away for murder, since Concho killed so many of my men."

"That good," Joe said.

Dane folded the cardboard back over the promissory note and put it in his pocket. He shoved the bills in his front pocket and put the tobacco pouch in his back pocket.

Montoya and Alicante rode up.

"He's dead, no?" Montoya said.

"Yes," Dane replied.

"Can I take his pistol and his knife?"

"You can take anything Concho owned, Carlos," Dane said. "And the both of you can strip the dead rustlers of their guns and personals and stow 'em in the supply wagon. And add their horses to the remuda."

"We will do this," Alicante said, and saluted Dane.

Then Paddy rode up, his face puffy and red from exertion. But he was smiling.

"Would you believe we got prisoners,

Dane? They just up and surrendered."

"Where are they?" Dane asked. "I want to talk to them."

"Jim and Donny are herdin' 'em over to the chuck wagons. We got their guns. They're a surly bunch, but they got their tails tucked atween their sorry legs."

"Joe and I will ride over. How's the herd?"

"They're ready to drink at the river, and when you give the word, we'll run 'em acrost and head for Kansas City."

"Let's make sure we account for all the strays and get Wu and Barney to butcherin' the dead cows, as many as they can take on."

"Wu's already sharpenin' his skinnin' knife and Barney's got his butcher's apron on."

"How many men did we lose, Paddy?" Dane asked.

"Two or three that I know of, boss. I got Steve and Whit checkin' on it. Don't know if we got any wounded or not. Your idea to stampede the cattle worked real good."

"But we did lose some men," Dane said. He seemed to be in a momentary daze.

"Yep. We got graves to dig. Charley's goin' to pick up our dead and take them to a nice place under some trees over at the river."

Dane rested his forehead in his hand and

seemed to be shaking off his grief. "Thanks, Paddy. I'll be over there soon."

"Don't take it too hard, Dane," Paddy said. "It could have been worse. At least we took down Concho and got all his men corralled. We ought to line 'em all up for a firin' squad."

"Let's not sink to their level, Paddy. Now, get on with what you have to do."

"Sure, boss." Paddy rode off, skirting the cattle that were being driven back to the river.

Dane looked at Joe. "Those men counted on me, Joe. Now some of them are dead."

"You no give life," Joe said. "Great Spirit give life. Some lives long. Some lives short."

"I can't look at it that way," Dane said. "I'm responsible. In some way, I'm responsible."

"Good men die. Bad men die. You kill one bad man. Good men go to star path. Bad men die many times, for long time."

"You believe that, Joe?"

Joe nodded.

"I wish I knew for sure," Dane said, more to himself than to Joe. Death was not something he liked to think about. Once he had asked his father whether or not he was afraid to die.

"I ain't afraid to die, son," Thor had said.

"Way I look at it is we were put on this earth for a good reason. When we die, we leave this life knowin' more'n we did when we come into it. If there ain't nothin' after death, no more life for us, then we won't know it once we quit breathin'. If there is, then we will remember what we learned and maybe get the chance to rub out our mistakes. Either way, ain't nothin' we can do about it. We live and we die, and dyin's just one more part of life."

Dane wished he had some philosophy about death. He wished he could let grief wash over him and drip onto the ground like water. But he knew he could not. He didn't want to bury any of his men. He didn't know how to face death and lived in dread for the day when his father would die. It seemed to him that when a friend or a relative died, the person left behind a hole in the world, an empty place that no other person could ever fill.

He watched the Mexicans strip Concho's corpse of gun belt and boots. He turned away, ashamed of himself. He had killed a man and now there was a hole in his heart that would never fill up, never heal.

Yes, Concho was a bad man. He probably deserved to die. He was a killer and had taken many lives.

But Dane didn't want the job of executioner.

Yet he knew that this was the way of the world. When threatened, a man had the right to defend himself.

Concho had meant to kill him.

It could have gone either way. He might be lying there, dead, instead of Concho.

There was just no way he could make any sense out of it.

Except it felt good to be alive and know that he now had the proof to send Throckmorton to prison.

He might even enjoy seeing Throckmorton hang for his evil deeds.

He shuddered at the contradiction.

But that was how he felt at that moment.

And it made him ashamed of himself for just a few long and introspective seconds.

Chapter 44

Dane and Joe rode over to where the rustler captives stood tied to one of the supply wagons. Their hands were bound behind them. They all glared at Dane with sullen expressions on their faces. Some of them appeared to have been dragged after their capture, since their pants and shirts were torn and caked with dirt.

Charlie Moss stood behind them in the wagon and was handing down coils of rope to some of the Circle K hands.

Maynard Cuzzins already had one of the manila ropes. He had uncoiled it and was looping the bitter end around the rope.

Chad Ransom also had a length of rope. He watched Maynard and duplicated his actions.

"What in hell are you doin', Maynard?" Dane asked.

"Makin' a hangman's knot in this here rope," he said.

"What for?"

Maynard stopped coiling the rope and stared blankly at Dane.

"Well, we're aimin' to hang these here rustlers," he said. There was a belligerence to his tone, and the other men crowded around Maynard and Chad. Chad too had stopped wrapping one end of the rope around the long line.

"Yeah," Charlie said, "that's what we do with cattle rustlers. We hang 'em. Same as horse thieves."

Dane's eyes flashed with anger.

"You're not hangin' nobody, Maynard," he said. "Nor any of you. Do you hear me?"

There were shouts of protest from all the cowhands gathered there. One or two raised their fists and shook them.

"How come?" Maynard asked.

"Well, first of all, these men didn't rustle any of my cattle. And second, I aim to turn them over to the U.S. Marshal in Kansas City. You'll all be witnesses and will sign depositions."

"They tried to rustle the cattle, Mr. Kramer," Charlie said.

"But they didn't," Dane replied.

"Well, they're guilty of murder, then," Maynard said. "We can hang 'em for that."

Dane shook his head. "We aren't going to

do that neither. I'll file murder charges against them in Kansas City, and attempted cattle rustling to boot. They'll probably hang, but they'll be tried in a court of law. We aren't vigilantes, men. I'd like to shoot every one of them right between the eyes, but we're not the law. We don't have that right. Or that privilege."

"Shit," some of the men said.

"We want justice," Dewey yelled above the din of the others who were grumbling.

"They'll be brought to justice," Dane said. "But not here. In Kansas City."

The men all glared at him. The rustlers all stared at Dane as if they were watching a madman. Their faces reflected disbelief.

"Throw the ropes back in the wagon," Dane said. "We've got men to bury and we still have to drive these cattle across the Caney and up to Omaha."

Nobody moved.

Dane's right hand dropped to his side and gripped the butt of his pistol. "Now," he said softly, and stared down Maynard, Chad, and Charlie.

Maynard swallowed and unwound his hangman's knot. He tossed his rope up to Charlie. Chad did the same.

Paddy rode up a few seconds later.

"What's goin' on here?" he asked.

"Nothing," Dane said. "It's all over. Get these men to work and get some graves dug. I don't want Concho or any of his men we killed buried anywhere near my men."

"We was just goin' to bury Concho and them others out on the prairie," Paddy said.

"Yeah, not too deep," Maynard said, "and fill up their graves with cow shit."

"Maynard," Dane said, "you'd better get a shovel from Charlie and start diggin'. Maybe it'll take some of that anger starch out of you. Chad, you get to diggin' too."

"Yes, sir," Chad said. "Charlie give me a shovel. But I ain't buryin' no rustler."

"Me neither," Maynard said.

"Paddy, show 'em where to dig and let's get this over with."

"You boys foller me," Paddy said, and rode off toward the tree-lined river.

Montoya rode up. Concho's pistol hung from his saddle horn.

"Light down, Carlos," Dane said. "I want you to take a look at these prisoners, tell me if you know 'em."

Montoya dismounted and walked over to the bound prisoners. There were four of them. Dane had never seen any of them before.

"Sure," Carlos said. He looked at each man's face.

The prisoners glared at him. There was anger on their faces and something else that Dane not only recognized but felt, as if they were burning inside with it. Hatred.

"That first one, the tall one, he is called Leroy Eckersley. The man next to him is Frank Groves. The short one they call Whiskey Bill, but his name is Bill Vickers, and that last one, with the knife scar on his face, is Bart Norman. They call him 'Blackie' because of his black hair and beard. You are going to hang them, no?"

Dane shook his head. "I'm not going to hang them, but I'm going to turn them over to the U.S. Marshal in Kansas City and charge them with murder and attempted cattle rustling."

"They should hang," Carlos said.

"They probably will hang. I want you to give a deposition, Carlos. You and all the other men who were here today."

"I will give the deposition," Carlos said.

Blackie spat at Carlos. His eyes burned with hatred. "Ain't no damned Mex goin' to —"

"Shut up," Dane said. "All of you are prisoners. My prisoners. You'll ride in one of the wagons to Kansas City. If any one of you, or all of you, tries to escape, my men will have my permission to shoot you down

411

like the dogs you are."

"You can't scare me, mister," Frank said. "It's a long way to Kansas City."

"As far as I'm concerned, you and your pards are the lowest of the low," Dane said. "If you have any prayin' in you, you might make your peace with whoever you pray to because I'm going to see to it that you all hang."

Whiskey Bill snarled as he cursed Dane and Carlos.

"I got friends in K.C.," he said. "You just might get a knife in your back before you can make out a deposition, or get your head blowed off with a Greener."

Dane turned his back on the men. He grabbed Carlos by the arm and led him away. "I'd like to shoot every one of them, Carlos, but we want to do this right."

"They would not give you quarter, Mr. Kramer."

"I know. I should shoot them, but that would be something I'd have to live with for the rest of my life."

"Your kindness will get you killed one day," Carlos said.

The cowhands buried Concho, Lyle Fisk, Mitch Markham, Logan Heckler, Skip Hewes, and Will Davis in a single grave. It was a hole, really, shoveled out of what might be called a ditch. Wu and Barney added the entrails of the cows they butchered, along with the heads and tails, and the hides. To them, it was a final insult to Concho's rustlers.

As for the hands who were killed, they were buried in separate graves on the west side of the Caney River, beneath some large cottonwoods. Most of the men wept when Dane said a few words over their graves. He was one of the men who had to wipe his eyes when dirt was shoveled over the bodies of men he worked with and liked.

The captured rustlers rode in Charlie's supply wagon after he had put all the guns in the other wagon. Their feet were bound as well and they had to lie on the hard wagon bed as the team pulled the wagon over rough ground.

They crossed the meandering river with ease. The water was not high, but the banks were steep.

The herd moved to the Missouri River and turned north to Kansas City.

When they reached Kansas City, Dane and Joe Eagle took several hands with them, along with the captive rustlers, and turned them over to the sheriff. They went before Judge Harlan Evers and swore out affidavits, charging the four outlaws with murder and attempted cattle rustling. The judge called in a deputy U.S. Marshal and had them formally arrested and charged for their crimes.

When Dane and his men, including Joe Eagle, went to the stockyards to pick up the cattle being held for Otto Himmel, Dane paid off the boarding fees and drove nine hundred head of cattle to the west of the city, where they joined his herd.

To his dismay, the cattle Himmel had bought and boarded in Kansas City were all Mexican longhorns. So he had to keep the longhorns separate from his own cattle and trailed after Paddy some two miles in the rear, with Len acting as trail boss.

"Not much meat on them longhorns," Len observed.

"Himmel paid enough for their feed," Dane said.

"Didn't Himmel tell you the breed?"

"No, he did not," Dane said.

"Would you have taken them on if you had known?"

"Probably. Cattle are cash and that's what we all need at this point."

"I wished I could have paid off Throckmorton," Len said.

"Well, you may get your ranch back, Len. I think I can have Throckmorton sent to prison and maybe the court will give you back your deed."

"Throckmorton did it all legal," Len said. "I don't see how I could get my land back."

"If I can prove that the bank acted out of greed and foreclosed on a lot of folks without giving them a chance to pay off their loans, the court just might let you buy your land back for pennies on the dollar."

"You think so?"

"There is a strong chance that the court will bend over backwardss to right a wrong. To right a bunch of wrongs."

Dane didn't know if he could get the courts to look at Throckmorton's banking practices, but there was a good chance that they would. If they became outraged at how Throckmorton had hired killers to murder his men and steal his cattle, the judge or judges just might side with the landowners and return all the lands Throckmorton had grabbed just to teach other unscrupulous lenders a lesson.

The longhorns were no trouble. They were trail-savvy animals, big and rangy, with large frames.

"You know something?" Dane said to Paddy and Len one night when they were drinking coffee around the campfire after supper. "If we crossbred our Herefords with longhorns, we might produce a bigger and better beef cow."

"Ah, it would never work," Paddy said.

"Why not?" Dane asked.

"Never been done before."

"Maybe it's time somebody tried it. I just might go down to Mexico or the Rio Grande Valley in Texas and buy me a couple of seed bulls and give it a try."

"You know," Len said, "when I look at them longhorns, I see they got long legs and larger skeletons. You fill 'em out with Hereford meat, you might have a big old cow that would bring top dollar."

"See, Paddy?" Dane said. "Len agrees with me."

"All you'd get, Dane," Paddy said, "would be a whiteface with real long horns."

They all laughed, but the idea settled in a corner of Dane's mind. He believed in cattle and with a new crossbreed, he might wind up a wealthy man.

It was a thought he carried with him all the way to Omaha.

CHAPTER 45

On the last leg of the drive to Omaha, Dane and Joe Eagle rode well ahead of the herd. Paddy and the whitefaces were a couple of miles behind him, with Len and the longhorns less than a mile behind Paddy. The wagons and the remuda followed well to the rear of the longhorns.

He was tired but oddly exhilarated. The miles seemed to drop off him like water off a duck's back when he saw the distant buildings shining in the sun. It looked like a city out of a fairy tale, a magic kingdom rising out of the pages of a book. His pulsed quickened and he thought he could smell the fragrance of a garden filled with beautiful flowers.

"There it is, Joe," he said. "There's Omaha."

Joe grunted.

As they approached the southern edge of the city on the hard-packed road, they began to see stock pens and smell, not the fragrance of flowers, but the heady, musky scent of cow manure. They rode on, and saw more and more pens that looked like a maze and they heard the bawling of cattle. They saw men on horseback who waved to them.

Within a few minutes they were in the midst of the labyrinth of stock pens and saw men, women, little children lining the road on both sides. They all waved at them as the two men approached.

"It looks like they're waiting for a parade," Dane said, amazed and mystified at seeing so many people standing on both sides of the road. The women twirled their parasols, and the kids jumped up and down and shouted greetings to them.

"I wonder why they're all here," Dane said.

"They wait to see cattle," Joe said.

"They didn't do that in Kansas City," Dane said.

Beyond the stock pens, Dane saw the outlines of large buildings. They were painted with names he had never heard of: Cudany, Rath, Swift, and many others.

Smoke spewed out of tall chimneys and trailed out over the city in an ashen pall. Dane smelled the smoke and felt the powerful allure of a city with its sleeves rolled up and its hands covered in grime.

There were other smells too. There was the smell of hay and the indefinable aroma of blood and cattle innards.

A man rode out from among the log corrals that formed the pens. He met them and said, "Howdy, gents."

"Howdy," Dane said.

"You with the herd from Oklahoma?" the man asked. He pulled a small notepad from his shirt pocket and flipped it open to a page. "The Circle K?"

"We are. Herd's about two miles back."

"Thanks. I'll ride out to guide them to the feedlots. You two can turn in at that road just past the pen yonder." He pointed to railings, and Dane saw a wide thoroughfare that ran in between cow pens.

"Then where do we go?" Dane asked.

"There are some men waiting for you just before you get to that big gray building among the pens. If you're Kramer, that is."

"I am," Dane said.

"They're waitin' for you. We knew there was a big herd comin."

"Why are all those people waiting along the main road?" Dane asked.

The man laughed. "Oh, they heard about the big herd of cattle comin' into town too.

They're here to welcome you and your boys. My name's Claude, by the way. Claude Lomax."

Claude and Dane shook hands.

"See you by and by," Claude said, and rode off down the road. The people alongside waved at him and cheered.

Dane and Joe rode past pens that held hogs, and others with cattle. There seemed to be no end to them. They saw a couple of trails leading from chutes. The trails were enclosed with cement walls on both sides. It appeared to Dane that these trails led directly to the slaughterhouses.

They approached the gray building Claude had told them about and as they rode up to a hitch rail out front, the door to the building opened.

Three men stepped out.

The tallest one, in the middle, was Otto Himmel. He wore a smile on his face. He was dressed in a business suit and wore a gray derby.

He raised his arms in greeting.

"That you, Dane?" he said.

"Sure is, Otto."

"Did you make the drive all right?"

Dane nodded and swung his right leg over the saddle and touched the ground. Joe dismounted as well. They wrapped their reins around the hitch rail, and both stepped over to where the three men stood.

"Dane, this is Hank Strimple, my office manager, and let me introduce you to Vic Padios, my accountant."

Dane shook the hands of both men.

"This is my friend, Joe Eagle," Dane said. Both men shook Joe's hand. Vic carried a fat satchel that looked heavy. The tan leather was shiny. Hank carried a clipboard. Both men wore ties. Only Otto wore a vest, but they all had on white shirts that bespoke neatness and precision. Dane took an instant liking to both men. They both had open, honest faces and neatly trimmed hair. Both wore small hats that looked like fedoras.

"Claude will guide the herd to the pens and I have two men waiting to tally them as they pass through the gate. Your trail boss can keep a tally too," Himmel said.

"Oh, they will, Otto. I have two trail bosses."

"Then you picked up the cattle I had waiting in Kansas City?"

"Yeah. The longhorns. You neglected to tell me the breed."

"Oh, did I? So sorry, Dane. Were they any trouble?"

"No. The only trouble we had was after

we crossed over the Kansas border. We were jumped by a gang of rustlers."

"Oh, I am sorry."

"We killed several and captured four of them alive. They're cooling their heels in the Kansas City Jail if they haven't already been hanged."

"Do you mean to tell me that rustlers tried to steal three thousand head of cattle?" Himmel said.

"Yep. They was hired by Throckmorton, the banker in Shawnee Mission."

"Why, that's outrageous," Padios said.

"The nerve of some folks," Strimple said. Both men seemed genuinely surprised.

"Throckmorton, eh?" Himmel said. "I didn't much care for the man when I met him at the bank."

"I don't think he'll be sitting at his desk long," Dane said. "When I get back, I'm charging him with murder and attempted cattle rustling. I've got proof to back me up."

"Good for you, Dane. Shall we go over to the pens and see what the herd looks like?"

"Sure. We had good grass and plenty of water on the trail," Dane said.

"This is going to be a big boost to Omaha's economy," Otto said.

"It probably won't hurt your wallet none

either," Dane said.

The three men laughed.

Himmel led them to a large corral with gates and chutes to other surrounding pens.

They all heard the people cheering along the road, and after the five men perched themselves on a top rail, they could see Claude and Paddy leading cattle down the road to the cattle pens.

Two men wearing cowhand boots and denims, dressed in chambray shirts, one blue, one red, sat on a top rail a couple of pens away from them. Another man on the ground swung open the gate.

"I'd better go over there," Strimple said. "Your trail boss, or bosses, might want to use this clipboard."

Hank slid down off the fence.

"Yes, Hank, show the Circle K men every consideration."

Hank walked over and said something to the man at the gate. Then he climbed up to the top rail and sat near the two men who were going to tally the cattle as they entered the pens. Both had pencils and clipboards as well.

Claude rode up and waved an arm to show Paddy the gate. The two men spoke.

Dane saw Paddy dismount and tether his horse to the bottom rail. He walked over to

Hank and took his clipboard and pencil. He looked over at Dane and Joe, then waved. Dane waved back.

"Here they come," Otto said as the cattle began to stream through the open gate. "They look fine, just fine."

"Fine and fat," Vic said. "Otto, you made a good choice when you bought this herd from Mr. Kramer. I've never seen finer cattle."

"Thanks, Vic," Dane said. "I appreciate it."

"I meant what I said. We see a lot of cattle in these stockyards, but most of them are puny. Some of them show their bones, they're so lean."

"The longhorns are a bit leaner," Dane said. "But they've got bigger frames and probably have good meat on their bones."

"That was all I could find when I went to south Texas," Otto said.

"I'd like to know where you got 'em," Dane said. "I'm thinking of crossbreeding some longhorn bulls with my whitefaces."

"I'll give you the name of the rancher and directions to his spread," Otto said.

Claude saw to it that the cattle came through the gate at a steady pace, four or five wide. He carried a quirt that he used to detain or to urge the cattle through. Dane was impressed with the smoothness of the operation. The two tall men and Paddy were counting heads as they came through.

It was a long and tedious process, but exciting to Dane. He wasn't counting, but he had allowed for lost cattle, and they might have lost a few strays during the gun battle. But they hadn't lost any head to drowning or to rustlers.

People began to crowd around the pens as they filled up with Circle K cattle. Small boys pointed out steers and cows that they liked, while their mothers twirled their parasols and tried to keep the youngsters from teasing the animals. Men stood at the fences with their boots resting on the bottom rail, and chewed tobacco or straw, smoked pipes or cigarettes, and commented on the stock.

"This will likely last up to dusk or nightfall," Otto said. "If you want, Dane, we can go into the cattleman's building where your horses are tied and have a drink. We have a full bar in that building."

"I'd like to see it through, Otto," Dane said. "And then I've got to take care of my hands. You know, find a hotel, a place where they can all eat and such."

"I've taken care of all that, Dane," Otto said. "When we have the tally, Vic here is going to pay you off in cash. That's what he's carrying in that Italian-made satchel he's carrying."

"Oh, by the way, I owe you money, Otto," Dane said. "The bank draft you gave me for the longhorns more than covered the bill at the feedlot in K.C."

"Well, Vic can figure that all out, when the time comes. I think you're due a bonus for getting the cattle up here ahead of time."

"I don't even know what month it is," Dane said. "Nor what day of the week it might be."

Vic and Otto both laughed.

"Well, it's 1879," Vic said, "if that helps."

"And I think it's June already," Otto said.

"We left Oklahoma sometime in April, I think," Dane said.

"Well, you'll be glad to be back home, I expect," Otto said. "Be sure and tell your father I said hello."

"I will," Dane said.

He missed his father at that moment. He looked over at Joe and saw the impassive expression on his face. Joe had no one to miss or come home to, except him. It made him feel awkward to talk about his father in front of Joe.

When the last of the cattle streamed into the pens, the man at the gate closed it. All of the hands gathered there and lined the fence looking at the Herefords and long-horns they had delivered.

The chuck wagons and the two supply wagons were parked in a separate pen.

"We'll put armed guards on your wagons," Otto said to Dane as they climbed down from the fence. "And tell your men to follow us to the cattleman's building. There's food and drink for everyone."

Dane walked over to Paddy and told him to gather all the men and walk over to the gray building.

"What for?" Paddy asked.

"There's a bar in there and a bunch of cooks hard at work."

"Whooeee," Paddy shouted, and walked over to the hands standing at the fence.

The hands all whooped and shouted, and some threw their hats into the air and stomped up and down as if they were dancing Irish jigs.

Then Paddy came back and handed his clipboard to Dane.

"I didn't add up the lines," Paddy said, "but there's a whole bunch of pages with lines crossed out."

"I'll take that," Hank said, and reached for the clipboard.

Paddy handed the papers to Hank.

"Oh, and one more thing, Paddy," Dane said. "But keep it to yourself."

"Sure, Dane. I ain't one to flap my jaw like a washerwoman."

Dane leaned over and whispered something in Paddy's ear. Then he clamped a hand over Paddy's mouth.

"If you let out a yell, I'll choke you, Paddy," Dane said aloud.

"Mum's the word, boyo, mum's the very word."

Dane laughed.

"Get all your boys and follow us," he said.

As they reached the gray building, Otto stopped and asked Dane a question. "What did you whisper to your trail boss, if you don't mind me asking?"

"I told him that tonight was payday," Dane said.

"You no tell me," Joe said.

"Your payday is next week, Joe," Dane said, then slapped him on the back.

"You make the joke," Joe said. "I know."

"You'll get paid first, Joe."

They all entered the building as dusk fell over the cow pens and the sky paled before turning black.

Paraffin lamps glowed in a large room. There were tables set up and candles lit. Men cooked on iron stoves and bartenders in white aprons braced themselves for the onslaught of men who had not seen anything like it for a very long time.

"Welcome to Omaha," Otto shouted as the men stomped onto the hardwood floors.

The men let out a loud yell and headed for the bar.

"Follow me, Dane and Joe. We have our own private table over in that far corner. There's whiskey, rye, gin, and wine at our table, and waiters will bring us beefsteaks with all the civilized trimmings."

"I feel like whooping myself," Dane said. "No, I think I'll just have a swaller of whiskey to wash away the trail dust."

"I'll join you," Otto said.

For the first time in months, Dane felt right at home with all the men at his table. He would not sleep on stones or hear coyotes howl this night. He would not have to listen to the nighthawks singing off-key and off-tempo. Tonight, he would celebrate and maybe give a toast or two to the men he had lost on the long drive through grand country.

Chapter 46

Dane rode Reno into the mist of an autumn morning. It was quiet at that hour and there was a zesty tang to the air as he listened to the sussurance of the horse's footfalls in the dew-wet grass and the lowing of the cattle in the near pasture. The sun was just peeking over the horizon in the east, a golden red disk with the aura of an ancient god emerging from darkness to peer over the windowsill of the waking world.

He headed for the creek where the trees were sporting their autumnal garb, the maples with their deep magenta leaves, the poplars and dogwoods with their pale mottled colors dripping from forlorn branches, the yellow leaves of the birches, the browning leaves of the oaks.

Joe Eagle rode away from the creek over fallen leaves, driving a cow and her frisky calf ahead of him onto pasture. The calf shook its tail and its body, throwing off sunlit beads of water. Dane had heard its cries from the stable while he was saddling his horse.

Joe's horse, Swoghili, pranced like a Tennessee walker as it tailed the cow and calf as if they were its special charges, nudging the air with its nose and whickering softly.

"Calf fell into the creek," Joe said. "Had to rope it and drag it onto the bank."

"I heard it," Dane said. "It sounded like a hurt child."

"It wasn't hurt, just scared," Joe said.

"I'm glad you dragged it out of the creek. It's running full after that rain yesterday."

Joe broke off as the cow and calf romped off to join the herd grazing a few hundred yards away.

"Poor little tyke," Joe said, with uncommon tenderness.

"Want to come up to the house? Pa's up and sitting in his chair. Ora Lee has made coffee and is cooking breakfast."

"Sure," Joe said. "Coffee would be fine at this hour of the morning."

The two changed course and rode toward the house.

"I noticed that since we got back, Joe, you're talking like a white man, not an Indian."

"I could always talk like a white man,

431

Dane. I just didn't want to."

"Why?"

"My talk set me apart. It was where I wanted to be."

"What changed your mind?" Dane asked.

"The drive. At night I would listen to the other men talking and I realized something. Something about them and about me."

"What was that, Joe?"

"They all spoke differently, but somehow all the same. They spoke like Americans. They all had different accents, but they talked the same language. I wanted to be like them. I was an American too. I spoke to Carlos and Alfredo and Rufio about their being Mexican. They told me that only their Mexican accents set them apart from other Americans. They were trying to fit in and overcome their Mexican accents because they said the minute they opened their mouths, other men looked down on them and called them names."

"I know what you mean, Joe. But the way we talk tells something about where we were born and raised. You can never shuck that."

"Yes. I am part Cherokee, and the Mexicans come from Mexico. The language, the way they talk, is like their skin. It cannot be shed. But I do not want to be looked on as odd or stupid, because I am neither."

"I think you're right, Joe. We can't help being who we are, no more than that cow and calf can help being what they are."

"The herd is looking good," Joe said. "The calves will be yearlings next year, and then the yearlings will grow into cows and your herd will grow large once again."

"It gives me a good feeling," Dane said.

They reached the house and stepped down from their horses, tied their reins around the hitch rail.

They both looked back at the pasture with its rising mists and the dewdrops sparkling on the grass. There was the smell of new-mown hay from the barn, and some of the hands were out of the bunkhouse and standing at the water pump to wash their faces and hands before breakfast.

"I own it all, Joe," Dane said. "And when we go to south Texas and look for a seed bull or two, I'll have longhorns to cross-breed."

"You paid off the bank, then."

"I didn't pay Throckmorton. I paid off my mortgage after he was arrested and taken to jail."

"What will happen to him?" Joe asked. "Will he hang?"

"I don't know. I just think how misguided he was. He thought that land was the basis for all wealth. But people can't eat dirt. They eat beef, and cattle represent the future for me. Oh, I'll buy more land, but only to raise more beef. We can feed the world, Joe. Land is meant to be tended, to grow things on, not generate money for fat bankers.

Joe laughed. "I am learning a lot from you, Dane."

"We all learn from each other," Dane said.

The two men walked into the house.

Thor banged his phallic cane hard against the floor as the two came through the door.

He was smiling, and so was Ora Lee, who stood next to his chair.

"Set," she said, "and I'll bring you both some coffee."

"Hens set; people sit," Joe said with a smile.

"My, my," Ora Lee said, "but aren't we takin' on airs?"

"We sure are, Ora Lee," Dane said as he and Joe sat down to hear what Thor had to say on such a fine morning in autumn.

ABOUT THE AUTHOR

Ralph Compton stood six foot eight without his boots. He worked as a musician, a radio announcer, a songwriter, and a newspaper columnist. His first novel, *The Goodnight Trail,* was a finalist for the Western Writers of America Medicine Pipe Bearer Award for Best Debut Novel. He was also the author of the *Sundown Riders* series and the *Border Empire* series.